She Goes By Many Names

Monique Kristine

She Goes By Many Names

Translated from the Polish by Translative Co-op

The bass reverberated in her ears, and the sound of a trumpet invaded her mind, effectively blocking the influx of ghastly memories. Music aided her in evading unwelcome thoughts. Despite the lapse of eight years, she still remembered every violation, every exploitation by her stepfather. She would awaken at night because she could still taste him. Though she had lived alone for years, she had installed locks on the insides of every room.

In group therapy, a participant mentioned that music helped her when intrusive memories returned unbidden. She decided to take this advice. She turned on the music. Loudly. As loud as possible to drown out the thoughts and focus on something else. Though the girl had recommended simple, memorable tunes, Magda opted for heavy house. It seemed only in this way could she rid herself of the intruding memories.

Her legs were often adorned with bruises. When the memory of the grimy, dirty touch returned persistently, she would pinch her thighs. She devised her own alert system. Sensing the oncoming wave of memories, she'd put on headphones, pinch herself hard and find a distraction – just as she was doing now.

Though it was only four in the morning, Magda knew sleep would evade her for the rest of the night. She flung the balcony doors wide open. The winter air refreshed her swiftly. She felt free. She fetched flour, vanilla sugar, baking powder, eggs and nearly three kilograms of apples from the cupboard. Quickly, she kneaded the pastry and placed it in the freezer. She peeled the apples, sliced them into small discs, placed them in a pot and added a touch of water. A teaspoon of vanilla sugar and cinnamon imbued them with a magical scent. Magda was always enchanted by how modest spices could craft such a perfect aroma. Just a few more drops of lemon juice for that zing, a touch of gelatine.

Serenity was slowly encroaching, and although it was still far, she felt its effect. Her breathing was slower and calmer, and she no longer glanced fearfully over her shoulder. Even though she was living alone and no one knew she had moved to the capital, the fear of her stepfather appearing at her doorstep haunted her. The aroma of apple charlotte lazily, as it was apt for a morning, filled her home. She smiled to herself. Alone, with no one's aid and without medication, she overcame the surge of fear. She stepped onto the balcony, scanning the neighbourhood. Warsaw had awakened! She took a deep breath of the morning air. Snow was lightly falling, casting a fairytale ambience upon the city. *This will be a good week*, she murmured to herself.

The week commenced with a calm, lazy Monday, typical for a winter holiday. The city seemed deserted, the roads remarkably clear. Traffic jams vanished, and the route that usually took an hour could now be traversed in less time than waiting for a meal in one of Warsaw's more popular restaurants. Monday morning greeted the residents with snowfall. The air swirled with descending snowflakes.

Warsaw boasted many iconic spots which, despite the passage of years, shifts in trends, fashions and tastes, still ardently clung to history. One such place was undoubtedly the doughnut shop in Górczewska, treating its patrons to unique, incomparable doughnuts once savoured by Piłsudski himself. To taste the essence of Warsaw, this place was a must-visit. One ought to also try the mushroom rolls in Old Town and dine at the nearby *bar mleczny* Rusałka. The taste was important, but so was the scent. The unique aroma of Hala Mirowska, precisely the spot in front of the hall where florists had been selling flowers for decades, was enthralling. Each season brought a different scent. Summer's scent was the most intense, with plenty of roses, freesias and peonies. Autumn carried the aroma of chrysanthemums, inevitably associated with All Saints' Day. Winter heralded the reign of poinsettias and fragrant firs.

A cavalcade of colours and fragrances exploded with the first spring tulips. Magda loved to pause here on her way to work and bask in the beauty of this place. For a moment, she'd indulge her senses with colourful bouquets, then she'd proceed towards the City Hall building.

Nestled beside Hala Mirowska, amid the glass wilderness of the urban jungle, stood a building that was in defiance of the developing city. Among the towering skyscrapers emerged an edifice, a relic from the days of *bambino* ice creams. Its ground floor housed a *bar mleczny*, one of the last ones, from which homely aromas wafted at all hours. In times of sushi, kebabs and phosphorescent drinks, one could still get Warsaw-style tripe, genuine tartare or tongues in horseradish sauce here. Summer saw strawberry *kompot* instead of coloured fizzy beverages, while winter brought its apple variant. The clamour of cooks shouted 'Dumplings and fried eggs, one portion!' It was a haven from bygone days, preserving its unique atmosphere and flavour. In the same building on the second floor functioned a division of the City Hall dedicated to projects that no other team would tackle. Comprising people whose passion rose to meet many a challenge, it was a place of mostly friendly relations, only occasionally interrupted by minor disagreements.

Among many rooms existed one, a favourite of those seeking good energy or a taste of home-baked delights. Four women worked in this room, different in every respect: appearance, age, marital status, dreams and expectations.

Yet they formed a team unmatched. They complemented each other professionally and were friends in private lives.

The longest-serving employee among them was Krystyna, ever so conservative and firmly grounded. She allowed no moments of weakness, her demeanour always shielded by propriety's veil. At work, she epitomised professionalism; every full stop was always in its place. A well-practised smile and attire were impeccably chosen to suit the occasion, the time of day and the mood. Privately, she was the wife of Krzysztof and mother of fourteen-year-old twins, Patrycja and Patryk.

The second inhabitant of room number 5 was Magda. Even though it seemed impossible, she was even more reserved than Krystyna, never sharing about herself, not dwelling in reminiscences, offering no explanations. The little her colleagues knew about her emerged slowly over time. She hailed from a small town near Poznań where she had worked for a while but moved to Warsaw after two years. And that was all. Only much later did they learn that her mother had passed away years earlier and her father did as well when Magda was still a child.

The third of the women was Gosia, who detested being called Małgorzata. Married for several years, she and her husband longed for a child. Sadly, no one could explain why their efforts bore no fruit. They had had two attempts at in vitro, with every pregnancy miscarried between the fifth and seventh week. Each attempt took a heavy toll on Gosia, who often sought solace among her colleagues after work.

The last member was Alicja, the most colourful bird in the flock. Usually adorned in vibrantly coloured, airy dresses, always smiling, brimming with charm, and, when necessary, sarcasm. Unattached, she revelled in her singlehood and enjoyed life. She vowed never to fall in love, to remain alone, letting no one seize control over her.

On this day, Krystyna was the first to arrive at work, impeccably made up as always. Short, elegantly styled black hair framed her face, while a dress in light shades of grey gave the impression of a formal uniform. As soon as she entered the room, she threw open all windows. It brought her joy that, in an era where everyone was stuck in open spaces within air-conditioned confines, they had a room where windows could be opened to welcome the morning breeze.

The water for coffee hadn't yet boiled when Magda entered.

'Hello, Krysia. As always, first on duty. I brought us a delicious apple charlotte, I baked it this morning.'

'Hey, didn't sleep again?' asked Krystyna, who knew that Magda had sleeping problems, though she didn't know the cause.

'Yes, but I used the time to bake an apple charlotte. I suspect, with some vanilla ice cream, it will go perfectly with today's coffee,' she said, showing a box of ice cream and a tray of neatly cut diamond-shaped pieces of cake.

'So, we're starting off with a little lounging around instead of closing the next phase of the project,' Krystyna remarked with a hint of irony.

'You could say that.' They both started laughing. A moment later, the door opened, and Gosia entered the room. She was a petite, slim woman, so fragile that one felt an urge to approach and hug her. She seemed like a delicate being in need of someone's strong support.

'I knew you were already at work; the whole corridor smells of your apple charlotte. I also saw the boss. He mentioned he'd visit us after the briefing and that we should save him a piece of the cake. Where's Alicja?'

'Where else? She's sleeping ...'

They all burst out laughing. It had become a habit for Alicja to be late at least once a week – the alarm didn't go off, there was a power outage, or the tram didn't leave. Of course, everyone knew these were just excuses, but in this – perhaps the only – place on earth, such explanations were treated with a blind eye. As long as she performed her duties perfectly, nobody made a fuss about a few delays each month.

'Knowing life, Alicja will call in a few minutes, ask to be signed in and announce that she's on her way with juices for us. By the way, these juice guys must be really handsome if Alka risks being late so many times a month just to treat us to litres of fresh juice. But honestly, I've got used to these vitamin breaks.'

No sooner had Magda finished speaking than the phone on Krystyna's desk rang. The smiling faces of the girls turned towards her.

'Damn it, Alka, where are you? The director's been searching for you all over the department; he knows you're late again. He's not thrilled. Get moving and come over fast.' Krystyna could be very convincing, and Alicja couldn't see Magda and Gosia who were doubling over with laughter at their desks. She hung up quickly.

'Do you think she believed you?' asked Magda.

'I'm sure she did. The crazy girl doesn't even know that I signed her in early this morning. It was obvious that she would oversleep as usual. She'll learn her lesson for a few days,' Krystyna chuckled. 'How was your weekend?'

'My weekend was calm. I went to a private view of one of my friends on Saturday, was supposed to go to dinner with her and her friends afterwards, but some lover appeared who believed no one could resist him and insisted I should go to his place after dinner,' Magda started, but Gosia quickly interrupted her.

'What did he look like? Handsome?'

'Quite the opposite. Handsome, yes, but you could immediately tell he had issues not only with alcohol but with other substances as well. And he apparently didn't like washing much, for he had greasy hair. And the amount of perfume he used let you guess that it wasn't just his hair that was dirty.'

'Ugh! I can't stand men who don't acknowledge such a thing as washing!' interrupted Gosia impatiently. It was clear that she couldn't wait to share her news with the girls. 'We are trying in vitro for the third time. Next Thursday, I won't be at work because I need to be at the clinic. I can't wait. I feel that this time it will be different, that it will work for us.'

'I'm keeping my fingers crossed for you both. You're right. You need to stay positive,' Krystyna hurriedly assured her.

'Do you really think I can have a child? That, despite everything, I'll get pregnant and give birth to a baby?' asked Gosia. The pain in her eyes was something Krystyna had never seen before. She herself had given birth to twins and had no problems getting pregnant – she simply wanted children, so she stopped taking birth control and after a few successful evenings with her husband, the test showed two lines. She didn't know the pain Gosia had to endure – not only going through a series of tests but, above all, experiencing miscarriages. For a moment, she looked into Gosia's eyes, wondering what to say, but concluded she could tell her anything except for what doctors had been repeating for years. *It's all in Gosia's head, she blocks herself too much, and that's why there are problems*, she thought.

'Gosia, there are thousands of confirmed cases where, despite the diagnoses of the best specialists, women got pregnant and gave birth to beautiful, healthy babies. But are you sure this is a good idea? I am only concerned about your well-being. Maybe you should let it go for a while and focus on something else?'

'I know about that. Piotr says the same, and our doctor confirms it. I know you are right, but this is stronger than me. I can't stop thinking about having a child. It drives me mad when I see pregnant women. It infuriates me when I see daddies in Auchan buying nappies for babies. I avoid friends who have small children and, God forbid, such tiny, fragrant babies. I know it's wrong, but I can't deal with this jealousy. What do these women have that they can have a child or even more than one, and I can't even make it to the tenth week? Either it's an ectopic pregnancy, a failed fertilisation attempt, or a miscarriage. Seriously, I've had enough! I can't imagine how I could work with you if any of you were pregnant.' With apprehension, she looked around the room where the four of them worked.

'Oh, I'm done after my twins, and I don't want more. Besides, you need time for that, and Krzysztof and I don't have time for anything. Magda, what about you?' Krystyna asked. She knew her position well. Although Magda never spoke loudly about her problems and didn't share her experiences, Krystyna sensed that there had been traumatic moments in her life, and she simply wasn't ready to talk about them. Magda smiled grimly.

'Sorry, but from what I was taught at school, a male specimen is needed for that. And I haven't had one by my side for several years. And I do not intend to change anything. I'll remain the old maid with a cat, seated on a rocking chair with knitting in hand, gossiping about everyone and everything. So don't count on me. Well, unless Alicja ...' They all started to laugh at the mere thought of Alicja giving up her singleton's life to take up housekeeping, laundry and cleaning with a child in tow.

'You see, Gosia, you are safe here. By the way, where is Alka?'

The girls chatted about something else, but Magda stopped listening. She felt a strange chill that penetrated her body. Although she was warm, she couldn't shake off the feeling that something sinister lurked around the corner. She glanced at Krystyna, who, being the oldest among them, always had a calming effect on her. Perhaps it was because she was always so composed, not volatile like Alicja, didn't curse other people and could find a solution to every problem. The age difference wasn't large, but enough for the three of them to agree that Krystyna was their biggest support.

'Shall we meet for our usual Saturday gathering? I'm just on juice, but with you guys, I can sit even with juice,' Gosia suggested. They referred to their monthly Saturday get-togethers as 'witches flight.' They usually met at Alicja's place, which was easily accessible for all.

'Absolutely. I'd love to have a leisurely Saturday with you all. The twins are hitting puberty, and Krzysztof is often away on business trips, so I'd happily delegate to him the task of dealing with the teenagers in their growth and rebellious phase.'

'Is it that bad?' inquired Magda.

'Not really, but sometimes I get fed up when for the umpteenth time I hear a squabble over blue headphones or a yoghurt eaten from the fridge. It'll do him good to spend a whole Saturday with them. At noon, I have an appointment with my dad. We'll have lunch somewhere in the city, and then I'll come over to you.'

'Do we have any plans? Or is it just jazz, wine and us?'

'Jazz, *juice* and us,' Gosia added.

The door opened, and Alicja ran into the room.

'Where's the director? Do I need to see him now?' She seemed scared, but even in such moments, she looked charming and very feminine.

'Shall I go to him now? Just take these shakes from me. Apparently, they are the winter hit.' She placed plastic half-litre cups with lids on the desks. 'Here you go, straws, and enjoy, darlings. Now I'm off to face the music with the head.' She was about to dash out of the room when first Gosia burst into laughter, followed by Magda and Krystyna.

'Hey, you tricked me, right? You monkeys, never ever will you get shakes from me again. I thought I'd die running here to you.'

'You'll learn not to be late so often,' noted Krystyna. 'But I must admit, it's good working with you guys. Magda bakes heavenly cakes, Alka brings delicious shakes, and it's a delight coming to the office.'

'If only there was no director, manager or accounting,' Alicja added sarcastically. 'It would be nearly perfect. But speaking of accounting –' she made a serious face to give a more dramatic effect to what she wanted to say '– an idea struck me about that flawed questionnaire. Actually, not me, but a guy named Jacek.'

'Which Jacek now?' asked Magda, slurping her shake. She relished observing Ala, who was a stark contrast to Magda. Alicja carried a joy, a vitality, always with a smile gracing her features. Her storm of blond curls seemed to bounce around her every time she sauntered sensuously through the office corridors. All in all, there probably wasn't a chap who wouldn't take a second glance at her. Tall, slender and mostly clad in dresses, she looked the epitome of femininity. It wasn't a wonder that she often found herself on romantic dates. However, none of the acquaintances lasted long enough for Alicja to venture into a more committed phase of a relationship. She insisted that not a single one, absolutely none, had swept her off her feet. Either the butterflies didn't flutter long enough, or merely the suitors turned out to be just handsome, well-built chaps, offering nothing beyond good looks. Thus, months and years rolled by. Alicja had amassed an impressive list of acquaintances, which she often made use of. For instance, if something broke at home, a call to an acquaintance who owned a renovation business would do – soon enough, one of his employees was on his way to Ala's. The same went for times when she needed a driver, an accountant and a police officer (a small fine for speeding). No wonder she found a chap for Excel sheets as well.

'Jacek is Krzysiek's brother. Anticipating your next question, Krzysiek is the neighbour from across, the taxi driver who always ferries you home from gatherings at mine. Getting back to the matter at hand, Jacek said we should review every line item again. Seems someone input a figure manually instead of letting the form do the maths. We need to show those gals that we are right, not them,' she said cheekily, glancing at the ladies in the room. 'We have over a thousand records to check. How shall we divide? Two hundred fifty each? I'll take the first, Krystyna up to five hundred, Gosia to seven hundred fifty, and you, Magda, to a thousand?'

'So columns G and L in every record, right?'

'Exactly, Gosieńka. If we don't find it, I'll share the sheet, and Jacek can have another look.'

'I can already imagine the looks on the faces of those accounting gals when we point out their system error,' Magda daydreamed.

'No daydreaming, only action! We know where to latch on.'

A few hours of perusing the sheets later, it was Alicja who broke the silence.

'I don't know about you, but I've had enough of these figures, tables and records. I'm hungry and dreaming of a proper lunch.'

'Good idea,' agreed Magda. 'I could do with a bite too. What shall we have? Chinese, kebab, sushi?'

'How about some croquettes with beetroot borscht? I've been craving some canteen flavours,' Alicja suggested.

'Are we all going downstairs, or is one of us fetching the grub? Great idea, it's been ages since I had such lunch,' Gosia chimed in.

'Better for one of us to go,' Krystyna added. 'The boss hasn't been around since the meeting, he could drop by any moment with updates.'

'I can go. Need to stop by the cashpoint for some cash anyway,' said Magda. 'Besides, I'd love to step out for a bit. Wonder why the boss isn't back yet. Could the meeting still be on?'

'If so, that only means one thing – another project and more work which we so dearly love.'

'Ala, don't scare us, alright?'

Krystyna looked towards the door as footsteps resonated just beyond. Moments later, the door swung open and in strode the boss. A man in his fifties, his grey hair emphasised his age. Tall and lean, his pronounced cheekbones rendered a somewhat grotesque appearance. Yet as soon as he spoke, his voice made everyone want to listen, and the unimpressive first impression gave way to a pleasant surprise. Though he knew how to harness the power of his voice, he quickly earned a nickname. Everyone called him HenRYK. For when Henryk roared, it set everyone to attention, and even the photocopier seemed to spring to life.

'Good afternoon, ladies. Don't think I've forgotten you, but the meeting ended later than expected. And you can surely deduce what that implies. A new project is on the horizon, which means more work for us. In two weeks, we have a meeting with the new partner. By then, we need to organise and divide the responsibilities. Primarily, we need one person responsible for contact. The director has an idea of how it'll be structured, but since he's already on annual leave, we'll have to wait for the meeting. A few words about the project: we are to create an online database for all municipalities in two provinces, which will be digitally connected.'

'Sounds straightforward … I guess. What are we tasked with?' queried Magda.

'Magda, I'd like you to handle the contact and information flow. It's crucial, and since you are never late –' he grinned at Alicja '– you are the most suitable person. Krystyna will handle the legal agreements, while Alicja and Gosia will provide support. Okay?'

'Sounds good, our favourite boss,' Ala smiled warmly.

'Ha ha ha, please, I won't fall for that charming smile of yours. One more tardiness and I'll report you to the director.'

'Even if I give you a piece of the best apple cake you've had in a while? A juicy apple charlotte, fragrant with cinnamon, which melts in the mouth and tantalises the senses …' Ala coquettishly smiled at the manager, handing him a plate with the cake. As she walked away, she swayed her hips more than usual. He stood there, oscillating his gaze between the tempting view of Alicja's backside and the cake, before regaining his composure.

'Alicja, Alicja … You are absolutely impossible. Thanks for the cake. If you need anything, I'll be at my desk.' He once again gazed at her lingeringly before exiting the room.

Shortly after, Gosia burst into laughter, followed by the rest of the girls.

'You've spun his head for the next few hours. The poor chap will have wet dreams. Now, what shall we get for lunch since he interrupted us? I fancy some *kopytka* today.'

'I've got an idea, let's have a Polish spread like we did with the sushi last time. We'll get four different dishes and share.'

'Brilliant. What shall we have besides croquettes and *kopytka*? Pork chop, cucumber salad, potatoes and ...?' inquired Magda, who offered to head to the *bar mleczny*.

'Let's go all out – add some fish, sauerkraut salad, and potatoes with dill. Sounds good?' Krystyna looked at the rest of the girls.

'World class. A feast fit for champions. I'll be back in a bit. Get the plates and cutlery ready.' And with that, Magda was gone.

A few minutes later, Alicja suddenly exclaimed, startling the girls.

'Yes! He's a genius!'

'Don't scare us! What did you find and who's brilliant?' Gosia asked.

'I found the error. Normally, when you change a cell in the formula, a series of digits, brackets and other gibberish shows up. But in the G247 version, only the amount appears. Someone manually removed and input the amount – precisely the difference reflected in the final balance.'

'You're right! It seems we'll triumph over the office this week. Let's not tell anyone until Friday. At 1:30 p.m. on Friday, we'll upload the corrected sheet with a note saying if someone doesn't know how to use the forms, we'll teach them, but they must not enter changes manually, as we'll identify every such manoeuvre and point out the mistake,' Krystyna proposed with a secretive smile.

'Why 1:30 p.m.?'

'Because the accounts department always wraps up at two o'clock on Fridays. If we upload it at one thirty, they won't have time to cook up anything new.'

'Vicious and clever. I like it. Krystyna, you've impressed me with this plan. It's a bit unlike you, but shrewd!'

'When it comes to the accounts department, I have no qualms anymore. They're nasty. Instead of coming over and saying something is wrong, they run straight to the director with complaints. Alright, if they can't talk it out again, we'll deal with them with their own weapon. We'll send the sheet to the main server with an appropriate note to everyone. At 1:30 p.m.'

'Divine in its simplicity,' Gosia noted. 'Where's Magda? I'm starving.'

After a moment, the door opened and Magda entered, carrying a bag stuffed with polystyrene containers full of warm food.

'Hey, you were supposed to have everything ready! I run for grub, and you can't even set the table? That's not fair ...'

'Alicja found the error in the spreadsheet, and we got a bit carried away devising a plan,' Gosia explained.

'Alright, honour restored. If that's the case, I'll set everything up.'

'No worries, we'll do it together.'

A few minutes later, they sat around the table at lunchtime, plotting Friday's revenge on the accountants and planning a feast for Saturday evening.

Krystyna stepped out of the clinic. Hunger gnawed at her. She had been undergoing tests as recommended by her doctor. Every year, she went through a series of pricks and scans, humorously dubbing it the 'service'. She believed birthdays were the best time to gift oneself a check-up to ensure everything was in order.

The February weather wasn't inviting for a stroll. A strong wind blew. The snow falling lightly turned into a swirling cloud that found its way into every uncovered nook of the body. She hunched over, pulled up her collar and marched forward. She knew that in a few steps she'd be greeted by a familiar scent. The Doughnut Shop, or rather the patisserie called Zagoździński's, was a legendary spot-on Warsaw's map. Ever since she could remember, this place had been familiar to her. Her father used to come here for doughnuts with his parents, then he brought his daughter, and now Krystyna came here with her children. There were thousands of such stories in Warsaw. Everyone who visited for the first time came on recommendation and remained a fan of the doughnuts from Górczewska Street forever.

Krystyna reached the crossroads. To her left, in the distance, there was an old building that still bore the memories of the Warsaw uprising. Bullet marks were still visible on its walls, a stark reminder of Warsaw's tumultuous history. The aroma of fried doughnuts hung in the air, another signature scent of the city. The chair placed beside the entrance was a clear signal for regulars that doughnuts were on sale. Krystyna confidently walked in, bought two dozen doughnuts, devoured two on the spot, and, thus laden, headed to the office.

'Good morning, lovely ladies. I have something for you,' announced Krystyna as she walked into the office.

'Let me guess, doughnuts from Zagoździński's? Nothing smells quite like them,' remarked Alicja, standing up to brew some coffee. 'Admit it, how many did you eat on the spot? I always get two because one is never enough. And though I know it's a gazillion calories, I just can't help myself,' she chuckled, spooning coffee into mugs. Gosia approached the table and began arranging the doughnuts.

'One box for us, the other I'm taking home. Do you reckon the accounting department suspects anything?' probed Krystyna, sipping her hot coffee in small gulps.

'I doubt it. They looked quite pleased with themselves this morning. I ran into them while signing the list. One of them muttered something like "Oh, it's Friday already, and the error still hasn't been found",' said Magda. 'But I didn't let on anything. Let them think what they want. Have we got the note ready for the server?'

'Hand me a piece of paper and a pen; with this sugar rush, I am in the mood for preparing a lovely card for those nasty women,' Alicja was in a combative mood. Gosia handed her the requested items.

'Let's write something like "If you can't use the form, don't, or come over for training. We'll teach you",' Magda quickly chipped in.

'Oh, come on, too weak. They won't grasp the irony. Let's be sarcastic: "Working in accounting, one should be able to handle spreadsheets. In the twenty first century, it's as basic as the abacus once was. If your room is still stuck in the medieval era, we invite you for tutorials. We'd love to introduce you to modern technology so that no record will keep its secrets from you."'

'Alicja, it's supposed to be a work memo, not a declaration of the World War III,' Krystyna laughed.

'There's no fun with your lot,' Alicja said, feigning a pout. 'It would at least be amusing; something would be happening.'

When the long-awaited hour arrived, Krystyna uploaded the latest file version to the server – along with the memo. The memo was pleasant enough not to cause another earthquake in the office, but it still clearly stated that the error was due to the accounts department's actions. The note was crafted by Krystyna, who apparently wasn't too sugar-rushed.

Alicja stood on the balcony, looking out for her friends. They had planned a gathering for the evening with wine, jazz and gossip. Occasionally, they would include their partners in these meet-ups, but it wasn't the best idea as the evening got dominated by the English league matches. So, they stuck to the tried and tested formula – just the four of them and wine, jazz and a break from all the games, projects and problems. After a moment, she saw a taxi pulling up to the block and the girls getting off. As was customary for such get-togethers, they quickly ordered some food, made themselves comfortable on Alicja's sofa and chairs, and dove into gossip. Once everyone had been discussed and a momentary silence descended, Alicja spoke up.

'We absolutely must make a toast!' She leapt up and headed to the kitchen. After a short while, she returned with a chilled bottle of champagne and four tall, slender glasses.

'Phew, that's a real Möet. What's the occasion? Or do you simply want us to have a giant hangover tomorrow?' inquired Gosia, sipping cranberry juice in the meantime.

'No, sweetie, I just want us to be happy, close all unnecessary doors and open up to new experiences.'

'Something in the form of a resolution one makes at the end of the year?' Magda chimed in, approaching the chest of drawers where candles were. She lit them and looked at the room through half-closed eyes. 'Now it's okay,' she remarked and walked towards the large corner sofa occupying half the room. 'I reckon you got such a colossal sofa so we could all fit on it.'

Krystyna burst into laughter.

'Not at all! She got it so she could shag in any arrangement! Alka will do anything to feel good.' Saying this, she turned to Ala and stuck out her tongue.

'You lot are wicked, so the first toast is mine.'

'Does this mean each of us will say a wish and it will come true?' Magda cunningly looked at her friends and with a faux-serious expression, proclaimed, 'In that case, I want to eat cakes for a whole month, not just on the first day of my period, and not gain a single gramme.'

'I wish for a sale at Molier's once a month,' Gosia followed.

'Ha, ha, ha, then I want men to pick up all their socks lying on the floor and toss them in the laundry basket,' added Krystyna, laughing out loud.

Alicja swept her gaze over everyone, rested her hand on her hip and addressed them in a no-nonsense tone.

'While I believe they'll invent a non-fattening sweet cream and that at Molier's they will have sales on the latest Gucci collections at ninety per cent off, I'll never believe that guys will stop marking territory. You've had your chances and made your jokes. Now I'm starting seriously.' She lifted her glass and looked at them but seemed to see nothing.

'I want things to remain as they are. I am not ready for all those declarations, steady relationships, or all that comes with them. I can't even imagine it. Everything should stay as it is. Let it be!' She drained her glass.

Krystyna rose from her seat with a glass in hand.

'I want it to be like it used to be. To bring back what was, but got lost along the way. Let it be!' She, too, drained her glass.

Magda quizzically looked at Gosia, who, with a nod, signalled it was her turn.

'I'll drink to have peace in my life, for the past not to return, to memories fading and giving way to new, good thoughts.' Seeing the genuine interest of the girls, she stretched out her hand to signal that it wasn't a good time for questions. 'I promise I'll tell you, but I'm not ready yet. Let it happen!' She drank her toast and looked at Gosia.

'Now it's my turn.' They saw tears rolling down her cheeks. 'I want my one and biggest dream to come true. I want to hug my child. I want to feel its scent, have sleepless nights, sore nipples and stretch marks on my belly. I want to experience everything every mother experiences, but it's not given to me,' she added almost whisperingly. 'Let it be! No, don't hug me now. I'll fall apart,' she protested softly yet firmly when she noticed they wanted to comfort her. They respected that and gave her time for all the tears that needed to find their way out that day to flow calmly. After a moment, she wiped her eyes, smudging mascara on half her cheek.

'Now you've gone too far. You look like an Ethiopian emerging from a rainforest after a victorious battle,' Alicja remarked, glancing at Krystyna.

'An Ethiopian from a rainforest? Do you even know where Ethiopia is, Alka?' inquired Magda, and Krystyna nodded in agreement.

'Don't you challenge my comparisons and terminology here.'

'I can never stop wondering where you get these comparisons from,' Magda said, laughing as she walked to Gosia. She handed her a mirror and a tissue. 'Wipe off your victorious makeup, Ethiopian.'

'Oh fuck! I do look as if I had been in some battle. This was supposed to be waterproof mascara. What the hell did this idiot buy me?' Gosia grabbed her bag, searching for the culprit. In a moment, she pulled out a beautiful pink mascara package.

Seeing this, Magda burst into laughter.

'Surely, this is water-based mascara. I bought the same for Krystyna's daughter so the young one could practise. But whatever it is, it's certainly safe for the eyes.'

'First and foremost, we should wish that guys learnt to read the shopping lists we give them,' Krystyna declared, sipping her champagne.

'I'll sooner believe that my Aunt Geńka will come to terms with my spinsterhood than that men will start to do exactly what we ask them to,' Alicja pointed out sharply, getting absorbed in her thoughts.

Single womanhood. The stale word knocked her off balance. She despised it. It carried a fatal tune. It reminded her of an old, eccentric woman dressed in faded dresses, talking aloud to herself or to cats. She always referred to herself as single, which sounded much more pleasant, even cosmopolitan to her ears. Yet this term, frequently used by her family, suddenly painted a picture of an old, lonely woman in her mind, and it frightened her. Did she really want to be alone forever? She glanced at the rest of the girls. Gosia was engrossed in a conversation with Magda and didn't catch her questioning gaze. Krysia had her back turned to everyone while browsing through Alicja's rich record collection. It was more than certain that Armstrong would be played in a moment. As the first notes of 'What a Wonderful World' filled the room, Ala smiled to herself. Wonderful world. Was it really as wonderful as they had wished for? Was the toast they had raised truly what she wanted, or yet another attempt at tilting at windmills? To prove to everyone at any cost that she could be both alone and happy? *On top of it, I got drunk in a gloomy mood*, she thought. She glanced at the clock on the wall, ticking away every fleeting second of her life.

The morning greeted Gosia with a snowstorm. It must have been snowing for several hours, as the entire city was enshrouded in a white quilt of fluff. The snow-covered trees added a fairytale aura to the scene. Gosia stood by the window, waiting for Piotr to emerge from the bathroom. She was ready. Or at least she appeared to be.

'Gosieńka, are you ready?' asked Piotr, examining her sideways.

'Yeeeah …' she drawled, but after a moment, with a more lively voice, added: 'Yes, I'm ready. Let's do this. Why do you keep asking?'

'You seemed lost in thought? I thought you had drifted off somewhere.'

'That's true. As I looked out of the window, I remembered when I was little and I used to imagine being like Snow Queen. And it's almost like a fairytale …' Her voice trailed off as she gazed at the white trees.

'Why almost?' Piotr asked, moving closer.

'Do you think any girl dreams that she'll have a prince from a fairy tale, but to get pregnant, she'll have to undergo another round of in vitro?'

'Darling, if you think you're not ready for this, just tell me. We'll call everything off. Do you need more time? Want to change the date?'

'No! It's just that not everything can be like a fairy tale or how we dream it to be. It's these medications and hormones making me so sentimental. I'm ready, we can leave.' She buttoned up her coat and looked at Piotr expectantly. He looked at her for a moment but then briskly walked past her and opened the door.

'Let's do it! And then we'll go for a delightful lunch, a stroll, some shopping, whatever you fancy! Unless you'd rather stay in, that's fine, too. We'll lie in, order some food and watch a film. Okay?'

'We'll see how I feel,' she decided, and without waiting for the lift, they both descended the stairs to the car.

Driving through the city in the morning hours was a tiring experience. Especially on a day when a significant amount of snow had fallen and when half the residents were suddenly trying to reach the other end of Warsaw. On the way to the clinic, they remained silent. Everything had been discussed in every possible way, leaving nothing more to be said. The only thing left to do was reach the destination, step into the office, undergo the procedure and wait for the test result in three weeks. They knew the order of the procedures, they knew exactly what to do and how to proceed. Yet, on the day of fertilisation, they became silent. Each was in their own world, guarding access to their thoughts meticulously. So it was on that day. They arrived at the clinic and parked the car. Piotr paid the parking meter, and shoulder to shoulder, they walked inside, where their doctor was already waiting.

An hour later, they were sitting in the car, wondering what to do next. Both had taken the day off from work and had a few hours of free time ahead with virtually no idea of how to spend the day. According to the doctor's assurances, the procedure went by the book. After the fertilisation, Gosia rested on a recliner for half an hour with Piotr sitting beside her. They held hands yet stayed silent. They understood how it might look. They were going through this whole process for the third time and knew that what initially had the potential of elating might turn into a terrible pain of loss a few weeks later. After forty minutes, they said goodbye to the doctor and headed to the car.

The silence in the car was broken by Piotr.

'It's so beautiful outside. Since we're playing truant, why don't we head to Łazienki? We'll stroll around the park, feed the squirrels with nuts, and if we get hungry, we can go somewhere for lunch. You mentioned today was like a fairy tale. And with a fairy tale comes a palace and my princess,' he said tenderly to Gosia.

'You know what? You surprised me, but that's a brilliant idea. Probably the worst thing we could do is go home and remain silent, pondering on what will come out of this. Let's go to Łazienki. A walk will do us good.'

After a few minutes' drive through the city, Piotr parked the car at the entrance to the park. They stopped at a nearby kiosk to buy some nuts for the squirrels. Although it was noon, the park was full of walkers who had come with the same intention to this enclave of peace and quiet, an oasis of white and purity in the middle of a bustling city. Walking around the park, they bought hot chocolate, and with steaming cups, they roamed the paths, tossing nuts to the squirrels every few minutes.

'I don't know about you, but I'm hungry. I forgot how tiring it is to walk through these snowdrifts,' said Gosia.

'What are you in the mood for? Which cuisine?'

'Polish cuisine. I fancy traditional Polish cuisine. Can we afford a meal at the Belvedere?'

'I think our budget can handle it, but till the end of the year, it's bread and water for us. Ha, ha, ha, don't worry, it was planned. I heard they have delicious tartare and sturgeon here. I am going to try them.'

'And I'll see what's on the menu.'

As they entered the restaurant, the waiter appeared as if on cue. He led them to a table and left menus, suggesting wine for the drink. They both opted for water and delved into the menus. Gosia spoke first.

'I'm so hungry I could eat everything, but for starters, I'll go for duck and plum dumplings. Sounds delightful. I hope it comes quickly. What about you, tartare?'

'Definitely the tartare, followed by lamb shank with white beans, tomatoes, vanilla and sauce.'

'I'm even hungrier now. So with the duck dumplings, I'll also have the sturgeon sirloin with brussels sprouts, bacon, buttery potatoes and Breton sauce. And for dessert, gingerbread with sour cherries, dark chocolate and almonds.'

Seeing Piotr's amused face, she added, 'What? You said I'm a princess. You should have the cheesecake with white chocolate, mandarins and pistachios. We'll see which one is better.'

An hour later, as they exited the restaurant, Gosia was in high spirits.

'I haven't eaten so well in a long time,' she said. 'World-class. They truly know how to host and serve real culinary artistry. I give them a ten on my six-point scale.'

'A ten?' Piotr chuckled.

'Yes, a full ten. I enjoyed it very much. You can take me here for dinner every week.'

'As you wish, Your Highness,' he bowed before Gosia and offered his arm on the way to the car.

'Now you're talking sense, sir. That's how it should be every day.'

The afternoon and evening passed in a pleasant atmosphere. They knew the procedures; they knew that for the next few weeks sex was off the table, so they snuggled up to each other and fell asleep.

In the morning, there was even more snow, and the frost decided to have the last word in this winter season that was coming to an end.

As they drove to work, Piotr asked Gosia, 'How are you feeling? After the day off yesterday, I don't really feel like going to work today, especially just for one day. I could have taken two days off. Even the boss suggested it. Maybe we could call in and figure something out?'

'Very responsible for future parents,' Gosia chuckled, reaching for her phone. A moment later, she heard Krystyna's voice.

'Hey, Krysia, am I particularly indispensable today? I'm asking sincerely because, one, we want to play truant, and two, we don't feel like going to work for just one day …'

'You're not indispensable; I'll mark you on leave and you can drop the application at the secretariat later. No stress. Everything okay?'

'Yes, everything's fine. Just sometimes we don't feel like being adults.'

'Have fun, say hi to Piotr for me.'

Gosia passed on Piotr's greetings to Krystyna and hung up. 'Now it's your turn.'

Piotr chose the number and within a few sentences, the matter was settled.

'So what do we do on such a beautiful Friday? Where are we going?'

'Since we have three days off, why not somewhere further? What does your highness desire?' Piotr asked.

'Fish, and since we have plenty of time, I want to eat that fish by the sea.'

'You're taking this fairy tale too far, you know? I just asked, and you immediately have me drive halfway across Poland,' Piotr noted, turning onto Wisłostrada. 'As you wish, Your Highness.'

'You brought this on yourself, now you deal with it. I've grown accustomed to my role. And stop at a petrol station on the way for a hot dog. There's no seaside trip without a hot dog from a petrol station.'

'Damn, I should have called you Cinderella yesterday. It would have been cheaper.'

'You pig, ha, ha, ha!'

A few hours later, they arrived in Sopot in high spirits and checked into the Grand Hotel.

After checking in, they went shopping as they had arrived at the seaside completely unprepared. They bought two pairs of jeans, sweatshirts and some underwear, and then they headed for fresh fish at a restaurant. Unfortunately, the weather wasn't encouraging for a walk by the sea, so they spent the evening in bed, watching TV and eating cake from a nearby bakery.

'I think I'll take a shower. The air here has worn me out. I feel sleepy,' Piotr said, rising from the bed. 'Do you want to use the bathroom?'

'You're inviting me?' Gosia asked with a playful smile.

'We can't make love …'

'Who's talking about making love? I'm just asking if I should come with you.'

'Why ask when you know the answer?' Piotr said and pecked her on her forehead. He walked into the bathroom; shortly after, Gosia heard the shower running. She undressed, put on a hotel robe and stepped into the steam-filled bathroom, struggling to make out shapes. She slipped off her robe and joined Piotr. Seeing her naked, he smiled and extended his hand, pulling her under the warm water stream.

'We can't …' he started as Gosia's hands caressed his penis.

'I just wanted to remind you that I didn't have the procedure done on my mouth. And it's warm and moist in there, just the way you like.' She rubbed her bare bosom against his torso. Her firm breasts and erect nipples teased him. Getting on her knees, she brushed her breasts against his stomach and manhood before kneeling and taking him into her mouth, her hand making gentle strokes. Piotr moaned loudly. He placed his hands on her head, guiding the rhythm. She looked at his face. Even in the steam, she could see and feel that the end was near. Piotr's climax came swiftly. He needed a moment to recover, then helped Gosia to her feet. She wiped her mouth with the back of her hand.

'From now on, call me goddess.'

She put the hotel robe back on and left.

When nearly two weeks later the pregnancy test turned out positive, they decided to approach the early stage of pregnancy with less euphoria. They were well acquainted with the procedure and knew that weeks of anxiety lay ahead. Anything could happen. They only informed their parents and Gosia's girlfriends about the pregnancy. They believed that the joy and celebration of pregnancy had to wait a while longer.

Krystyna was on the tram to work. She had once again quarrelled with Krzysztof. She just wanted to cuddle up to him in the morning. She missed the closeness, the tenderness, let alone the real intimacy. Once again, she was pushed away and called names. She felt powerless. She wanted to find out why Krzysztof behaved the way he did. Why he pushed her away without saying a word. He avoided the conversation; he avoided her. The phone rang. Gosia needed a day off. She was grateful to be able to focus her thoughts on something other than her marriage for a while. She was the first to arrive at the office. She put the kettle on. Before the water had boiled, Alicja walked in.

'Hey, how's it going? Did you put more water on? I'm knackered. I spent half the night texting this bloke. We'd met a few times before, but he had to leave Warsaw for a contract, and long-distance relationships are a parody,' said Alicja.

While Alicja was talking, Krystyna pretended to be interested, but her thoughts were still far away, with her own problems.

'And almost six months passed until suddenly he texts me saying he's back in Warsaw for good and would like to meet up. We'll see how it goes.' Alicja smiled to herself. 'But I guess I'm boring you? Something happened?' She took a closer look at Krystyna.

'Just a morning argument with the husband. A trifle. It threw me off balance, but I'm steadying myself,' Krystyna quickly added, trying to change the topic, 'Gosia took today off. They decided to de-stress and went for a weekend to Sopot.'

'Alright. I won't pry further. Getting back to Gosia, I wish I could do the same. Lounging in a hotel and doing nothing for a few days. Just think about it. Where's Magda? I'm here, but she's not?'

Alicja didn't have to wait long; Magda appeared in the doorway moments later.

'Oh my, what a crash happened on Aleje Jerozolimskie! Trams derailed, blocking the entire roundabout. I thought I'd be late, but our director happened to be driving by and gave me a lift.'

'Oh darling, you've got some nice connections!' Alicja began teasing Magda, mostly trying to cheer Krystyna up. 'Do you also carpool after work?'

'You're nuts, you know?' Magda laughed. 'Where's Gosia?'

'She's jetted off to Sopot. Without us, said nothing to us.'

'That swine,' Magda winked at Alicja. 'We must send her a picture to make her jealous that she's not here.'

'Then she'll send us a picture from Sopot, and we'll be even more jealous that we're not there. This stick has two short ends.'

'True … So, shall we start work?' Magda said, taking a sip of coffee.

'Must do,' Krystyna nodded and delved into the abyss of contracts.

Friday passed by calmly and Krystyna left work in a significantly better mood. She called her dad and they decided to go on a day trip to Kazimierz together. Krzysztof, as always, had other work-related plans and couldn't reschedule them. On one hand, she was concerned about their drifting apart. On the other, she was getting used to his absence.

On Saturday, from early in the morning, Alicja was preparing for the evening date. Every face mask and body scrub she had was employed. Even her hair received special treatment. She cleaned her house, lit a set of her favourite candles and dispersed the essence using a diffuser. Her apartment was to resonate with her persona. At the stipulated hour, she hailed a cab and rode to one of the finer restaurants in town for dinner with a long-unseen acquaintance. The place, as always, was bustling with people. She recognised a few faces from the first pages of newspapers. They were allocated a table somewhat on the side, away from other tables, yet its seclusion lent a sense of intimacy. The waiter poured them wine and left them with the menus to leisurely make their choice. Alicja observed Kamil. He was well-built, almost athletic. His dark hair was tied back in a ponytail, and the perfectly shaved beard accentuated his immaculate appearance.

'What do you fancy?' Kamil inquired, examining Alicja closely.

'I've heard they do perfect steaks here. I'll have a medium-rare steak, salad and seasonal vegetables. What about you?'

'I'll take a steak too, rare, with Hollandaise sauce and asparagus.' Kamil hailed the waiter, placed the order and turned to Alicja.

'Now, tell me, what's been happening with you over these last months? Are you still the independent, enigmatic Alicja as in the past?'

He gazed at her with undisguised curiosity.

She smiled flirtatiously and said, 'Well, being Alicja, I must play the part. But in all seriousness, nothing has changed. I'm still single by choice and have no plans to change that. Things are good as they are. Perhaps I haven't met anyone who could enthral me enough to leave my solitary life.'

'That's not the answer I was expecting. I thought since we are dining together, there might be something more,' he calmly retorted, though Alicja detected disappointment in his voice.

'Mhmmm, we agreed to have dinner as good friends, nothing more. You know me, you can't pressure me into anything,' she said, emphasising the latter part of her statement. She felt disappointed with Kamil's stance.

'Beautiful Alicja, don't get riled up, please. I was just asking. I find you quite appealing, and I don't want you to pull another stunt like the last time.'

'What do you mean by "pull a stunt"?' She put down her cutlery. Her appetite dwindled, and so did her desire for Kamil's company.

'We were supposed to go away together, and you left me right before the trip!' His voice became coarse, and he looked at her with angry eyes. Alicja, wishing to calm herself, looked around the room. In the distance, she recognised a colleague from another department who she frequently collaborated with. She smiled at him. Kamil didn't miss that.

'We are dining together, discussing our future, and you are shamelessly flirting with others?' he said, increasingly raising his voice.

'Discussing our future? What are you rambling on about, man? What future? I've always told you that I'm not interested in any steady relationship. And after tonight, I am even more certain.' She frantically looked around the room and upon spotting the waiter, she hastily beckoned him over.

He approached briskly and addressed Alicja, 'Anything else, miss?'

'I'd like the bill for my meal. Can my food be packed to go?'

'Of course. I'll bring the bill and pack your meal right away. Anything else?' said the waiter, and was about to take her plate when Kamil sharply reacted.

'Alicja, don't make a scene! And finish your meal immediately, I will pay for it!' His aggressive tone reverberated throughout the hall.

'Could I wait in the back for a taxi? I don't feel safe with this Neanderthal from Wąchock.'

She stood up from the table. So did Kamil, but at that very moment, two bouncers appeared and escorted Alicja to the back. She glimpsed that two waiters were keeping an eye on Kamil.

In the back, she paid for her dinner, collected the packed steak and, accompanied by a security guard, got into the taxi. Only back at home did she discover that she had received a fresh portion of meat and vegetables and a piece of cake with a note from the head chef. Walking through her living room, she saw her phone on the table. There was a blinking envelope icon and several notifications. She picked up the phone and, with one swipe, dismissed all notifications from Kamil. She blocked his number. She hesitated slightly, but after a moment, she called Magda.

'Hey darling, what are you up to?' she asked.

'Nothing exciting. Watching some silly game show. Aren't you on your date?'

'I fled from it, escorted out by security. It's a long story. Fancy spending Saturday evening with me, with a tub of ice cream and a bottle of wine? I am not feeling too secure after my escape and wouldn't fancy being alone now. Could you come over?'

'Oh, I see, an evening filled with stories lies ahead. Sure, I'll pack a second bottle of wine and will be right over.'

'Thank you, and could you stay over till tomorrow?'

'Of course, I won't leave you alone. I'll pack my pyjamas, get some more wine, and head over to yours. Don't open the door for anyone. If I need to buzz the intercom, I'll call you from below first.'

After nearly forty minutes, Magda called Alicja to say she was downstairs and would buzz the intercom shortly. As soon as she came in, Magda was surprised at Alicja's distress. They opened the wine and the ice cream, settled on the sofa and Alicja began recounting her tale. Magda was a good listener. She waited patiently for her friend to finish her story before she started asking questions.

'Was this Kamil always so possessive?'

'No, he was assertive, but never possessive. Or perhaps, I never noticed.' Alicja mused for a moment. 'He may have had a choleric streak, but not to this extent.'

'Scary to think of what could have happened next. Have you deleted his number from your phone?'

'I have. Deleted, blocked, and when I entered the building, I asked the security not to tell anyone where I lived. Luckily, he had never been to my place before. I only mentioned which neighbourhood I live in once. There are over sixty blocks here. He can search all he wants. The security will surely not disclose where I live. Besides, I don't think he would remember.'

'What a twit he turned out to be. I can't imagine living with such a control freak. Actually, I can't imagine living with anyone at all,' she looked at Alicja. She had always admired her for her courage, zest for life, and everything she herself never had. And today, she got to see another side of her friend.

'I said something to that effect when I left.'

'Can imagine, one of your famous analogies?' Magda inquired further.

'I called him a Neanderthal from Wąchock.'

'Ha, ha, ha, Neanderthal? Alright, but, blimey, where did you get Wąchock from?' Magda was clearly amused. 'If not an Ethiopian from a rainforest, then a Neanderthal from Wąchock!'

'My imagination doesn't concern itself with such absurdities as geographical boundaries,' Alicja slightly relaxed.

'Definitely no boundaries there.' Both burst out laughing.

After a few minutes, Alicja placed her hand on Magda's and said, 'Thank you for coming, for listening to me. You are lovely. And if you want, you can choose any film we'll watch together.'

'Alright, but it needs to be a film that's a feast for the eyes.'

'We have limited choices then because you never see the entire bloke in any film. Just their chest and perhaps their arse. And pornography might be better watched on your own,' Alicja pointed out cheerfully.

'You're spot on. By the way, whoever came up with the rule that peckers shouldn't be shown must have had a microscopic one himself.'

'True. When they show a woman in a film, it's no problem; they show all of her naked body and that's fine. But when there's a scene with a naked man, the shot goes only down to the abdomen. God forbid they show hair below the belly or even the arse. I, for one, would like to see what a Wesley Snipes looks like from the front, not just from behind. Although, he does have a really nice arse,' Magda mused.

'Where did you see Wesley Snipes's arse?' Alicja probed. 'I want to see too! We'll pause on the right frame and admire. Who knows, maybe something might jiggle?'

'We can always watch the appropriate scenes in slow motion. The film is *Money Train*. Jennifer Lopez and Woody Harrelson also star in it.'

'She's so pretty. There's another film that's on my mind … and there you really see a lot, because, for a moment in a pool, you see Bruce Willis's penis. Or his stunt double, but you see it,' Alicja assured earnestly.

'I haven't seen that film. What's the title?'

'*Colour of Night*. An old film. A classic of the nineties, in my opinion.'

'So now we have two. I'll get the ice cream and you get the wine.'

'You know what, I have an idea,' said Alicja, stopping Magda. 'Come on, let's get into our pyjamas. We'll be more comfortable, we'll settle in our spots and cover ourselves with blankets. It'll be like a mini pyjama party.'

'A mini pyjama party with a background search for peckers?'

'If we aren't getting any action today, we might as well look,' said Alicja, laughing.

'Speaking of which, going back to the whole Kamil thing …' Magda had already settled in her chair, dressed in her pyjamas. She wrapped herself in a blanket and waited for Alicja, who was just starting to set up her spot and of course had to comment on it in her own style.

'I'm fussing with this wine and ice cream like a hen on a perch after a morning cock-a-doodle-do with the rooster. What about Kamil?'

'You were divine. Intriguing, mysterious, slightly cruel, but mega classy.'

'I know! Let's get sweatshirts with GODDESS printed on them,' exclaimed Alicja, leaping to her feet. 'Brilliant idea, Magda!'

'It wasn't my idea, and honestly, as always, I can't keep up with your ideas.' Magda watched with interest as Alicja, in her skimpy pyjamas, paced around the room. The shorts barely covered her firm buttocks, enticingly swaying to the rhythm of her steps.

'But you said I was divine, intriguing and mysterious. Krystyna has a very good taste, you have perfect facial features and Gosia … Mhmmm, she's inspiring.' Alicja looked at Magda until she got the hint.

'I fear I'm still not getting what you're on about,' Magda observed Alicja, who in turn was studying Magda. Eventually, they both burst into laughter.

'One more time. Focus! We are divine, cruel, brilliant, inspiring, unpredictable, intriguing. Who's that?' Alicja bore into Magda with her gaze.

'You? Sorry, I still don't understand.'

'All these words are attributes of a goddess.' Seeing Magda still puzzled, Alicja emphasised, 'We are goddesses.

We don't feel the need to be queens or princesses. I'll make us sweatshirts with that printed on them.'

'And mugs too?' Magda adored the cool mugs that Alicja designed herself and had made at a nearby studio.

'I'll make mugs, too, for each of you. And for myself, of course. But I'll focus mainly on the sweatshirts. I believe next month we will have a working Saturday, so we can wear less formal outfits to work. That's when we'll sport our GODDESS sweatshirts.'

'Rad idea, but I still have no clue how you came up with it. You're one in a million.'

'Madzia, so are you. Now, let's sit on our Olympus and gaze upon the divine *derrière* of Snipes.'

Several weeks later, the girls, wearing those very sweatshirts, crossed the threshold of the office. The sweatshirts came in different colours, matching their complexion and beauty. Alicja had gone wild with the design. The word GODDESS was placed vertically, and next to each letter, she inscribed a corresponding attribute. She also brought new mugs for each of the girls, with creative phrases of her own design.

Krystyna lazily rolled onto her other side, paying no heed to the alarm clock. She always set it a few minutes earlier than she had to get up. She liked to lie in peace instead of springing up at the last moment. She glanced at the sleeping Krzysztof. He lay on his back, his face turned towards her. She snuggled up to him gently, craving a bit of tenderness and closeness. She could not recall when they were really close to each other last, let alone had sex. The last quickie happened five months earlier, and it wasn't the most successful intercourse in the world. She couldn't remember the last time she had an orgasm. She realised it shouldn't be like this, but she lacked the courage to ask Krzysztof for reasons. It was an issue hanging between them, but neither broached the subject. Out of fear or concern? She couldn't define it. She laid her head on his shoulder and began to gently scratch his chest.

'Get up, sleepyhead, it's already six. Hey, snoozer!' Her fingers massaged him gently, dancing on his chest, circling lower and lower. 'Shall we make the most of this quiet moment while the kids are asleep?'

Krzysztof opened his eyes, looked coldly at his wife, pushed her hand away and hurriedly got up from the bed.

'I need to be at work early today. I don't have time for such nonsense. By the way, you could do with growing up a bit. Pretending to be a dignified office lady, yet you behave like a common floozy. I don't like it!'

'What? It's you who has been avoiding intimacy with me for months. It's surely normal for two healthy individuals to have sex, don't you think?'

He had hurt her. She didn't want to admit, even to herself, how deeply.

'Can you tell me why our bedroom has only been a place for sleep for the past few months? It used to be entirely different. What's going on? Why don't you want to talk about it?'

'I just don't want to make love with you. That's all. I've grown bored. And I don't understand why you can't accept that.' he looked at her arrogantly, checking to see if the words he'd spoken inflicted the pain he'd anticipated.

'You're bored?' She knew the meaning of the phrase, but it didn't resonate. She asked in a whisper, not wanting him to hear the pain in her voice.

'Yes!' he shouted. 'Now hurry up, get up, sort yourself out and prepare my breakfast and lunch for work. I'm off on a business trip today and won't be back until Monday, straight to work. I need to have something to eat today.'

'You must be joking? Since when do you go on business trips over the weekends? It was never like this! Do you have someone? Are you screwing some secretary at the company?' Krystyna was losing her composure.

'Can you think of anything else besides fucking?! You act like a whore!' he hissed and left the room.

She sat alone on the bed. She didn't recognise him. This wasn't the man she met a long time ago and loved. Lately, every conversation they had ended in a row during which he desperately sought to insult her, to make her feel like rubbish.

She approached the chest of drawers and pulled out clean underwear. At first, she grabbed the lacy knickers that came to hand, but a moment later, she switched them for old cotton ones that she kept for those days when menstruation was particularly gruelling, as they were ideal for large sanitary pads. To match, she chose a flesh-toned cotton bra and a plain navy dress, which had been hanging in the wardrobe for several years now. While brushing her teeth, she looked in the mirror as if to confirm that the woman she was now was real. Perhaps she expected to see someone else? But she saw a faded woman whose best moments in life were already behind her, and now only a blanket in the living room and no entertainment awaited her. With difficulty, she emerged from the bathroom, already dressed. In the kitchen, the twins were already waiting and, as usual, quarrelling over their seats at the table. Surprisingly, this time, Krzysztof reacted to their whims. The morning passed peacefully from that moment on.

'Mum, what are we doing this weekend?' Patrycja asked. 'Are we going anywhere?'

'No, Dad's going on a business trip and won't be back until Monday after work. We'll be on our own. On Saturday, we'll go to Grandpa's and take him for a walk. Maybe we'll go somewhere for ice cream or pizza baguettes.'

'Super duper,' said Patryk.

'Don't talk silly,' Pati snapped irritably.

Krystyna's twins differed in every way. In appearance, as for fraternal twins, they were a textbook example of how vast the differences could be. Patryk was a dark-haired boy, well-built for a fourteen-year-old. He preferred spending his time outside with friends or at various sports clubs. This was his passion, and Krystyna and Krzysztof supported him in it. Sport, besides building up fitness, also fortified character, which was a desired trait. They preferred him to spend his free time outdoors, even if just playing football with his mates, rather than sitting all day in front of the computer playing virtually. He was keen on studying, finding no trouble in learning. They suspected that if Patryk devoted more time to his studies, he would receive more A's and A* grades. However, their son claimed that he was spending enough time at school and didn't need to dedicate more of it to studying at home, reading unnecessary things. He was completely satisfied with an average grade of B – as long as he had the merit badge, his mum and dad were pleased and didn't restrict him in any way when it came to sports.

Patrycja enjoyed studying and attending most of the thematic clubs available at their school. She willingly participated in all sorts of competitions and 'Olympiads', which she often won with ease. She was short, slender, with ashy blond hair. Her favourite pastime was engaging in discussions, especially with Grandpa, who adored his little smarty, as he called her. The twins argued about everything, giving the impression that it was their additional hobby. Yet, a moment later, they would shut themselves in a room to share secrets.

'I'll talk however I want since I'm older than you.' said Patryk.

'By a whole three minutes, you donkey!'

'Could you two calm down? I don't fancy listening to your quarrels first thing in the morning!' Krystyna, after her morning squabble with Krzysztof, was not in the mood for the idle chatter of teenagers.

'How can you talk to the children like that? You don't want to listen to your own children? What kind of mother are you? Wonder what you're in the mood for? But we cleared that up earlier this morning, didn't we? Maybe it's time to focus on something else?!'

Krzysztof glanced at Krystyna from the corner of his eye. His look was cold, almost aggressive. The children fell silent, surprised, not knowing what was going on. Krystyna tried to compose herself; she didn't want to burst out in front of them. She got up from the table to clean up after breakfast and tucked the dishes into the dishwasher while the twins stored the food in the refrigerator. Only Krzysztof sat there, observing the whole situation with an arrogant smile on his face, which Krystyna didn't even want to analyse.

'So, if Dad's going on a business trip, how will we get to school? Are we taking a taxi?' Patryk inquired.

'No need, my boy, I'll gladly drive you both to school and Mum to work,' Krzysztof said with a smile as though nothing had happened.

'Super duper.' The son beamed.

'Ass,' Pati chipped in.

'Only calm will save us. Grab your backpacks. Darling, are you ready?' The last thing Krystyna was dreaming of now was a drive across half the town in the car with Krzysztof. She was astonished by his erratic moods. *I'll just hop out of the car before I murder this eunuch*, she thought. With an ironic smile, she looked at Krzysiek and said, 'I am just grabbing my little bag, and we'll jump into the car.'

The ride to school wasn't without verbal skirmishes between the twins.

'Mum! He's sitting on my side and breathing on me!'

'I'm not breathing on you! This part of the air is mine!' With a flamboyant gesture, Patryk showed his sister where his share of air was.

'Don't come near me. Mum, he's encroaching on my seat space to ogle that busty blonde walking by on the pavement!'

'That's not true! I'm too young to be interested in women. I was just looking at the car. It was a Ford Mustang!!!' Patryk retorted swiftly.

'Stop bickering. It's unbearable to listen to. I'm off on a business trip, so you'll be staying with Mum. When you get off, I'll give you money for kebabs; you can grab some on your way home. That way, Mum won't have to stand in the kitchen right after work to cook you dinner. But the rest of the drive must be peaceful.' Krzysztof glanced at the rearview mirror to see if the twins had obeyed. Each sat on their side, noses glued to the window. They told him a polite goodbye at school and waited with hands stretched out towards their father. He pulled out a note for each and handed it over. 'Just make sure there's peace at home over the weekend, understood?'

'Yes, Dad', the twins replied in unison and waved their parents goodbye.

The drive to Krystyna's work was enveloped in perfect silence. Neither of them spoke a word. A thousand questions swirled in her mind, seeking answers, yet she asked none. For the day, she had had enough humiliation and savoured the moment of respite. Near the office, Krzysztof stopped at a no-parking zone, indicating no intention to explain anything from his side. He merely threw in a dry tone: 'Get out quickly; you know I can't stay here. Have a nice weekend and see you Monday evening.'

'Bye!' she said ironically and got out of the car. Krzysztof sped away with a squeal of tyres. Krystyna lingered outside the office for a moment, and only after a few minutes she entered the building. She was looking forward to catching up with the girls. Despite the mound of work awaiting her that day, she knew she'd spend it in pleasant company.

The room had been cheerful since the morning. Alicja surprisingly arrived on time, and Magda and Gosia were teasing her, joking that since she had recently turned thirty-five, her time was up, and she had no energy left for all-night parties.

'Do you have time tomorrow? I thought we might get together for some wine at my place. I know it's Friday, but I thought it'd be nice to have a quiet chat,' Krystyna suggested.

'Don't you have any plans with Krzysiek? Does he know about this?' Gosia inquired.

'Turns out he urgently needs to go on a business trip, not returning until Monday evening. Tomorrow morning, I'll take Dad for a walk and lunch, then leave the twins with him for the night. He's been nagging for a while that the kids don't spend enough time with him, so I'll have a free evening. What do you say?'

'I'm always in, have no obligations and would happily spend time with you, even if these monkeys can't make it,' Magda said.

'I can easily meet up with you all. After all, as an ugly old maid, I have nothing better to do.' Alicja declared.

'You nut! I'm also up for it. There's some match or something tomorrow, and Piotr wants to hit the bar with the guys. I even thought about suggesting a get-together, only I'll be on juice. I'm in,' Gosia said with a smile.

'Well, we have a plan. Chinese and wine? I won't be cooking; we'll just order something when you get to mine.'

The rest of the day passed in a calm work rhythm. As is often the case in large offices, Friday was for gossip and counting down the last hours before leaving work. Coffee and lunch set the pace of the day. It didn't bother them at all; they had submitted the project on time and could now laze around. They found time to devise the menu for Saturday evening and to order it for the appropriate time. Krystyna left the office in a much better mood.

Saturday morning greeted Krystyna with beautiful sunshine. After weighing all the pros and cons, she felt something akin to relief due to Krzysztof's absence over the weekend. Lately, they have spent time together less frequently. More often than not, he had some matters to attend to and had to head to the office on Saturdays. Krystyna often spent Sundays at her father's.

Just a few years ago, they used to go to her dad's for dinner together with her husband. Krystyna's dad rarely visited them. There was never open warfare between him and Krzysztof, but the chill in their relations had become more noticeable over recent years. At Christmas, she had hoped something would change in her relationship with her husband. They spent the entire holiday together in the mountains. Alicja and Magda stayed in the cottage next door. It was a truly successful trip, or so it seemed, until they had to return home. On the way back, she argued with Krzysztof, and they got out of the car with sullen expressions. Her dad noticed and asked what her husband had said to her. Hearing the question, Krzysztof reacted very violently, shouting at his father-in-law that it was their business what they said to each other, and he had no right to interfere. Since then, Krzysztof hadn't seen Krystyna's father once, and the father-in-law didn't insist on his son-in-law's presence. The already difficult relationship between the men had reached an irreconcilable stage.

Krystyna rang her father and arranged to meet him in the Old Town at their favourite ice cream parlour. The twins were very fond of these shared moments with their grandpa, and the news that they would spend the whole weekend with him was received with grandchild-worthy enthusiasm.

Krystyna's father sensed at once that something was amiss.

'What's the matter, darling? Have you two had a falling-out again?'

'How did you know, Daddy?' she asked gloomily.

'Because I can see, because I've known you since birth, because I've been around for quite a while, and I know how women react. Your sadness is apparent in your eyes. I'd much rather see them filled with smiles and joy, not disappointment.'

'We've been going through a rough patch. Actually, it's been like this since December. We live together, raise the children and when he is at home, we have breakfast together. And that's about it.' Krystyna was surprised at how short this list was. In fact, she hadn't planned on telling her dad everything, but that's how it played out.

'Have you had a heart-to-heart since the holidays? Has he told you?' Her father's question puzzled Krystyna. It sounded as though he wanted to reveal something to her.

'What was he supposed to tell me? Or is there something you want to tell me?'

'No, just asking,' he replied quickly. Too quickly. And he changed the subject as soon as the children approached. 'Shall we go to Bazyliszek's for lunch and have some duck?'

As could be expected, the twins joyfully ran up to their grandfather, grabbed his hands as they used to when they were little and headed towards the restaurant with him, Krystyna trailing behind.

The lunch, as always, was delicious, the duck fresh with a crisp, well-seasoned skin, and the beetroot that was served hot had the perfect beetroot taste with a slight tang. Even the baked potatoes were perfectly done. When it came to settling the bill, they were treated to the best cherry liqueur. It was a tradition in this restaurant that adults got a shot of cherry liqueur with the bill while the children got lollipops.

'I have a feeling that time has stood still in this place. Everything always tastes divine here, and the liqueur tastes the same in summer and winter. I remember when the twins were little, we would come here for dumplings and chicken broth,' Krystyna's dad reminisced.

'Grandpa, but we're almost grown up now, and we eat schnitzels for dinner,' the twins retorted.

'Oh yes, eating a schnitzel definitely attests to your adulthood,' Krystyna said with a laugh.

'See, Grandpa, the kind of daughter you have? She's making fun of us!' Patryk stated emphatically.

'Indeed, I raised her wrong.' Krystyna's dad joked, chuckling. 'I think it's time to bid your mum goodbye, and, on the way back to mine, stop for ice cream in bulk quantities.'

'Grandpa, you're the best in the world,' Pati replied and was about to turn away from Krystyna to go with her grandfather.

'Hey, young lady, who's going to say goodbye to Mum?' Grandfather pointed out. He approached her first and hugged her tightly, as if wanting to transfer his strength to her, yet not wanting to explain why. Then, the children ran up to Krystyna for a brief goodbye before departing with their grandfather. She stood for a moment by Zapiecek, watching her children walk away with her father, then headed towards the tram. She suspected there was something her father didn't want to tell her. It troubled her, but she realised that no one would solve her marital problems. Only she and Krzysztof could do that. She decided to talk to her female colleagues later that day, for even though they were younger, they had already provided good advice on more than one occasion.

Just minutes after she had returned home, the intercom buzzed, announcing the arrival of her friends. Krystyna's mood instantly lifted. Bottles of wine for the ladies and juice for Gosia had been chilling in the fridge since morning. They poured themselves drinks, settled into the living room and cranked up some Aretha Franklin.

'I immediately feel relaxed in moments like this,' Alicja said with a playful grin directed at Krystyna. 'But you, dear, don't seem all that relaxed. Is a weekend without some shagging really getting to you that much?'

'Alicja!' Gosia protested, her face turning a shade of crimson. Magda simply chuckled.

'A weekend without shagging? Come on, I can't even remember what my husband looks like without a shirt,' Krystyna quipped, dripping with irony. 'He hasn't touched me for almost six months. Believe it or not.'

'Are you telling me that you haven't done anything at all? No little kisses, no action, not even a blowjob?' Alicja asked, her astonishment evident. 'Absolutely nothing for half a year? One hundred and eighty nights spent in the same bed and no desire for sex? You do know that's not normal, right? Have you talked to him and asked him why it's like this? I don't want to worry you, but it doesn't look good. Sex is like a second nature for men. I can believe everyone has a bad day or week, but not half a year! Maybe he's become addicted to pornography and is taking care of himself, or perhaps he's found a comforting companion on the side?' She glanced around at the girls, noticing their alarmed faces, and decided to approach the topic from a different angle. 'I'm not saying that's the case, of course. It's just a bit strange that a guy doesn't want sex for over half a year. Okay, if he doesn't want it, it's his loss. But Krystyna also has her needs and, as her husband, he should take care of them. How is it with you? Does anything happen when you want to make love? Do you tell him that? Do you initiate intimacy?'

'Alka, believe me, I've done everything,' Krystyna replied, her voice tinged with frustration. 'I've worn beautiful, sexy lingerie, the kind he liked. I've sent the kids to my dad's for the weekend so we could have some time alone. It was never a whirlwind of passion, but there was sex. And now, nothing. Nothing stirs him. The day before yesterday,

I thought I'd go crazy. We were watching some movie, and there was this steamy scene that could've revived the dead. I started making advances, placed my hand on his cock –' she winced at the memory' – and he told me to stop acting like a horny bitch.'

'What?' Alicja nearly leapt from her chair. 'And how are you supposed to act after half a year of abstinence? Hey, maybe he's ill? You know, testosterone levels drop in men at a certain age. I think there's even a disease for that, from what I remember. Although, I don't know anyone who has it. Have you asked about it? Maybe he's seen a doctor or made an appointment with a specialist? Although around here, waiting for an NHS doctor can take ages.'

'No, I haven't asked him about it. Do you think it might be some illness?' Krystyna inquired with a hint of hope, although she knew well what it looked like from the other side.

'I would primarily check that. We women can make love anytime; they need their equipment to be operational. Speaking of equipment, I understand you have a "friend"?' Alicja asked Krystyna and winked at her.

Gosia didn't conceal her indignation. 'Alicja! Don't you think that whether she's seeing someone on the sly or not is a private matter? Besides, Krystyna isn't the type to fly into another's arms at the first minor problem.' She tilted her head and looked defiantly at Alicja. Magda smiled at Alicja.

'Gosia, don't get worked up, darling. You shouldn't right now. Alicja is referring to a different kind of friend, one you can hide under the bed or in the drawer of your bedside table …'

'Under the bed?! What if Krzysztof …'

When Gosia realised what kind of friend was being discussed, she began to laugh.

'This pregnancy has altered my sense of humour. For a moment, I was wondering how Krystyna could hide a friend in a drawer, ha, ha, ha! And what would happen if Krzysztof caught them.'

She turned to Krystyna. 'Which kind do you have? Waterproof or glow-in-the-dark?' Seeing the curiosity in the girls' eyes, she continued, 'Yeah, we ordered a glow-in-the-dark one, but Piotr started laughing so much when we began using it. He said he could swear on anything that he saw the light seeping through my skin, and on my belly, he saw the shape of Leonard.' Of course, we never used the glowing Leo again.'

'Glowing Leo, a good one … I have brutal Jan. Krystyna, what about you?'

'I don't have one. None at all. And honestly, I've considered it. But if I order one home, the kids will immediately be curious about what it is. I don't want to order it to the work address either, as I might just bump into the manager. He'd definitely ask what I had ordered. And what would I tell him? Oh, nothing much, just that my speedy Zdzisiek has arrived, and I intend to arrive quickly, too?'

'Can you imagine the manager's face? If Krystyna pulled out a vibrator from the box and began showing him how it works and how to use it? And that engagement on his face? He'd lean slightly over her, fingering his beard … "Could you tell me about the power consumption and the safety certifications? Were there tests conducted? Of course, I hope not on animals …"' Alicja often imitated the manager when they were alone, and they always had a great time. 'But seriously, if you want, you can order it to my address. It doesn't bother me, and if it makes it easier for you, you're very welcome.'

'Thanks. I'll think about it, okay? I don't know how I'd feel about it yet, but I could always imagine I'm with Mr A again.'

'Phew, phew, this is the first time I'm hearing of Mr A. Will you lift the veil of mystery?' Alicja inquired.

'Alka, I think it's "lift a corner of the veil of mystery".' Magda had a habit of correcting all Alicja's sayings, which she invariably got wrong. This twisting of words used to bother her, especially at the beginning of their friendship when they started working together. After several months, she laughed it off, pointing out Alicja's incorrect phrases.

'Corner or veil, call it what you will. Don't you want to know who Mr A is?'

'Well, I do,' Magda confirmed in a theatrical whisper.

'Then silence!' Ala whispered as well, and as if on cue, they both looked at Krystyna.

'There's nothing much to tell. He picked me up on the tram. He was looking at me for half the journey, and when he really had to get off, he came up to me, handed me a note with his phone number and said that I should call him when I had the time.'

'Wow! You'd never told us about this. What happened next?' Gosia inquired.

'Do you really want to hear about it? It's an old story.' Though, she actually found herself wanting to share it. She never allowed herself moments of weakness, a wander back through memories of past situations, events, or people. If someone was absent from her life now, it was evidently meant to be. Perhaps it was the moment of doubt in the marriage institution or the lack of closeness with her husband that made her want to share this brief romance. A story of true love, which sometimes seemed surreal, and the handsome Antoni with his fervent lips that now seemed like a dream.

'Are you asking? I'm already opening another bottle of wine. Gosia, juice for you?' Alicja refilled everyone's glass to the brim, settled into an armchair and looked at Krystyna.

'You know, sometimes all of it seems so unreal … as if it had happened in another lifetime, as if it hadn't been me who lived through it, but someone else. That day, I was on the tram. The route was dull, as I had to travel it from start to finish. I had even brought a book along to keep me from getting bored. I didn't read a word that day.

'At the next stop, an incredible man got on. Dark, closely cut hair, blue eyes, nicely built. The type of a well-built bear with beautiful, full lips, whom you immediately wanted to cuddle. He entered the carriage, looked at me and there he stayed. The tram rolled on, and people came and went, but we just stared at each other. It was the first and probably the only time I ever felt that way. The chemistry between us was palpable. Later, he told me he was supposed to travel for only five stops, but he travelled for twenty-five.

'Near the end, he began asking around if anyone had a piece of paper and something to write with; someone handed him a scrap of paper, someone else a pen. He wrote down his number, approached me with that scrap of paper and said that I should call him if I wanted to. And he got off.'

She closed her eyes, suddenly seeing herself in a completely different light. This was Krystyna who didn't need to control everything, her emotions or feelings. She smiled to herself and continued with her story.

'You know that I remember his number to this day? He got off, and I, like a fool, was staring at that piece of paper. A few hours later, I sent a text and he replied right away. Then I replied too and so it went on the entire evening.

'We arranged to meet the next day. I remember I had some training that day. I don't remember anything from the training, but I can recount what he was wearing and how he smelt. It rained. It always rained whenever we met. We joked that the rain was our fairy godmother. For many years, every summer rain reminded me of him. I remember how we stood under this gigantic tree in Krasiński Park to take shelter from the raindrops. With a commanding gesture, he pulled me close and kissed me. Until then, I didn't think a single kiss could evoke such desire. Seriously, it never happened to me again.

'And so days and weeks went by. Sex with him was absolutely fantastic. We could make love all night, laugh, talk and make love again. We met in June, and at the end of August, he came to me one evening and said that actually, there was something I should know, as he was getting married two months later.'

'What the fuck?' Alicja exploded. 'What do you mean, "getting married"?'

The rest of the listeners were also spellbound. They probably expected every kind of ending, but not this one.

'Yes, he got married in October, and for a long time, I couldn't pull myself together. I was alone for over a year. I couldn't forget him until I met Krzysztof.'

'After he told you he was getting married, did you see each other again?'

'Just one more time. I wanted to hug him one more time, feel him close. I was madly in love with him. Everything reminded me of him: a walk through the city centre, the park, every rain. It was only with Krzysztof that I felt secure; maybe he didn't kiss as passionately, but it's not about the kisses. It's about everything. I fell in love with Krzysztof for real. It was, and still is, such a mature love. At least, that's what I thought a year ago. Now I don't know what to think.'

'Did you ever wonder about how Antoni was doing? What did his life look like?'

'Now comes the best part of the story. I met him once more in my life. Guess when?' she looked around. 'Two weeks before my wedding with Krzysztof. We bumped into each other in town completely by chance. He begged me to at least let him say something, to give him a few minutes. I was scared to be alone with him, so I chose the nearest crowded cafe.'

She became lost in thought, transported back to that day when, from a distance, she saw him approaching even before he saw her. She remembered every detail. He was dressed in a blazer and a white tee, with dark jeans that perfectly accentuated his well-built muscles.

She saw him stop at the pedestrian crossing and then move on. And his expression when he spotted her in the crowd. He was just as surprised as she was but also visibly elated.

To this day, she remembered the scent of the cologne he wore. She remembered that one moment when he hugged her close, and for a nanosecond, she felt at home as if his wedding and her tears had never happened. It frightened her immensely then; she quickly pulled away from him, and he asked for a moment to talk.

'As we sat at a little table, we ordered coffee, and he began to speak. It turned out that his parents had forced him into the marriage. They desperately wanted him to marry the daughter of their friends, pressuring him heavily. They used to be a couple, but just before the wedding, he met me and fell in love just as I did, but by then, it was revealed that his fiancée was ill with leukaemia, and they practically forced him to marry her. After the wedding, it turned out that suddenly, his wife had miraculously recovered. Supposedly, the happiness and love had healed her. Antoni realised he had been deceived. Later on, a few more unsavoury truths came to light, confessed by his wife and in-laws. He first fell apart and, for several months, battled with depression. After finishing therapy, he filed for divorce. The day he bumped into me was the day he got his divorce.'

'Blimey … And you were just about to marry Krzysiek … Didn't you feel like calling off the wedding to finally be with Antoni? God, it's hard to believe such stories actually happen! And here I was, thinking my story with Piotr was romantic. I'll tell you guys later on. Maybe we could use tonight to share these romances?' Gosia suggested.

'Gocha, me and romantic stories? Please, I don't believe in that; I either like a guy or I don't. If I like him, I can go on a few dates with him, of course only if, besides good looks, he also has a brain and knows how to use it. But romantic stories are not for me.' Alicja smiled with irony. 'But I'll listen to you with pleasure. I can only support you and bore you with stories of my next conquest.' She grinned and they all burst out laughing.

'Please don't count on a romantic story from me either. I've never experienced one and I am not planning to. That's a totally different universe. I'll tell you one day, but I am not ready for that today. Even though my therapist thinks the opposite. I will tell you about that one day too. Not on a far-in-the-future day, but on a near-in-the-future day.' Magda seemed very determined. They were very curious why she was so cautious, nearly withdrawn, but they respected that she needed time and they waited patiently. Well, nearly patiently.

'There's no such an expression, "a near-in-the-future day". And you always laugh at my phrases.' Alicja even managed to make an 'I am sulky' face, but a moment later they all started to laugh. 'Okay, okay, Krystyna, tell us what happened next! What happened next?'

'Yes, it was right before my wedding. Exactly ten days before the wedding. Everything was ready; all that was left to do was get dressed and go to the church. I didn't tell him that straight away, I wanted to enjoy the moment. The only moment I could still have with him. When he was done talking, we just sat there and looked at each other. I wasn't thinking about anything, I was just sitting there, enchanted, and I was gazing into his navy blue eyes. As if I wanted to extract from them all that I had seen within. His palm touched my cheek. I don't know if you know what it is like when a potent current goes throughout your body; a shiver of exhilaration and enormous desire.

'And then, indeed, I felt it that way. I was frightened, I stood up weeping. I told him that ten days later would be my wedding. I never told Krzysztof about that. He never found out about Antoni. But even on the morning of my wedding, as I sat at the hairdresser's, I pondered what it would be if I could be with Antoni. But don't think that I didn't love Krzysiek; yet it was an entirely different love. And then, when I was dressed, with my hair done, and I was walking to the altar with Dad and saw Krzysztof, I was certain it was the right decision, that I was doing the right thing by choosing him.

'That summer got buried deep in my mind for ever, and I go back to it very rarely. It's only the second time I've unearthed it from the abyss, from the "What once happened and shall never return" section. And this is the first time I've ever told the story. Thank you for listening. It helped me immensely, and now I know what to do with Krzysiek. I am certain there must be something wrong, given his reactions, and I, preoccupied with the children and work, have drifted away from him. I didn't notice that he had been suffering.

'I've rambled about myself so much. Now it's your turn, Gosia. Because these two vipers won't share anything beautiful anyway.'

'With us, it was infatuation at first sight, too. Only we had to overcome my parents' opposition. Initially, they were vehemently against our relationship. They did not wish for me to marry a lad from an orphanage. I know how it sounds, but they believed, for the first few weeks, that I had committed a terrible misalliance, marrying a boy from an orphanage.'

'What? But your Piotr is the most diligent, responsible chap one could meet. I'd never have guessed he was from an orphanage.' Astonished, Krystyna shook her head. It seemed surreal to her that someone like Gosia's husband could be from an orphanage.

'How did you two meet?' Magda inquired.

'Piotrek was an IT technician at my parents' clinic. I went there as I had planned to go shopping with Mum. I walked into her office, and there sat Piotrek by the desk; the feeling was so sudden that we still laugh about it today. I entered the room and was dumbstruck – Piotrek, too, for that matter. We just gazed at each other in silence. Only my mum, who was there at the time, uttered any words. Of course, she had been in the room all along, I just hadn't noticed her. And so I stood there, he was seated, and we stared at each other like kids looking at a dream toy in a shop window. My mum couldn't help but laugh, and it was only then that I realised she was in the room. Naturally, I had to blurt out something silly and embarrass myself right from the start, telling her, "I didn't notice when you came in," to which she replied, "It was you who entered my room." Can you imagine the embarrassment? To this day, we all have a good chuckle about it. From the very outset, Piotrek and I knew this was it. I hadn't even made it to the city centre with Mum before Piotrek managed to get my number and texted me. Actually, he looked through my mum's computer calendar and simply nicked it from there. I don't think I had ever selected a dress – which Mum was going to buy me – that quickly before, and within two hours, I was sipping coffee with Piotruś. Do you know what he wrote in that first text? I quote: "I never thought love could strike so unexpectedly. I saw you for five minutes, but those five minutes were the most significant time in my life. In that brief moment, I experienced the most beautiful and intense emotions I've ever encountered. I know nothing will ever be the same. It's as if I've suddenly found the other half, perfectly fitting me. The question is, do you feel the same? Perhaps we could meet for a coffee and see if our goals and dreams align, if our eyes are set in one – in a mutual – direction?" End of quote.'

'He wrote that? Good heavens, it gave me chills,' said Magda, pulling up her sleeve to show her goosebumps. 'I don't blame you for memorising such a message. It was quite direct from the get-go.'

'Didn't he scare you off with that message? I probably wouldn't have dared to meet up if a guy wrote to me in such a manner right away. But well, that's just me,' Alicja smiled at Gosia.

'When did you learn that Piotrek was from an orphanage? How did he end up there anyway?'

'His parents died in a car accident. And they had no family. Or rather – no one claimed him. Piotrek was five at the time. And to answer your question, Ala, he told me right away. That he was from an orphanage, that he had nobody in the world, that he was completely alone. He never lied, always told me the truth. Right from the first day, he shared all this with me, just as he shared his dream of building a home. He had a flat, but, he said, he couldn't call it a home until there was love there.'

'He said that?' Krystyna asked.

She had been silent until now, still immersed in her story with Antoni. On one hand, she was mad at herself for raking up the past, yet on the other, she wanted to bask in it. She yearned for that closeness, the kisses, the unparalleled desire. Delving into the past allowed her to revisit the times when she truly felt loved. Krzysztof was a good husband, but she never felt as much of a woman with him as she had with Antoni. In her relationship with Krzysztof, control was always paramount. Control over emotions, feelings and touch. According to him, there was a proper place for such things, namely the bedroom, and they should not take it outside. Thus, they never held hands or showed affection in public. They were perceived as a stiff couple. Krzysztof never spoke openly about his feelings.

'Yes. We both knew from the very first moment that there was no point in dragging out dates indefinitely. We knew we wanted to be together, to live together. After three weeks, Piotrek came over for dinner at my parents'. That's when we told them about our plans, that we wanted to be together, that we intended to get married. And then the question arose about what Piotrek's parents thought. He then told them the truth, that he had no parents and barely remembered them. They seemingly took it in their stride, but as soon as Piotrek left, they began filling my head with doubts, saying he was an irresponsible man, an unknown entity, probably after their money. I got so infuriated that I packed a few essentials and moved in with him that very evening. It was a Saturday. Of course, I told him everything, and he just held me close and assured me that we would sort out such issues in a day. I didn't know what he had in mind, but I trusted him. On Sunday, he printed out bank statements to prove he had money, gathered his tax returns from the last few years, took the cash he always kept at home for emergencies, and we drove to my parents. They were quite taken aback but remained calm. Piotrek then showed them how much he earned, how much he spent, colloquially speaking, on life, how much money he had saved up, and how much cash he had at home. He assured them he would sign any paper to confirm he didn't want any money from them, as he had plenty of his own. He mentioned his two university degrees, how he worked in both professions, and could provide well for his family. Honestly? That was the first time in my life I saw my parents utterly speechless. He had knocked down what they thought was their biggest argument. Even my mum, who always had some retorts ready for her defence, had absolutely nothing to say this time. She looked at Dad, who smiled, approached Piotrek, shook his hand, and said he was entrusting his most precious treasure, which was me, to his care. Three months later, Piotruś gave me a ring, and then we started planning our wedding. It doesn't mean my parents gave in, especially my mum kept subtly hinting that I could have more, better, with another man. But I ignored her effectively. You know the rest. Two miscarriages, thousands of doctor appointments.

'Piotr is quite an insightful bloke. Seems to always know what to say, how to act … a real man, in my eyes,' asserted Magda and the others nodded in agreement.

The alarm had been ringing for a good few minute. Alicja tried to ignore it, but the sound irritated her so much that she could no longer disregard it. To turn off the alarm, she first had to catch it. She had bought it online after yet another morning when she overslept. Silencing the alarm in the morning bordered on a miracle – it rolled around the entire flat, emitting horrendous sounds, until she caught it and switched it off. She always had trouble waking up in the morning. Ever since she could remember, her parents would wake her up, sometimes a dozen times, before she would rise for school. No matter how early she went to bed, she always faced the same issue in the morning.

She lost count of how many times she had been late for work this year. She felt like she'd only shut her eyes for a tiny moment, and when she opened them, an hour or two had passed. But since she bought that dreadful alarm clock and left it in the other room, she finally started waking up on time. As soon as she got out of bed, she had to rush to the toilet, then grab something from the fridge to nibble on, and the urge to sleep would pass.

She walked over to the coffee machine. It hummed pleasantly, and moments later, the kitchen was filled with the aroma of freshly ground coffee. *Mondays have a way of brimming with good energy. Maybe something really cool will happen?* she thought. *What bizarre ideas come to my mind. And they say waking up early is so beneficial. Bloody hell, now I'm talking to myself. Fucking brilliant. The quintessential old housekeeper.*

It hadn't been an easy weekend for her. She spent it entirely alone at home. She was supposed to visit her parents but changed her mind at the last moment. She knew that extended family would be there, and she didn't want to explain to them once again that she was single by choice. She wouldn't desperately search for a husband just because most of her peers already had grown-up kids. She felt no pressure to hastily become a wife and mother. Out of the roles dictated by society, the only one she was willing to play was that of a lover, and that, too, for a very short time. She steered clear of married men as if they were the plague, forging no relations with them. Should one approach her, they received a clear and concise message to keep their distance. She rang home, apologised to her parents, blamed it all on work and promised that as soon as her project was completed, she would visit for a few days. Then she buried herself under a blanket on the sofa and mindlessly stared at the television screen.

She ordered dinner from a nearby restaurant and lazily whittled away the entire weekend. She needed this. She had to mull over everything. Somewhere between a bag of crisps and a chocolate bar, a thought nestled itself firmly within her.

She dubbed herself an old housekeeper. On one hand, it amused her; on the other, it made her feel profoundly lonely. For a long while now, she had grown weary of fleeting dates, quick flings that added nothing to her life. She felt as though she were living as a hermit. Suddenly, it dawned on her that she truly didn't want to be alone but feared being with someone even more.

Her first real relationship ended in the hospital – she had been beaten up, which led to a miscarriage. She decided never to get involved with anyone again. She would treat men as a means to an end. The moment they showed greater interest, Alicja vanished. She deleted their numbers and blocked them. Yesterday morning, she woke up around noon and began wondering what it felt like when someone woke you up in the morning, brought you coffee in bed, kissed you good morning and cuddled you before sleep. She tried to shun these thoughts, but the image of a supportive male arm persistently resurfaced.

She couldn't complain about a lack of attention. A tall, slim blonde with long, curly hair cascading down almost to her waist. A pretty face, almost always smiling, attracted glances. But the icy gaze she shot at men automatically deterred potential interest. She decided whom she would spend moments of passion with and set the terms: where and how. Typically, two or three meetings would occur before Alicja disappeared. The forsaken men often tried to find her, dubbing her 'Enchanting Alicja'. She had a charm that was hard to resist, yet she seldom exploited it.

After breakfast, she dressed and calmly set out for work. She was glad it was another Monday and she wasn't late. The tram arrived on time, which was rather peculiar considering the traffic jams in Warsaw. She sat down, took out her phone and delved into the gossip of the high society. Suddenly, she felt a tap on her shoulder.

'Excuse me, madam, may I see your ticket?' came a robust, slightly raspy male voice from above.

'Oh fuck … You're certainly not going to believe me, but I always, always have a ticket, only today I utterly forgot to top up my card …'

Determined to use all her seductive skills to avoid a fine, she looked up at the inspector, intending to enchant him with her beautiful smile. But what she saw made her heart race. Standing over her was a handsome man, around thirty-five, tall, well-built, with the greenest eyes she had ever seen. *At worst, I'll sleep with him*, she thought, gracefully rising from her seat.

'I actually need to get off here. Can we continue this conversation outside? You see, I don't want to be late for work, and at the same time, I don't want to be seen as a runner.' She smiled mischievously and brushed his hand as if by accident. Unperturbed, she walked towards the tram doors, which opened momentarily. She stepped out. Immediately, she felt someone grasp her wrist and stop her.

'Madam, I believe our conversation is not over yet.'

'Oh, certainly not,' she said, turning to him with a smile. 'So what shall we do with a day that has started like this?' she asked, blinking conspiratorially.

'I must issue you a fine. My superior was on the tram; he would hold me accountable for every check. And although you have the most beautiful smile I've seen, I unfortunately need to ask for your ID and issue the fine.'

Without much haste, she took out her ID, handed it to him, and unabashedly began examining him. In the brief moment, she noted his beautiful, strong fingers and sharply defined shoulders, and he significantly towered over her, even though she was in heels. She saw his long eyelashes and beautiful, navy blue eyes.

'Just the phone number, please, and we'll be all done.' He said, his smile so charming that without much thinking, she handed over her number.

'Here is your form; you have seventeen days to pay the fine. Have a nice day.' He handed her the fine folded in half, smiling at her with incredible charm. She took it, smiled back and headed towards the office.

She was the first one in the room. She took off her spring coat and hung it in the closet. Any remnants of the gloomy weekend filled with sad thoughts were gone – the ticket adventure had filled her with good spirits. Shortly, Gosia entered the room.

'Good morning. Astonishing, Alka, you're at work five minutes before eight. It's a miracle!' Gosia smiled at Alicja.

'I would've been here even earlier, but, of course, I forgot to top up my travelcard and got caught by an inspector. But the most handsome one I've ever seen. Well, none of the guys I've dated looked like him. Masculine, fragrant, with beautiful, strong hands. And he was the one who fined me. Such bad luck. I tried every trick in the book, but nothing worked. Damn it, one less appointment with the beautician this month.'

The door opened, and Magda walked in.

'What happened? Why can't you go to the beautician? That's all I heard. But you know what, wait a moment. Krystyna will join us shortly; she's talking to the manager, and you can tell us everything over coffee. Oh, do you have coffee? Damn, I forgot to buy some, and now I've run out.'

A moment later, Krystyna entered, carrying a tray with a cake.

'Good morning. I baked a cake for our morning coffee. Anyone fancy some cheesecake?'

'Cheesecake, coffee and Alka's testimony,' said Gosia, arranging the cups while Magda was pulling out plates to serve the cake. 'I'll have just tea, already had coffee, and now I need to take better care of myself.'

Alicja glanced at Gosia, then quickly at Krystyna. They were so saddened when Gosia had miscarried previously. Alicja feared that another attempt would cause her friend even more pain. They cheered her on ceaselessly but feared that this time, too, it might not end well. After all, the doctor had warned there was such a risk.

'What happened? You've had another wild sex escapade or, on the contrary, decided to join a convent?' Krystyna, knowing Alka's aversion to the Church, often teased her that, given her lifestyle, anything could be expected, even becoming a nun.

'Hello, I'm here, so please don't impute various things to me. After today, a convent is the least of my worries. I met such a ticket inspector that literally, my knickers could've dropped on their own,' chuckled Alicja, grabbing a cup of coffee and casually beginning to savour its taste.

'Don't be a hog. Share the details!'

Alicja narrated her adventure to the girls about the handsome ticket inspector who had fined her. And how he was one of the few men in the world who piqued her interest to the extent that she wouldn't mind going on a few dates with him.

'I don't understand one thing: why would the ticket inspector need your phone number? They never ask for it. My Piotrek also got fined recently because he forgot to take his card from home, and nobody asked him for his number. It's quite suspicious. And also, that you have seventeen days to pay the fine. You get seven days. Show us that little form. Maybe he was just trying to pick you up in an inspector's guise?'

'Do you think so, Gosia? Mhmmm, that would be an interesting experience.' Alicja grabbed her handbag and started rifling through it, looking for the form. 'He chose quite an original way, though,' she mumbled to herself, almost diving into her bag. 'Ah, found it!'

A moment later, she began to laugh. 'You know what's written on this form? "You're so pretty that I couldn't miss this opportunity. My number is 602 333 111, call me when you have a moment. Aleksander. P.S. My mate is the ticket inspector, not me." Not only sweet but also so handsome ...' Alicja smiled to herself and got lost in thought.

'Alright, let's get back to work. The manager will barge in for cake any moment now and will interrogate us on whether we have the contracts ready. And here we are, gossiping as usual instead of catching up on the project,' Krystyna said and started browsing through the catalogues on her desk. Shortly, a resonant voice and brisk steps echoed through the corridor. The door swung open with gusto, and HenRYK marched in.

'Greetings, ladies! I presume the contracts are ready, and that's why you're indulging in cake. The question is, are they in my inbox already?'

'Let's say it's as likely as your Legia winning the Champions League this year,' retorted Krystyna.

'You're quite the spiteful one, aren't you? And Legia will snatch that cup someday. What cake do we have? Cheesecake? My favourite? Maybe I'll indulge in a slice. Or three ...' He was about to approach the table where the cake was, but Alicja stood in his way.

'You'll get the cake, even five pieces, and trust me, this cheesecake is so moist, fragrant with vanilla, softly melting in the mouth ... and then you hit the raisins, so soft, having been soaked in whisky earlier. Did I mention that the glaze wonderfully cracks with each bite?'

'Alka, you're as spiteful as you are pretty. What do you want in return?'

'Five slices are yours and we get time for the contracts until Friday.'

'Are you mad? The director will have my head if they aren't ready by Wednesday morning.'

'We can't make it by Wednesday morning since not every client has sent us the documents. We'll hurry them, call them, but we need time. Thursday, end of the day.'

'Thursday, twelve sharp. One day, I'll fire you. You'll see. Not today or tomorrow, but someday I will.'

'Boss, it wasn't you who hired me, but it's the thought that counts. Here you go, sunshine, cake and coffee, and we'll get back to work.'

'Alright, alright, I'll leave you spiteful lot. By Thursday at twelve, I want those contracts in my inbox.' Saying this, the manager opened the door and exited with a smile on his face, carrying a plate of cake and a cup of coffee.

As soon as the door closed behind him, Alicja looked at the rest of the girls in the room and, with a smile, asked: 'So, how was your weekend?'

She couldn't concentrate on work the entire day. The thought of the faux ticket inspector, aka Aleksander, kept interfering. Right after lunch, she received a text:

Beautiful Alicja, would you join me for a coffee today? I've been thinking about you all day. Aleksander

She smiled to herself, replying:

I hope you have more to offer than a phoney fine. What's your proposal?

The response came very swiftly:

4:30 p.m. at the same spot we met this morning, at the stop?

OK. See you there.

After work, Alicja dashed out of the building to take refuge in the alleyway adjoining the stop, there to wait for Aleksander's arrival. From here, she had the perfect vantage point and impatiently scanned the surroundings for the man. She herself was astonished by her approach. There was something captivating about him, something she couldn't quite put into words. She was oblivious to anything happening around her. Aleksander surprised her – he approached from an entirely different direction than she had anticipated, hands brimming with a huge bouquet of tulips.

'You're beautiful,' he said, handing her the flowers.

'Where did you come from? I thought you'd come by tram,' Alicja said, trying to hide her nervousness.

'Oh, not at all! I drove by earlier today and spotted you from my car as you were heading to the stop. I sped up, parked at the next stop, and hopped onto the tram you were on. As luck would have it, I bumped into a mate who really is a ticket inspector. If it hadn't been for me, you'd have copped a fine.' He smiled at her with a tenderness she had never encountered before.

'So, do I owe you a coffee or even a meal? You saved me from a fine …'

'I'd rather take you out for dinner. I've been thinking about you all day.' Saying this, he took her hand. His hand was warm and dry. His grip was firm, as if he wanted to provide her with a sense of security and support. Alicja's hand almost disappeared within his large one. She glanced sidelong at Aleksander's fingers. They were long and strong. *Wonder what else these fingers can do*, she thought as they made their way towards the restaurant. Moments later, he opened the door, allowing Alicja to step in first. They settled at the first available table and ordered their dinner.

'I suppose, given that we're sitting here together, you're not tied to anyone else, just like me?' he asked.

'No. Over the past few years, I haven't been inclined towards anything serious. There have been some fleeting acquaintances, but nothing substantial enough to stand the test of time.'

'It's quite like me. No woman has evoked such emotions in me as you have, although I hardly know you. It's a total surprise for me,' he admitted.

'Welcome to the club then. I always used to wait a few days before replying to a text. Today, something happened; I don't even know what exactly. If I were a little girl, I'd say it's some kind of magic,' she said with a smile.

Their conversation was interrupted by the waiter bringing in their dinner.

'I feel the same,' said Aleksander once the waiter had left and they were alone again. 'Do you think there could be something serious brewing here?'

'If we give it a chance, yes, I believe something might come out of this. God, what am I saying,' said Alicja, laughing. 'Just a few days ago, I was swearing off relationships, telling myself they weren't for me. And now, sitting here with you over dinner, it feels as though we've always been meant for this. Don't think this is a proposal or anything, but there's something absurdly ideal about this moment that I can't quite articulate.'

'I know what you mean. I feel exactly the same way. Let's see if our outlooks on other matters align as well.'

'A joint checklist?'

'Something like that. Let's start with a rapid-fire round. One question from you, one from me, and we'll see where it leads. You go first.'

'Fish or steak?' blurted Alicja, as nothing else came to mind.

'Steak, medium done. Romance or thriller?'

'Thriller. You nailed it with the steak. Sea or mountains?'

'Mountains. I like hiking. Shower or bath?'

'Both, it depends on the situation and who's with me. I like hiking too.' She hesitated for a moment before continuing, 'Quickie or a passionate evening?'

'A quickie, followed by a passionate evening. Good question,' Aleksander smiled at Alicja. 'Sex in the evening or in the morning?'

'Morning and evening. Contraception or spontaneity?'

'Contraception. Is sex after dinner also on the table?'

'Sex is always on the table. Especially by mutual consent.' Alicja began laughing. 'Our questions are becoming increasingly one-track. Jelly or custard?'

'Ha, ha, ha, you caught me off guard. Custard with raspberry sauce.'

'Perfect. I prefer custard with sauce, too,' she looked at Aleksander. 'It seems our tastes align. What now? Shall we make that checklist?'

'Absolutely, why wait? I don't want to waste any time unnecessarily. Do you have any fixed obligations?'

'Work. I live in Białołęka and work in the centre, which you know about. And that's my only obligation. How about you?'

'I also work in the centre but live in Ursynów. We need to figure something out. The whole city stands between us. Every now and then, I visit my parents and grandmother.'

'I, too, visit my parents at times, though perhaps not often enough. But I'd rather not discuss that.'

'Alright, I respect that. The fact that you don't want to discuss it, Alicja.' The way he pronounced her name, the way he looked at her, made Alicja's cheeks feel warm. 'It feels like I've known you forever. It's strange because I can't recall what it was like before you entered my life.'

'I can't imagine having dinner after work with anyone else but you now. I don't know. Someone must've spiked our drinks this morning. Well, except maybe with my girlfriends. They are brilliant. All three of them. You'll love them as much as I do.'

'Close friends?'

'Close friends and colleagues. Without them, I'd probably have switched jobs. I've been there for over three years. And seriously, I'm there primarily because of them. I adore them. Each one individually and all together. They are utterly unique.'

'So, I'll get to meet them, which means you're entertaining the thought that this isn't our last meeting?' He gazed at Alicja lingeringly.

'I can't imagine this being our only meeting. It took me by surprise, but I'm not going to hide my feelings. Though just a few weeks ago, I was swearing off this kind of connection.'

'I know what you mean. Last Friday, I met a buddy from university. He's settled down, has a good job, wife, kids … He asked when I planned on settling down. You know what I told him? Not in this century. And now? Less than a week later, I can't imagine the moment when we'll have to part ways.'

'Why should we part? We're adults. There's no need to play hard to get. I don't know why, but I don't want to miss a single second that I could spend with you.'

'I dreamt of you saying that, Alicja. If you hadn't said it, I was about to suggest the exact same thing. How did this happen? How have I suddenly lost my head over you? Where shall we go, to mine or yours?'

'To mine.'

'Then I'll need to buy clothes for tomorrow. I can't go in the same shirt. I have loads of meetings.'

'Where do you work, by the way? What do you do?' Alicja asked as they left the restaurant, heading towards a nearby shopping centre.

'I am an analyst at a financial corporation. So I always have to be in a tie and a suit. I hope that's alright with you.'

'I can't stand neglected guys, so your style suits me just fine. You'll also need a toothbrush. I have everything else at home.'

'This morning, heading to work, I had no inkling that I'd be late for the most important meeting of the year, that I'd meet someone like you, and after work, from which I'll practically flee, I'd be buying clothes to have something at yours.'

'All because, for the first time, I had chosen to take a route I never travel. It couldn't have been a coincidence.'

'So, we were destined to meet and fall for each other.' He paused, drawing Alicja closer, cradling her face in his hands, and tenderly brushed his lips against hers. They began kissing passionately as if the world was about to vanish. They heard nothing; only they existed. After a while, the noise started seeping through. Only then did they realise they were standing in the middle of the street, with car horns blaring around them. A few people started applauding. Laughing, Aleksander grabbed Alicja's hand, and they dashed across the street.

'Do you feel it, too?' she asked. 'A total earthquake, a colossal surprise. I wasn't prepared for this, but it feels like a tsunami wave had just enveloped me. Goodness, I come up only with catastrophic comparisons.'

'I was taken aback too. And now I've just been assured that this is something extraordinary. You, your touch, the kiss … You're right; it feels like an earthquake.'

In the shopping centre, they quickly shopped for Aleksander. They also ventured into the grocery section and bought prawns, mussels, wine, yoghurts and fruit for breakfast. Walking towards the car, they held hands. Once inside, Alicja gave the address, and they slowly navigated through the clogged city. Arriving at the block, they took out the bags of groceries and walked into the building together. The moment they closed the door behind them, they literally pounced on each other. As they meandered towards the bedroom, they shed their clothes. They tripped over them, laughed and began kissing again. In the bedroom, Aleksander laid Alicja on the bed, stepped back and looked at her with a desiring gaze. At her naked body, long legs and large, firm breasts.

'You are so beautiful! I never thought I'd fall for a woman as perfect as you …'

'I'm not perfect.' Alicja began to laugh. 'You'd better come to me here.' She reached out to him. He didn't hesitate for a moment. He jumped into the bed and with a decisive movement he spread her legs. As he entered her, he looked into her eyes. In no time, the fever of desire consumed them again. Quickly, they found their rhythm. Aleksander made love to her the way she liked the most. Intense sensations permeated every part of her body. Fulfilment arrived faster and more intensely than they had anticipated. They lay together on the bed, cuddled up to each other.

'Tea, water or coffee after sex?' he asked.

'Definitely water. Do you have sparkling?'

'Of course, I always buy a few packs.'

'Are you hungry?'

'Yes. Shall we make the prawns?'

'I love you, woman! Your replies to my questions are perfect. You make love divinely and look like a million dollars.'

'Good! So, I satisfy you intellectually, sexually and visually. Nice sequence. I like it. It's mutual …'

'Mutual?' asked Aleksander, putting on his trousers.

'I still need to see how you cook.' Alicja exited the bedroom with a laugh.

'Come on, come to the kitchen, let's see how you handle it.'

'Am I to cook? Super, I like that,' said Aleksander, following her into the kitchen. 'Just tell me where you keep your spices.'

'In the drawer under the coffee machine. I'll go get the groceries from the hallway. You grab the wine glasses from the shelf above the bar.'

'Yes, ma'am,' he replied playfully.

Alicja moved to the hallway. Bending over to pick up the shopping bags, she saw her reflection in the mirror. Her cheeks were flushed, her eyes smiling, hair tousled. She looked genuinely happy. Out of the corner of her eye, she saw Aleksander. He grabbed her by the buttocks and pulled her close. She felt Aleksander was ready again. He rubbed against her backside a few times.

'You can't even imagine how incredibly tempting you look in just a shirt. And knowing that it's all you have on drives me wild. I love watching you walk ahead of me so I can admire your bum in all its glory,' he whispered in her ear, teasing her neck with his warm breath. His hands fondled her breasts as he rubbed against her with his hardened member. Alicja moaned loudly.

'Take me here,' she said softly, arching her back more. There was no need to tell him twice. Aleksander dropped his trousers, put on another condom, and entered her forcefully. They made love standing up. Alicja, looking in the mirror, never took her eyes off Aleksander. She liked the picture she saw. He moved within her with quick motions, making increasingly wider circles. Another orgasm took them both a moment later.

'Attempt number two to reach the kitchen for the prawns,' said Alicja as she put on her shirt for the second time that afternoon.

'There's a chance we might make it this time. I'm really hungry now. You'll wear me out, woman …'

'So, it's a good thing you can cook; you'll be useful to me in some other way.'

'Excuse me?' Aleksander began to laugh. 'Am I needed for lovemaking and cooking only? Is that all?' He feigned great horror. Alicja approached and nestled against him, almost disappearing in his arms.

'And for cuddling, talking and kissing too,' she kissed him ardently. They kissed for a long while, growing more passionate, and might have tested the sturdiness of the kitchen counters had Alicja's phone not rung, jolting them out of their passion's grasp.

'I have to take this,' whispered Alicja to Aleksander, who was fervently kissing her breasts.

'I know we should eat something, rest a bit, but damn, I can't control myself around you. What are you doing to me?' He looked tenderly at the departing Alicja. He went to the sink, turned on the cold water and splashed his face for quite a while. After a moment, he heard her laughter.

'Thanks for calling, Magda. No, darling, you're not interrupting. We're preparing dinner. Yes, just the two of us,' she said and laughed again. 'Put me on the attendance list for tomorrow morning, just in case the tram doesn't show up again. Kisses, love, see you tomorrow.'

'My friends were worried about me, and Magda called to check if everything was alright.'

'That's sweet, they care so much about you.'

'No one else could provide them with such comparisons as I do. I'm the best at this. And every time I sleep in, I bring them the finest shakes. So, quite often.'

'You won't be late now.'

'How do you know?'

'Do you think I'd let you sleep through entire mornings that we could use for lascivious sex?'

'You promise? You know, I just want to make sure that morning sex is ticked off on our checklist. Oh, that smells nice. Seems like you cook just as well.'

'I need to ask you a somewhat private question. Do you rent your flat?'

'No, I'm cunning like a fox and bought this apartment as soon as I found out about this complex being built. Obviously, I'm paying off the mortgage, but it's still mine. What about you? Renting or owning?' Alicja inquired.

He looked at her for a moment as if contemplating something, but evidently, it wasn't anything urgent. 'Well, I'm renting because I couldn't settle on anything. Besides, I had no one to live with, so a bachelor's pad was enough for me.'

Alicja sat on a high stool, watching Aleksander cook for her. She was amazed at how well he and her flat meshed. How easy and pleasant it was to talk to him. And before she could think it through, she said, 'I know what I'm about to say is crazy. But I don't want to wait for anything. Since you're renting, and I own my place, why don't you move in with me? I know we've only known each other for a few hours. But it feels like I've known you forever. And I can't imagine you not being in my life.'

'It's not madness. I, too, can't imagine life without you. It's as if I've suddenly discovered that what I considered a successful life has suddenly taken on colour intensity. We are two souls who found each other in a city of millions merely because we trusted our intuition,' he said as he put the prawns on the plates.

'Madam, dinner is served.'

After dinner, they quickly tidied up and rushed to the bedroom. They didn't sleep much that night. And when they ran out of energy for further frolics, they simply lay next to each other and planned their future together. Living together from now on forever, lots of sightseeing, few obligations, Aleksander will cook and Alicja will tidy up. They didn't plan on having children in the near future.

When Aleksander woke her up in the morning, Alicja was sure that such mornings were something she couldn't live without. They had a quick breakfast together, and Aleksander drove her to work. They made plans for the afternoon, and Alicja got out of the car right outside her office.

With a smile, she entered room number 5. By the kettle stood Krystyna and Magda.

'Good morning, dear ladies,' she said and nonchalantly sat down at her computer.

'Hey, spill the beans quickly! What happened yesterday? What's he like? And tell us everything!'

'There's not much to tell, really. We had a nice dinner, went shopping, drove to my place, had supper. Laid out plans for the rest of our lives. Quite mundane,' she said with feigned indifference as if she planned a future with a man every week.

'Eh? What shopping, what "we went to my place", what "planning the rest of your lives"?' Magda looked at Alicja and burst into laughter.

'Oh my God, you're in love! Alicja's in love! I can't believe this. You, the leading singleton of the capital city Warsaw?'

'Is it so odd? It can happen to anyone, even you.' Alicja pointed at Magda. 'You never know the day nor the hour.'

'Did I hear right?' Krystyna inquired. 'You've got plans for the rest of your lives? What have you done to Alicja?'

'Very amusing, yes, indeed we have plans for the rest of our lives. Well, a detailed one for the first ten years anyway.'

'Someone's switched our Alka,' Magda said, examining Alicja as she blushed at the mere memory of last night.

'Alka, don't mess about. Just tell us about this chap. Who is he, and how in the world are you so smitten already?'

'Alright. Aleksander is a financial analyst in one of the corporations. He's not from Warsaw, but he's lived here for years, just like me. From the moment we met, we knew it was it! We don't want to wait. Aleksander is packing his stuff today and moving in with me tomorrow after work. We've got plans. We don't want to waste time waiting needlessly. We want everything right away. Well, almost everything, as we aren't planning on kids for the time being. We want to enjoy each other.'

'I must say, you've surprised me. On the other hand, I would more likely expect this scenario than you dating someone for years. You are too spirited for the conventional track. I wish you a lot of luck on this new journey.'

'Thank you very much. I've told him a lot about you,' Alicja said, looking at Krystyna as if seeking approval.

'Alka, this bloke has had a rare stroke of luck, indeed. I wish you both a lot of endurance. I'm sure you will give it your thousand per cent.'

At this moment, the door swung open and in walked Gosia.

'Hey, girls! These morning sicknesses are killing me. Seriously, I've had enough. What's going on here? A quick recap?' She glanced around the room and fixed her gaze on Alicja. 'And why are you so chipper today, had a little romp last night?'

'Oh, she romped alright and fell in love and planned half a lifetime with Alek,' chimed in Magda.

'What? Impossible! Just six months ago, she wanted to be the most famous singleton in Warsaw.'

'Well, now I'm a ticking bomb labelled LOVE.' Alicja said and giggled.

'Alka, you and your metaphors …' Gosia burst into laughter.

The ringing of Krystyna's desk phone interrupted the morning giggles. Each delved into her work.

Around noon, the manager burst into the room, his face indicating that something was amiss.

'Remember, don't shoot the messenger!' he yelled from the doorway, apprehensively looking at the women.

'You're forgiven, courier. What tidings do you bring, good sir?' Alicja inquired in their favourite jargon.

'The director "forgot to mention" that he had accepted another project, and we – I mean, you and I – are assigned to it, and meanwhile, we have to complete the project we're working on now.'

'Ahh, no worries, before this new one kicks off, they'll initiate a tender and all that jazz. Because, you know …' Gosia halted, seeing the increasingly horrified look on the manager's face.

'You see, this project was tendered a while ago, only …' the manager took a deep breath.

'Only no one wanted to take it because it's a ticking bomb?' finished Krystyna with an ironic smile.

'Wait, is this the one? The one that the director of our director's director was talking about recently? The one that's unfeasible in such a short time?' asked Alicja and all four looked at the manager in the hope that he'd deny it, but the longer they examined his face, the more certain they became that this was indeed the project no one, absolutely no one, wanted to work on.

'And the worst part of it all is –' the manager began.

'No, don't tell me there's something worse than a year-long project to be completed in three months,' Krystyna said, gazing expectantly at her superior.

'In fifteen minutes, there's an introductory meeting with the investor, which we all are to attend. Everyone.'

'Cool, it's a piece of cake. On Friday, we have a conference for five hundred people, and today, we start a new project we know nothing about! Bloody hell! Is our director sane? Does he have some sick ambition to be the best at everything? What an idiot! Shit, I need a drink! Krystyna, do you still have that whisky? Don't look, just pour. My nerves are about to snap. And you, turn the key so no one comes in.' Alicja motioned to the manager while heading to the cupboard for five glasses. 'Lock the door! Jesus, have you never drunk at work?' Alicja looked at the boss with slight mockery. 'If you behave, you'll get some too, you know? Pour it.' she turned to Krystyna.

'I'll pass. A glass of water will do for me.' Gosia managed to say before Krystyna poured the amber liquid into the glasses.

'If we're to take part in this farce, remember we set the schedule, and you nod along and keep the director at arm's length, or we might not hold back and do or say something to him,' Krystyna meaningfully looked at the manager.

'I agree to whatever you find appropriate. By the way, I wonder what else you have in your lockers.'

'You'll never know unless you need tampons or sanitary pads. You owe us two dinners, actually three. The first one is on Friday after the conference, the second to top up the first, and the third … damn, you'll really have to pull out all the stops for that one, as it's for the end of the new project,' Magda declared, with the rest of the girls confirming.

They each had a glass of whisky from the girls' stash. One of the partners in the previous project had brought the alcohol as a thank-you for the girls, who had discretely pointed out a few mistakes that could have impacted the delivery of the project. Instead of running to complain, as often happened, they informed the project partner, giving him time to rectify the damage. Of course, they never told anyone about it. After the project's closure, the man came to them with a special thanks for the cooperation, handing over a basket of goods. Inside, there were chocolates from the manufactory and a 0.7-litre bottle of twenty-five-year-old Chivas Regal. His gratitude made a huge impression on the girls, and they fondly reminisced about that day. The whisky was kept in the office for special occasions. It was only later that they discovered the value of the bottle they had in their stash.

'Where did you get such whisky for the office? I saw it in a shop recently; it cost over a thousand zlotys,' the curious manager inquired.

'You'll find out someday. When you take us out for dinner,' Alicja retorted unyieldingly.

'Alright, let's put away the glasses and go. Hopefully, everything will go smoothly without unnecessary surprises,' Krystyna instructed. At the word 'surprise', Magda felt a strange shiver. A chill ran down her spine, leaving behind an odd illusion that that's exactly what she should be wary of.

The five of them left the room, walked down the corridor and reached the conference hall. It seemed to shimmer with every shade of grey, navy and the soft colours of the women's clothing. The air was dominated by the scent of men's perfume, expensive and very charismatic. Magda knew this scent all too well; it matched one person and was associated only with them in her mind. It evoked the notion of olden days, gentlemen's meetings with politics, whisky and high-quality cigars. As is typical in IT projects, men made up the majority. And so it was this time. When they entered the hall, Magda, Krystyna, Alicja, Gosia and the manager saw their department director look at the conference table as if trying to quickly estimate if there were enough seats for everyone. After a moment, he asked everyone to take their seats. The table was meant for thirty-six people but could easily accommodate twice as many. The girls took their favourite spots near the window. They had experience with the air conditioning and knew that being near the window was advisable with such a crowd.

'I need to find the guy who wears that scent. You know which one I'm talking about?' Alicja quietly asked as the shuffling of chairs began.

'I can smell it too. Incredible. And I hope the owner of that perfume is too,' whispered Krystyna. Seeing the puzzled expressions on the girls' faces, she added, 'What, can't a girl look and reminisce later?'

'Kryśka, don't drink anymore,' Magda whispered, and the rest softly giggled.

'We may begin. Officially, good morning. I'm glad that Mr Henryk's team voluntarily stepped forward for the project and is keen on elevating the stature of our department in the IT arena of our country.'

'And you say I shouldn't drink at work! Listen to the director,' Krystyna whispered, covering her mouth to prevent anyone from reading her lips.

The director spoke about the history of the department, the accomplished projects, and the role he had played in each of them. He, of course, mentioned the employees, but from his narrative, it could be inferred that, without him, no project would have achieved such success. After a few words, the girls knew well that the director's self-praise would last a few more minutes. Thus, without losing anything, they began examining the newcomers. Most men were over thirty. Well dressed, some more or less handsome. One man was paying particular attention to the girls. Alicja noticed him first.

'Fourth to the right from the manager,' she whispered to Krystyna.

'To the right? You can't see him since he's seated on our side of the table. Perhaps you meant to the left?' Krystyna giggled, looking towards the end of the table where the manager sat. She hadn't noticed this man earlier. He seemed to dominate the entire gathering. The kind of person who didn't need to raise his voice to command attention. Charisma personified. He was looking in the direction of the girls, smiling amicably. As the director continued to extol his achievements, Krystyna turned towards Gosia and Magda and whispered.

'Fourth on the left from the manager, though according to Alicja, on the right.' The girls looked simultaneously towards the opposite end of the table.

'I know him,' announced Magda, looking at the man.

'You do?'

'Yes, he's the one with that scent, and he will be the project manager from the investor's side.'

'Thus, in brief, is the history of our project department,' the director concluded his speech, pleased that he could boast about unearned merits without being interrupted.

'How do you know him? And how do you know he will be the project manager?' Krystyna inquired.

'I've worked with him and some of his team before.'

'Then it's time our team introduced themselves,' the director continued.

'Alright, let's pay attention now. It'll be our turn soon,' noted Krystyna.

It was customary for the team to introduce themselves to avoid any unnecessary misunderstandings later stemming from someone not knowing who to approach regarding a particular scope of work. First, the lawyers, then the manager, and the girls.

'Our turn is coming up.' Krystyna softly gripped Magda's hand under the table and addressed the rest of the gathering, 'My name is Krystyna Dziekańska, and in projects, I am responsible for the substantive law, drafting agreements in consultation with the legal team, and handling all the project documentation. Seated next to me is Magdalena Jaśko, who is in charge of the contacts and information flow in projects. There's also Alicja Nowak, seated to my left, and Małgorzata Kowalska. These ladies are our support.'

'Excellent. Now, perhaps I might say a few words,' the man who had caught the girls' attention interjected. 'As it happens, I've worked with Magda on another project before, and our collaboration was nothing short of ideal. I'm all the more thrilled to work with her again. Oh, I haven't introduced myself, apologies. My name is Tomasz Ćwikliński, and I am the representative and project manager from the investor-executor's side. To not waste time, as time is of the essence, I propose that respective departments sit closer together and discuss the operation systems. The more we establish today, the smoother and simpler our road to success will be. Are we able to organise this?' He directed the question at the department director.

'Yes,' replied the director. 'Let the largest team take this room. The legal department can meet with the lawyers, and perhaps communication can convene in the social room?'

'In less than an hour, it'll be lunchtime, so the social room might not be a good idea,' the manager said.

'No problem, Magda and I will find an appropriate place. It's hard to determine how long it will take for the individual teams to settle all matters, so perhaps we could meet first thing tomorrow and present the action plan? Let's exchange email addresses and phone numbers so that, in case of any doubts, we can quickly ring each other. May I have a sheet of paper? I'll write down my phone number and email address. Magda will provide her details, too. Everyone else can jot down their contact information, and Magda and I will email it to everyone afterwards. We'll also establish a method for information exchange. Any observations, suggestions?' Tomasz inquired.

'That's a very good idea. We won't waste time, as from the get-go, everyone knows what to do. I like this approach. So now, each team will focus on their own scope. And we'll meet tomorrow at eight for the next gathering,' the director, seemingly pleased with Tomasz's suggestion, asserted. He was the kind of person who disliked sitting through endless meetings. He was keen on delegating anything possible to others, not exerting himself too much. He represented an old system where the leader reaped the rewards of others' work. He'd always mention it was a team effort, yet never distinguished anyone; he attributed all merits to himself. He fit perfectly with the whole building – a relic that should have long been reformed.

The meeting attendees rose from the table. Tomasz briskly walked over to Magda. He waited for everyone to write down their contact details, took Magda's hand and they silently exited the room. No one said a word.

Teams began congregating at the designated spots to flesh out the details of the collaboration. In Krystyna, Magda and Alicja's team, there were eight other people. It was apparent that they had worked on several projects. Each knew their worth, and they were well-versed in their duties. To Krystyna's surprise, she, bypassing the department manager, was appointed the project manager from the investor's side. Tomasz, who had already left with Magda, was the manager from the executor's side.

The workday was drawing to a close when all the arrangements were finally made and the girls could peacefully return to their room.

'Does any of you have a text or an email from Magda?' Krystyna asked as soon as the door closed behind them.

'How odd, did you see the way they looked at each other?' Gosia wondered aloud.

'No, I've got nothing. What do you make of it? To be honest, I was gobsmacked. She's never said a word about her personal life, and then Tomasz shows up and Magda goes soft as butter on a hot toast. Although, I'm hardly one to judge. Just a few weeks ago, I was adamant about staying single, and now look at me, my heart's a ticking pink bomb exploding with the sickening vomit of a love-trumpeting unicorn.'

'Oh Alka, I do love your analogies!' Gosia laughed. 'By the way, quite the surprising reaction from both of them. There must have been something strong between them. It was plain as day. But I forgot the most important thing: Krystyna, congratulations! I have a feeling this is a watershed moment for us.'

'Exactly, Gosia, I too offer my congratulations!' Alicja chimed in. 'Don't you feel that the roles in the project were decided even before the meeting started?'

'Thank you, we'll see how it all goes. What do you mean?'

Krystyna was pleased with the promotion. Krzysztof often chided her that despite years of service, she remained just an ordinary employee, while he climbed the ministry's hierarchical ladder, achieving new ranks. She felt a sense of satisfaction that this time she had been recognised too.

'You know, a new project comes along and it's really a big deal. And suddenly, bypassing the management staff,

Krystyna is appointed as the manager from the contractor's side? Henryk didn't even react, just hung his head. By the way, they must have had a good informant to know so precisely what tasks to assign to whom.'

'Alicja, you're sharper than a detective division.' Gosia, chuckling, packed her things into her handbag. It was nearly four o'clock, which meant the end of the workday. 'What are you up to after work? Piotr has meetings all day and won't be home until around 9 p.m.'

'Perhaps we could pop out somewhere? The twins are at a camp, and I don't fancy sitting at home with Krzysztof …'

'No improvement in your relations?' inquired Alicja. 'Actually, I could call Aleksander and tell him we'll meet later this evening.'

'Improvement? You mean his terse tone and the absence of sex, or his tirades if I so much as desire a modicum of closeness? He recently found a vibrator in my drawer. Do you know what he said? "I prefer you use that than to have you approach me." Nothing's changed, it's actually worse.'

'Oh, duck,' Alicja whispered, and seeing the smiles on her friends' faces, she added: 'You always say I swear too much, so I've coined my own gentle "duck" instead of you know what.'

'You can't imagine how empty my life would be without you, Alicja,' Gosia said with a laugh, drawing Alicja towards the exit. 'I adore working with you, spending my free moments with you. You're like my own colourful bird.'

'I love you too,' Alice quipped, then turned to Krystyna. 'I love you as well, just so there's no argument over my affections.'

'You're bonkers, you know?' Krystyna was looking forward to the evening with the girls. She took out her phone to text Krzysztof that she'd be home late. A message blinked at her. '

    I won't be home for a few days, back on Monday evening.

'Something wrong?' asked Alicja, as Krystyna caught up with them on the stairs.

'Krzysztof sent a text, he's gone away and won't be back until Monday evening. Such a dry message. Can we go to your place, Alicja? I don't want to return to my own home.'

'Certainly. We'll just nip into the deli for some wine and juice for Gosia, as I've not done the shopping. Would it bother you if Aleksander joined us around eight?'

'Not at all, it'll be nice to meet him,' Krystyna replied. She was curious about what it was about him that had been so fascinating, making Alicja change nearly all her rules for him.

'Shall we ring Magda, of course?'

'Of course,' Alicja and Krystyna exclaimed with a laugh.

A taxi that Alicja had ordered was already waiting for them outside the office. After half an hour of battling through the traffic, they finally arrived at the deli.

'What shall we rustle up for grub? Or should we order something?' Gosia looked around the shop, but it was clear she had a plan in mind as she glanced through the window across the street.

'Just say you fancy a kebab, no need for pretence. Krystyna, what say you to a kebab?'

'If they have lamb, I'm all for it. Let's just buy some wine, I fancy it with a spicy sauce this time.'

'Speaking of sauces, they've got their own mint sauce now and it's the bee's knees! Honestly, I'd never had a kebab this good. And the older brother has joined the team, so there's an extra dishy bloke to gawk at.'

They paid for the wine and crossed the street.

'Is he as hot as the other two?' Gosia asked. 'You know how it is, having your own stud at home, not on lease, but that doesn't mean I don't enjoy a gander at other models on display for demonstration purposes.'

'Good analogy,' Alicja said and laughed. 'High five. You'll make a fine person one day. And now, ladies, feast your eyes on the eldest of the kebab business brothers.'

She opened the door and let the girls enter first.

'Good day, Alicja, I see you've brought your friends,' said the man behind the counter. He was about forty, with a touch of silver at his temples adding to his charm. His dark complexion and Mediterranean accent were an intriguing variety.

'Hello, Abraham. We're setting up for a girls' night in and need some top-notch nosh. What have you got that's scrumptious today?'

'Everything's scrumptious. But perhaps you've not tried our chicken masala and lamb masala. That's our signature dish. Nicely spiced, aromatic, with freshly baked naan – you'll be over the moon.'

'What do you think?' asked Alicja.

'I must have a kebab with that mint sauce, and you, Krystyna?' Gosia replied.

'To be honest, I fancy a kebab with both the spicy and mint sauce, but I'd also like to try those masala dishes.'

'Let's get three kebabs with sauces and two masala dishes. Even if there's leftovers, Aleksander will have them when he gets home tonight. Maybe I'll take an extra kebab just in case Magda joins us?'

'Brilliant idea,' declared Krystyna, just as her phone rang. 'It's Magda calling.'

'Tell her to hop in a cab and come over to us.'

'Hello, lovely, where are you and why aren't you at Alicja's place yet?'

'I knew it. I am here, it's you who's missing from Alicja's doorstep, not to mention Alicja missing from her home. Where are you and how long will you be?'

'We're waiting for kebabs, yes, we've got one for you too, we'll be about ten minutes.' Krystyna glanced questioningly at Abraham, who was preparing their order. He simply smiled, displaying a row of perfectly white, even teeth.

'I'll wait for you then.' Magda ended the call.

'We do understand each other,' said Alicja, as they were leaving with their food in hand. 'Whenever one of us has a problem, we immediately know where to go, who to talk to, and that we'll always find support in each other.'

'I can't imagine not having you and not being able to share my woes and joys. It's great to have you,' said Gosia, and the rest concurred.

After a short walk, they arrived at Alicja's block and, from a distance, they could see Magda waiting, visibly agitated.

'Good that you're here. I couldn't wait for you to arrive. I've got so much to tell you,' Magda declared decidedly, while the rest of the girls looked on with intrigue. They had been waiting for Magda's story, knowing only that life hadn't been kind to her. They didn't press her, but now that the opportunity arose to learn the details, they weren't going to wait a moment longer. They entered the flat, shed their coats and settled into their favourite spots on Alicja's sofa, each with a dish and a glass of wine, waiting for Magda's tale. Only Gosia opted for orange juice, her constant craving since she became pregnant.

'You have no idea how relieved I am to be able to tell you everything. For you to be able to understand where Tomasz is from, how we met, and why I ran away from him,

I need to go back to the time when I lived with my mother. So ...' Magda took a deep breath, and after a moment began her story. 'I lived with my mum in a small town near Poznań. I never knew my father. He died before I was born. My mum was a cleaner, she cleaned people's homes. It wasn't a lot of money, but it was always enough for everything, and if we wanted to go on holiday, there was always enough for a short trip. Life was good until my mum met Franek. I was thirteen then, and my mum seemed very happy. After all, how long can one live alone? My stepfather first raped me a week after their civil ceremony ...' Magda's voice broke. 'From that point on, I never knew the day or hour when he would come to me again.'

Time seemed to have stopped; the girls were petrified. A silence fell, so tangible it was almost touchable. Gosia burst into tears. Alicja swore loudly and crudely, Krystyna wanted to approach her, but Magda emphatically objected.

'If you hug me now, Krysia, I'll fall apart and you'll get nothing more from me. Let me finish my story, and I'll answer questions afterwards, okay?'

Not waiting for a response, she continued. 'He raped me whenever he had an opportunity. When Mum went to work, to the shop, or to visit a friend. I don't know why I never told her. Perhaps I didn't want to upset her. I don't know. It went on for years.

'My mum passed away when I was eighteen. Right after the funeral, when I came home, Franek tried to rape me again. That's when I stood up to him for the first time. I started to hit him. I beat him for so long until he finally understood that he would achieve nothing, and he gave up. Then I packed my things and moved to Poznań. There, I managed to rent a room, found an afternoon job and during the day I finished school.'

'May I ask one question?' interrupted Alicja.

'Yes, the worst is behind me, thanks for not interrupting.' Magda smiled wanly, looking at the other girls.

'How on earth did you manage to live and coexist with someone so vile? I can't even begin to imagine something so repugnant ... To live daily with someone who commits such atrocities?'

'I can't answer that question. I mean, now I know from psychologists why it was so. Back then, I had no idea what drove me.'

'I don't want to say what I think about it just yet, because I can't process it in my mind. With a sick, twisted desire, I would gladly kill the bastard! Just like that.' Alicja grimaced with disgust and pain. Krystyna stroked her hand.

'I'm also at a loss to say anything wise, because I feel the same as Alicja, wanting to do the same to that –' she paused, searching for the word '– degenerate. That sick paedophile. I see it from a mother's perspective. GOD! I would kill the scoundrel with my bare hands. If I smoked, I'd burn through an entire pack right now. Pass the wine!' Krystyna stood up for the bottle. She poured for the girls, and wanting to shift the focus from the main topic, she asked, 'Whose flat was it?'

'My mum's. She inherited it from my grandmother,' Magda said, her voice swollen with pain.

'So after your mum's death, you inherited it?'

'Yes.'

'What's happening with that flat?'

'He lives there ...' Magda grimaced. 'I know I need to sort it out eventually, but I truly don't know how.'

'We must go there, chuck that swine out of your flat and report everything to the police. There's no guarantee he hasn't done it again. A paedophile is and always will be a paedophile. Simple as that.'

'It doesn't give me peace. I can't turn back the time. I'll always remember his touch, his smell, his taste.' She shuddered at the sound of her own words. 'But what's troubling me is that he hasn't paid for what he did to me, and there's a chance he might have done it to another child. Tomasz has offered to go with me, to settle this matter.'

'Oh yes. What role does Tomasz play in this story?' inquired Gosia, who had been silent until now. 'I kept quiet because I genuinely didn't know what to say to you. No words can now mend the damage and make up for the hurt you've suffered in your life. I reckon you should head to your flat as soon as possible and resolve this once and for all. Get the scoundrel out and definitely report everything to the police. Changing the subject for a moment – I can't remember the last time I had such a splendid kebab. I won't eat anything else today just to keep savouring that taste.'

'Yes, the food's bang on,' agreed Alicja. And she said to Magda, 'I can't imagine what you must have felt, but there's one thing that's nagging at me. I don't want to judge your mum, but really, over all those years, did she not see anything was happening to you? Didn't she notice you'd changed? Didn't she realise you were suffering? Surely it must have been evident. Nobody can hide something like that for so many years.'

'I never told Mum about what was happening. On the outside, we seemed like a happy family. There were moments when we were all together, it genuinely felt nice. I know how it sounds. My therapist has explained it to me in detail. But that's the truth. Each of us was so locked in her own world that we didn't see the other was unhappy. We both wanted to create a semblance of happiness for the other, so we sacrificed everything not to hurt one another. Contrary to what it seems, such situations do happen. And believe me, there are a lot of them. I've been in therapy for years and I hadn't realised how many people like me there were, living in a bubble. They construct their own reality to survive whatever is happening outside it. You have no idea how relieved I am now that I've told you all about it. I feel as if I've finally surfaced after a long, arduous dive.'

'I'm glad for you, darling, but for heaven's sake, where does Tomasz fit into all this? It's not that I don't sympathise. I don't even know how I would have reacted, what I would have done in your place. When did Tomasz come into your life and what exactly have you been doing for all those hours alone?' Alicja pressed.

Gosia also looked expectantly at Magda. Krystyna got up to refill the wine glasses. She handed Gosia her juice, sat back down in the armchair and looked at Magda. There was nothing left for her to do but continue her story.

'I met Tomasz on my first day at work, back in Poznań. It was several years ago, shortly after I had finished university. At that time, my life seemed to be quite in order. From day one, we caught each other's attention and I was immediately assigned to Tomasz's project; he taught me everything. We spent a great deal of time together at work, both of us were single. It was no surprise that we then began to meet outside of work more frequently. We grew closer, yet nothing ever happened between us. Until the project ended and we had an after-work party. You know how it is, a delicious dinner, plenty of wine, I don't recall at what point we ended up at Tomasz's place. I knew how things would end, and I wanted it. I was in love with him … But then something happened that he couldn't have anticipated. As we kissed and he undressed me, he said: "I've dreamt of this since the moment I saw you."'

'How lovely,' Gosia interjected.

'Yes, lovely. Except those were the exact words Franek had used when he first raped me. And back then, I wasn't in therapy and couldn't tell certain things apart. Anyone who spoke like that was a tormentor to me. I gathered my things and fled from Tomasz's place without an explanation. Come Monday morning, I handed in my notice and took immediate leave to avoid seeing him. I packed up and moved to Warsaw. Tomasz was in the dark about why it all happened. But since it gave him no peace, he looked for me over the years. Then one day, he noticed my signature on a client's documents. He asked where they came from. All it took was finding a project that our office could participate in. It turned out that the director of our director's director is a good acquaintance of Tomasz. The chief wants to get rid of our old one and was just waiting for a project that would expose the mentoring deficiencies of our elder, so the chief could use them to his advantage and dispose of him. He also wants to get rid of the manager, as he's the old one's confidant. So, we are under intense scrutiny. Everything was prearranged, even the fact that today we all would be working separately. So much gossip. And needless to say, these are strictly confidential matters.'

'Your Tomasz really knows how to pull strings. He knows precisely where to strike to achieve the desired effect. This could be an interesting project,' said Alicja. 'And what will happen with you two now?'

'I told him everything, the whole story from the beginning, just as I have told you now. He understands me and wants to be with me. He said that he's really loved me all these years and couldn't forgive himself for wanting to take me to bed so quickly. He thought that scared me off. It wasn't too soon; we'd known each other for about a year. But he took all the blame on himself and had been searching for me all this time.'

'Well then, that's wonderful. Perhaps you'll finally find peace and love. And on top of that, we'll have access to the contractor. Who knows how it will all unfold.'

'It might seem so, but is a workplace romance really a good idea? Won't it be frowned upon?' Magda asked, her voice laced with uncertainty.

'What's frowned upon is joining the mile-high club solo,' retorted Alicja.

Gosia choked on her juice on hearing Alicja's comparison.

'Alicja! I beg you, for the thousandth time: give us a warning before you drop another one of your similes. But really, what will people think?' Gosia countered, laughing.

'Attention please, no drinking or eating, for I am about to deliver a simile as successful as Rapunzel's wigs,' Alicja announced, unfazed.

'Alicja, I might start writing down your quips and publish them as a collection of comparisons for dreary days. The mere reading of a few will bring out the sunshine for anyone.'

'Sure, Krystyna, just don't forget to include me in the royalties. I'll have a lifelong supply for wine, makeup, and clothes,' Alicja replied calmly, taking a sip of wine as the girls laughed.

'If I understand correctly, the executive director has long wanted to sack our old man and the manager too, since they're in cahoots. He's been looking for a project on which they'd slip up, and that's why he's using Tomasz's project to achieve this? Whatever we gain from this project is ours, so we might even be up for a promotion. Or a spectacular failure,' Gosia summed up what had been said.

'That's exactly the situation, and even if things go south, the management will be blamed. It's dirty business, but what can you do when the top brass has their own agenda? And I've inadvertently dragged you all into this.'

'It could be an interesting experience. The key is to maintain our usual diligence in our duties. We've always put in a lot, never let anyone down, so I have no concerns for us. As for the old man, you see what he's like. He takes credit for everything, so I suspect that he's pocketed the bonuses for projects all to himself. The higher-ups have caught on, the word's out, and he'll have to answer for that too. From the finance department, I know they get bonuses for every project, but with us, it's always hush-hush,' Krystyna said with a hint of bitterness.

When the intercom buzzed, Alicja sprang to her feet. The smile that spread across her face was different. They didn't know Alicja in love; she was always just Alicja around them, but now they had the chance to witness her transformation within a minute. She stood in the hallway, eyes fixed on the door with anticipation. The bell rang and a moment later, Alicja found herself in the arms of a very handsome man. When she emerged from his embrace, blushing, she led Aleksander into the living room where the girls were waiting.

'Meet my dearest friends. This goddess-like one is our Krystyna. The beautiful curly-headed wonder is our Gosia, who, incidentally, is expecting a little one – that's why she's drinking juice. And this is Magda, the most enigmatic of enigmas I've ever known. Girls, I present to you my Aleksander, for whom I've completely lost my head.'

'We're delighted by such a charming introduction. Welcome, Aleksander, it's a pleasure to meet you,' said Krystyna. Magda and Gosia approached the introduction less formally, simply offering a 'Hey, how are you?' For a moment, they exchanged observations, casual social anecdotes, and the girls began to gather their things to head home.

'You don't have to leave yet,' Alicja said, but the rest didn't take her seriously. Laughing and chatting away, the girls left Alicja's flat, leaving the lovers in the only company that was right for them.

Spring that year encouraged everyone to go on trips and be in nature. It was green everywhere, and the air was fragrant with the scent of the trees and bushes in bloom.

It was to be a beautiful weekend. Krystyna planned to spend it with her father and the twins. Naturally without Krzysztof, who had to go away on business yet again. She was increasingly troubled by the growing distance between them as well as her husband's increasing secrecy. If someone were to ask her about Krzysztof now – where he was and what he was up to – she wouldn't be able to answer. She remained a devoted, faithful and loving wife. Only once had she allowed herself to share with her friends the whole story concerning Krzysztof and Antoni. On a daily basis, she was a loyal wife and did not entangle others in her affairs. She and Krzysztof had always believed that marital issues should be dealt with at home. But more and more, she wondered about one thing: why did she have the nagging feeling that this loyalty was only expected of her, and not of Krzysztof?

On a Saturday morning, Krystyna, accompanied by her children and father, set off for a stroll in Łazienki. They were aware that this weekend might very well offer the last chance for a sunny day to be spent outdoors, as forecasters had predicted a spell of rainy and cooler days ahead.

'Is Krzysztof away on business again?' Krystyna's father enquired, just as the twins had wandered off to a safe distance to marvel at the large carp swimming in the pond by the Palace.

'Yes, dad, but I'd rather not talk about it. I don't know what to make of it, and attempting a conversation with him always ends in a row where he tries to prove that I'm the one being irrational,' she replied, not wishing to admit to her father that they hadn't slept together for almost a year, and any attempt to discuss it resulted in insults from Krzysztof's end.

'Perhaps it's time to corner him? Maybe then he'll open up?'

'Dad, for some time now I've had the distinct impression that you know something but are withholding it from me.'

He looked taken aback, not because she was wrong, but because she had seen through him. Unfortunately, the twins returned, requiring them to cease their discussion, much to his apparent relief.

'Are there carp?'

'There are, Grandpa, and they could easily weigh twenty, maybe twenty-five kilos!' Patryk almost shouted.

'Don't yell like that, everyone can hear you,' Patrycja noted. 'Can we go to the stable? Maybe the horses will be out in the paddock?'

'Then let's go,' decided Krystyna's father, and they headed towards the nearby paddock. In high spirits, they shuffled their feet along the path so that the colourful leaves would be lifted as high as possible.

Having enjoyed watching the horses, they decided to head to a nearby restaurant for lunch. The children had run ahead when suddenly Krystyna's father stopped and clutched at his heart, struggling to breathe. She had the impression that he had looked somewhere and got frightened. Seeing her father's face, she was truly alarmed. He was almost grey, with terror evident in his eyes. Fortunately, at that hour the park was full of walkers, and it wasn't long before people ran to help.

'We need to lay your dad down on a bench so he can lean back. Please don't worry, I'm an ICU nurse; I know what to do,' said a woman, holding onto Krystyna's father's arm. 'Darling, call the ward, have them send an ambulance to us.' She then addressed Krystyna's father: 'I'll measure your pulse.'

The examination was brief.

'Is your father suffering from anything?'

'No, he hasn't mentioned anything to me.'

'Very high pulse, trouble breathing. Does your chest hurt?'

'Yeah …' he whispered. It was evident that every little effort caused him pain. Standing beside Krystyna were the twins. Patrycja was crying. Patryk was trying to show more restraint, but now and then he would stealthily wipe away tears. Krystyna took it all in. She felt as though a familiar face had flashed by in the crowd, but she wasn't in the mind to analyse what she had actually seen. She preferred to focus on the here and now.

'Daddy, help is on the way, you'll be taken to the hospital and they'll look after you. Be strong, please …'

'I will,' he whispered, but his rasping voice did not sound promising. At that moment, the ambulance arrived and a doctor and a nurse got off. The doctor exchanged a few words with the nurse who was on the scene. Krystyna didn't understand any of their conversation. When her father was lying in the ambulance, the doctor approached her.

'Madam, at this point, I can't say anything more than that we will do our best to see your father through this. We're heading to the nearest hospital on Wołoska. I think it will be another two or three hours after the tests that we will know more. Please stay hopeful.'

She nodded mechanically. Moments later, she heard the ambulance siren fading into the distance. For the first time in her life, Krystyna felt utterly alone, wishing someone would take care of her. Unfortunately, on that day, she had to be the adult and be responsible. She took several deep breaths and noticed the onlookers dispersing. She looked gratefully at the nurse and the man accompanying her.

'I don't know what to say or how to thank you …' she began, but her voice started to break. Patryk took her hand firmly, to give her strength, not to seek refuge.

'We know, both my husband and I work at the hospital. Please go home, calm yourself. Your father needs you in top form right now. That's the best thing you can do. Be strong for him.'

'Thank you,' said Krystyna. 'Goodbye.'

She moved towards the exit with the children. She told them to go home, but she decided to go to the hospital immediately.

On arrival, she was directed to the Intensive Care Unit. As she entered the room where her father lay, she was terrified by the number of tubes attached to the patient. A nurse was sitting next to him, looking at the monitors. She turned towards the entrance when she heard someone enter.

'You are …?' she asked coolly.

'I'm his daughter, I have the head physician's permission to sit with Dad for a few minutes.'

'If that is the case, please take a seat, and I shall step out for a moment. I ask you to not touch anything. Should anything commence, we have surveillance in the duty room. Your father has been induced into a pharmacological coma, but should you wish, you may converse with him. It is hard to believe, but such patients often do hear us. One must maintain hope.'

She approached the monitor, adjusted something, and exited, leaving Krystyna alone with her father. Krystyna sat in the chair the nurse had just vacated, took her father's hand, and wept. For several minutes, she could not compose herself. Only when she had cried out all the pain that had accumulated inside her during those hours could she view the whole situation more clearly.

'Daddy, I won't trouble you for long. You know what I am like. I just want you, well and healthy, to return home in a few days. That we might again take a stroll or share a meal together. Daddy, you are all I have, and I need you terribly. Rest here, sleep as much as you wish, but please, once you've rested and feel better, come back to me and the children. I cannot fathom a life without you by my side.'

She held her father's hand against her face, longing for him to open his eyes and assure her that all would be well. She yearned to see his smile again, the gentle look that had always soothed her. Instead, she saw the monitors, heard the hum of the machinery at work. After a moment, the nurse returned.

'Madam, I know you really want to be with your father, but I think it best if you return home. Your dad was specifically placed in a coma to allow his body to recuperate peacefully. It is standard procedure. Tomorrow should be better. Do you have children?'

'Yes, I have teenage twins.'

'They surely need you now. Being here, you cannot aid your dad; he needs tranquillity above all.'

'Yes, I think I shall go to them now.'

Krystyna rose from the chair. She wanted to lean over her father one last time but paused, looking at the nurse, waiting for her approval. The nurse smiled kindly, and Krystyna kissed her father on the forehead, just as he used to do.

'Until tomorrow, Daddy, sleep well.'

'Goodbye,' she said to the nurse and left the room.

She was eager to leave the hospital as swiftly as possible, to flee from it as one does from troubles. She felt overwhelmed by the events. She stood for a moment outside the hospital, pondering her next move. She took out her phone and decided to call Krzysztof. Unusually, he answered after the second ring.

'Hello! Has something happened? Because I'm at an important meeting and ...'

'Dad's in the hospital, he's had a heart attack, the doctors have put him in a medically induced coma and ...' her voice failed her, and she began to cry.

'OK. I understand that, but I can't get away to Warsaw right now. I won't be home until Monday morning. Can you manage until then? The children are grown, they can stay by themselves if you want to go to the hospital, to see your father ... I mean, your dad ...'

'Yes, of course, I'll manage, I just wanted you to know and I thought that ...'

Krzysztof interrupted her with a firm tone.

'I have a meeting that's important to me, can we finish this conversation at home on Monday?!' he asked sharply.

'Yes, see you then ...'

'Bye,' he said brusquely. Krystyna was about to move the phone away from her ear when she heard through the handset: 'I have the impression that our problems will resolve themselves ... damn, I haven't hung up ...'

The call was cut off. Krystyna was taken aback by the tone of that last sentence, which was certainly not meant for her. Now, however, she didn't have the strength to think about it. She shelved that problem under 'Krzysztof' for later consideration. This was not the time to dissect their marriage. She picked up the phone again and called Magda. Almost immediately, she heard her friend's voice.

'What's up, Krystyna? How did you know I was thinking of you? I mean, about our project, so about you too.'

Magda's voice was warm. It carried such genuine emotion that Krystyna burst into tears before she began to explain why she had called.

'Because I am at the hospital ... That is, outside the hospital and ...'

'My God, what's happened? Something with you, the children? Where are you? Which hospital?' Magda got to her feet at once.

'I'm on Wołoska Street. My dad had a heart attack, he's in a coma, and I don't know what to do ...' she sniffled. 'I called Krzysztof, but he doesn't have time, so I thought I'd call you ...'

'You did the right thing. I'm putting on my shoes now, there's a taxi stand just outside. I'm on my way to you. Don't move from there, okay? I'll be right with you.'

'Magda!'

'Yes?'

'Thank you for being here.'

'Oh, don't mention it! I'll be there for you shortly,' Magda hung up.

Krystyna sat on a bench by the hospital's entrance gate. The weather remained delightful. The sun shone just as it had several hours earlier when she had strolled through the Łazienki Park with her father and the children. It was only five o'clock, yet she felt as though her life had made several more turns of the clock than everyone else in the world. Thoughts she did not wish to access began to stir at the back of her mind. She was aware they existed but was reluctant to give them meaning and precedence. A taxi pulled up, from which Magda emerged. She hugged Krystyna quickly and asked:

'What's our plan? Are we staying or shall we go somewhere while we have the taxi?'

'We must head home, as the children are there alone.'

'Right, let's get moving then,' she said to the taxi driver and opened the door for Krystyna.

Magda spent the entire weekend with Krystyna, wanting to help and support her through this difficult time. Krzysztof did not call even once, nor did he return home. On Sunday, Alicja and Aleksander took the twins to the cinema. Only Gosia had not been in touch, but the friends understood that pregnancy brought varied days, and sometimes peace and quiet are simply needed.

Gosia awoke on Saturday morning with an unsettling feeling that something was amiss. She had dreamt of sinking into something damp. When she woke up and drew back the duvet, she discovered the sheet had been soaked with blood. She knew all too well what it meant. Another attempt at IVF had failed. She wanted to cry, but at the same time felt an immense emptiness inside. Quietly, she rose from the bed, careful not to wake Piotr. Yet before she could move away, she heard his voice.

'Gosia ...'
His voice was sleepy, but she detected a note of terror in it. It was a small comfort that he had discovered the miscarriage himself; she wouldn't have to tell him.

'I need to go get myself clean. Could you strip the bed and put the linen in the wash?' Her manner was nonchalant, as if nothing had happened, as if she hadn't just lost another pregnancy. 'Will you take me to our doctor after breakfast?'

'Yes, of course, I'll take care of everything. I'll get the washing started and call the clinic to let them know we'll be coming. Do you want to talk, Gosia?'

She heard the sadness in his tone. She knew this latest attempt had been a significantly emotional strain for both of them. Yet she didn't want to talk.

'What's there to talk about? About something that isn't there?'

She shrugged her shoulders and went to the bathroom to shower. She stood for a moment, listening as Piotr began speaking with the clinic. When she heard him start the conversation, she turned on the shower. She didn't want to listen. The shower took her several minutes. She just stood under the water, staring blankly at a point on the wall. When she decided the water had been running over her body for decidedly too long, she dried off with a towel.

From the cabinet, she took out a large sanitary pad and cotton pants she kept there for such occasions. Without a bra, she exited the bathroom. She looked around the living room and then moved to the bedroom. She could hear the washing machine in the kitchen drawing water. On the freshly made bed were her clothes. Without a word, she began to dress. She didn't look at Piotr once. It was only when she was putting on her shoes that she gave him an expectant look, signalling that she was ready to leave. She took her handbag with the documents and left the flat. Piotr caught up with her on the stairs, and they got into the car together.

In the clinic, the doctor was already waiting for them. Gosia maintained her silence. She seemed to believe that no words were necessary. She had been through this a couple of times before and was all too familiar with the procedures. This time, it was Piotr who chatted with the doctor. She reacted sharply when the doctor offered her a fortnight's sick leave from work.

'I don't understand. Why do I need a sick leave? There's nothing wrong with me. You yourself said, doctor, that everything had cleared out on its own and there's no need for curettage. I see no reason why I shouldn't return to work tomorrow morning.'

'Please listen, you need rest now, some peace. You should now …' The doctor tried to persuade Gosia, but she had no intention of listening.

'What should I do now, doctor? Sit and weep? Or torture myself with the notion that I've proved once again to be a woman of lesser worth? Or perhaps I should arrange another funeral for my … what shall I call it? Embryo, foetus, or has it become a child? Because I'm at a loss myself. That fragment of something that my husband so painstakingly collected from the sheet and brought here. Should I cradle it and name it Wiktoria?'

Her tone was cold, so detached from the one she knew. She heard herself speaking but did not recognise herself in the voice. She saw the tears in Piotr's eyes, which only infuriated her further. She wanted neither sympathy nor to be the central figure in yet another drama.

'Mrs Małgorzata! You can see for yourself that you need to rest, especially mentally. This is another loss of a child for you both, and your behaviour shows that. A short trip would do you good. Perhaps some organised holiday?' The doctor turned to Piotr with the question, but Gosia responded first.

'Perfect. A trip to Ciechocinek will fix everything, and in a week, I'll forget that another child of mine is dead. Even if you give me a sick leave, I won't use it.' She took a deep breath and turned to Piotr. 'Can we finally leave this place? Please …'

'Yes, of course.'

Piotr got up and approached Gosia, who was already waiting by the door. He opened it, allowing his wife to pass through first. She had the impression that he made some sort of gesture with his hands, but she didn't want to turn around. All she desired was to be home as swiftly as possible. From the car, she sent a text to her parents:

She then silenced her phone. The entire weekend was spent on the sofa in front of the television. Several times she heard Piotr speaking with her parents, but she had no desire to participate. She shut herself off from everything and everyone. At night, when Piotr thought Gosia was asleep, he went to the bathroom. She heard him crying. That's when she also began to cry, but when he came out of the bathroom, she pretended to be asleep.

On Monday, they got up for work as usual.

'Are you certain you want to go to the office today?' he asked, stirring his coffee.

'Yes, Piotruś. There's nothing I need more right now than to be busy. I must go to the girls, immerse myself in something. At home, I'll only dwell on what happened. I don't want that. Believe me, it's for the best, for both of us. It's better if I return to normal life quickly. I don't want to hear about children or pregnancies now.'

'Gosia, as you wish. If you think that's for the best, let's do so,' Piotr said.

Both were aware they were deceiving themselves, but neither wanted to show it. After breakfast, they got into the car together, and Piotr dropped Gosia at the office.

Alicja and Magda were already in the room, both appearing agitated, which caught Gosia's attention.

'Hey, what's with the tense atmosphere? Any issues with the project?' asked Gosia.

'We couldn't reach you over the weekend. Krysia's dad is in the hospital; he had a heart attack and is in an induced coma. Of course, Krzysztof didn't have time to come to Warsaw. Krystyna is completely alone with it all. And why was your phone off? Were you making the most of the weekend?' Alicja winked at Gosia conspiratorially.

'We spent half of Saturday in the clinic. I miscarried again, but I don't want to talk about it. And please, don't ask about anything. Will Krystyna be in today?'

Alicja and Magda exchanged swift glances.

'I don't mean to intrude, but shouldn't you be at home right now, Gosia?' asked a concerned Alicja.

'No, because I would just dwell on what happened. And I would blame myself for being utterly useless again, whereas now I can focus on the project. Krystyna needs me. That's what's important now, not my failed IVF attempt.'

Neither looked convinced by Gosia's words. Especially not her. After a few minutes, the door opened, and Krystyna entered. Her sombre expression boded ill tidings.

'How's your dad? The girls have told me everything. I'm sorry for not responding, but I miscarried and needed some time to myself. No need to discuss it,' she countered, seeing the sympathy on her friend's face. 'It was just a failed procedure with a minimal non-viable embryo.'

'Are you certain you don't need some time off?' probed Krystyna.

'And why are you at work today?' Gosia asked more sharply than she had intended.

'To avoid thinking. Alright, I understand. As for Dad, I called the hospital this morning. No change. And apparently no change is good. The most important thing is that his condition isn't worsening. Let's get to work. I need to occupy my mind.'

Though Magda and Alicja wanted to say something, they refrained and respected Gosia's and Krystyna's wishes. Around midday, the phone rang. Krystyna hesitated for a moment but answered.

'Good morning, this is Adamski from the hospital on Wołoska. I'm afraid I have bad news. Your father passed away fifteen minutes ago. I am very sorry. Please come to the hospital to complete the necessary formalities.'

The doctor's tone was matter-of-fact, detached. It sounded as if he was reporting a delayed tram. Krystyna was silent for a moment, stunned.

'Yes, of course, I'll be right there.' She hung up. 'I must go to the hospital to clarify a mistake!'

'What mistake? What's happened?' Gosia inquired.

'They've said my dad has passed away. But that's impossible,' she declared, scanning the room with a bewildered gaze. 'My dad couldn't have just passed away. Not my dad. We had yet to visit so many places together. We had so many plans. Oh God, Dad, please!' Her plea dissolved into tears which escalated rapidly into a hysterical sobbing. She wept like a small, lost child. Gosia rushed over, enveloped her in a comforting embrace and waited patiently for the initial shock to subside. When Krystyna had calmed somewhat, Gosia offered to accompany her to the hospital, which Krystyna accepted with immense gratitude.

The days that followed seemed to Krystyna a sequence of macabre dreams. Each day she harboured the hope that the next morning she would wake up to find it all a mere apparition, a falsehood, an illusion. She could not rely on Krzysztof. True, on hearing of his father-in-law's passing, he had come to the hospital and allowed her to cry on his shoulder, but he had to return to work shortly after. He offered some help with the formalities, but he was absent when she needed support during the visit to the funeral home. And it was Krystyna who had to help the children cope with the loss of their beloved grandfather. Her colleagues were a great support. Especially Gosia who was present during the funeral arrangements, choosing the flowers and planning the service.

On the morning of the funeral, Krzysztof went to work. He attended the ceremony, but by the next day, he was off on another business trip. Krystyna had a foggy recollection of standing over the casket. She saw faces but couldn't comprehend whose faces they were or why they had come. Snapshots of the funeral service were at times vivid and at other times completely blurred.

One thought tormented her incessantly. She couldn't forgive herself for not having the chance to say goodbye. A few sentences remained unspoken that should have been voiced. The final embrace, the last cup of coffee together – that's what was missing. Before the funeral, Krystyna had confided this to Gosia, who suggested she write a final letter to her dad. In it, she could enclose everything she had always wanted to tell him but never found the opportunity.

In the evening, after the funeral, once the children were asleep, Krystyna settled herself on the living room floor with a bottle of wine, a sheet of paper and a pen. Words began to flow forth of their own accord.

My Dearest Dad,

The act of writing this letter marks the closing of a beautiful chapter. I wish to express my gratitude for every excursion, for every joke of yours. For always being just there when I needed you most. I'm at a loss to grasp the sudden void of your absence. How will my life without you be? Without our shared meals, our conversations? It feels as if someone has ripped out my heart, severed it in half and then crudely stuffed what remained back inside me. This first week without your presence has been the bleakest I've ever endured. Once more, I am the little girl in dire

She remained there, over the letter, sobbing. By the third glass of wine, she realised she had not eaten all day. The combination of alcohol, hunger and tears induced a violent turmoil in her stomach. She rose abruptly and rushed to the toilet to be violently sick. It seemed as if convulsions sought to expel all her sorrow and grief. Coming to her senses, she found herself on the floor, her head resting against the toilet bowl. Rising from the floor, she grasped the toilet bleach and began to clean the bathroom. An hour later, when the room was almost sterile, Krystyna moved back to the lounge. Settling on the sofa, she wrapped herself in a blanket and fell asleep.

Several weeks after the funeral, Krystyna mustered the strength to visit her dad's grave. As she tended to the site, nothing registered but the withered flowers. Tidying the grave took her over an hour. She tried not to think about where she was or what she was doing. Acting on autopilot, she longed to finish her tasks swiftly and simply leave that place. She managed to hold herself together until she saw the plaque bearing her father's name. Seating herself on a bench by the grave, she allowed the tears to flow unabashedly.

When the sharpest pang of grief had subsided, she looked around. She noticed candles on the other graves and then recalled that she, too, had purchased one to light on her dad's grave. Reaching into her bag, she retrieved a small glass candle holder. It was tiny compared to other candles at the cemetery. This triggered a memory of a conversation with her father from years earlier, when Krystyna was still a student. They had gone to visit the graves of her grandparents, her father's parents. She had been curious why her father always chose such small candles. They weren't in need of economising, so she asked why they did this. His reply lingered with her to this day: 'No matter how fiercely we light a fire, it will never resurrect them nor provide them with warmth. It remains solely a symbol. A symbol of warmth, a smile, a touch. A symbol of what once was and will never return.'

In purchasing her single small candle, she had not noticed that she was doing precisely as her father had taught her. Nothing could change that now. Her father was gone and would not return; everything else was symbolic. A symbol of his life, their love, and her memory.

From the break of dawn, the air was thick with fog. It wasn't raining, yet moments after stepping outside, one felt besmirched by an unpleasant dampness. Gosia got into the car. Piotr had already started it. The engine's rumble, usually a source of solace, now seemed as intrusive as the buzzing of a fly. The morning traffic jam seemed interminable. They inched along in silence through the congested streets of the awakening city.

'What's the matter, Gosia? You seem rather distant today. Is it the weather?'

'No … I mean, I don't know what it is. But I feel an overwhelming heaviness, as if I'm bracing for a blow that's about to land at any moment. Do you understand what I mean? When you're in a boxing ring, and you know that your opponent is about to deliver the final punch, and you can't lift your arm, you just wait for his move that will inevitably knock you down.'

'Do you want me to slow down?'

'Could we go any slower? No, it's not that. But I have this odd feeling that something is going to come from an entirely unexpected direction.'

'I know better than to argue with you when you have these premonitions, but look, today the weather is so … destructive. It's warm, yet you feel as if you're sullied somehow. The pressure has dropped; have a coffee at work, and you'll shake it off. And if not, ring me. I'll take time off, and we can play truant for a while.'

She looked at him for a moment, pondering something.

'Really? If something's amiss, I call and we bail out?' she asked emphatically.

Although Piotr was taken aback by Gosia's question, he did not let it show. He found it hard to believe that Gosia would leave work early; she had resisted the idea ever since the miscarriage.

'I promise, besides, I've been thinking that we ought to escape, to cool down a bit. We haven't had any time for ourselves after everything that's happened.'

He glanced at Gosia anxiously, fearing she would break down in tears again, that she would withdraw into herself for days, as had happened with every attempt at conversation since the miscarriage.

'You know, that's a good idea. I've been considering what you suggested recently, what the doctor and my parents said. I can't keep burying myself in work and pretending nothing has happened. I'll file for immediate leave today. You're right, we should finally talk everything through and decide what to do next. I'm tired of being in limbo and pretending that nothing's wrong. Today will be my last day in the office and then we can go somewhere.'

She smiled at Piotr. When she got out of the car outside the office, she was in a better mood. She pecked her husband on the cheek as a goodbye – something that hadn't happened for a long time – and headed towards the entrance doors with zest. Piotr stood in front of the building for a moment longer, wondering what had just happened. Only after a while did he set off towards his own workplace.

Signing in, Gosia joked with the security guard and something resembling a smile appeared on her face. She was the first in the room. She placed her handbag on her desk and set about making coffee. Within minutes, the room was filled with the aroma of freshly brewed coffee. A fly buzzed quietly at the window, trying to find its way out. Gosia opened the window for it and stood for a moment, gazing at the treetops of the green trees. This is how Magda and Krystyna found her.

'Is Alka not here yet? I get the feeling that she's finally fallen in love and is about to settle down,' Krystyna said by way of a morning greeting.

'It's quite possible,' Magda said and, chuckling, approached Gosia. 'Hey, love, rest assured that we gossip about you as well when you're not around.'

'And quite right too, I'm a more intriguing topic than you lot,' Gosia bantered back. 'I'm taking a leave. A few weeks off. I need to rest after all I've been through lately.' Seeing their inquisitive looks, she quickly added, 'I'm not ready to talk about it, but I've grown to accept that I must go through my own little mourning.' With that, she turned away from the girls, strode quickly to her desk and immersed herself in work, oblivious to anyone else. The girls exchanged stealthy glances and got on with their tasks.

Around ten, Alicja arrived. Dressed in a colourful frock, her hair loose and flowing, she looked like the happiest person on earth. Her rosy cheeks and beaming eyes seemed to shout to everyone, 'I'm happy, I'm happy!'

'Good heavens, can't you look less happy just once? It's quite unsettling to see such cheerful folks,' Magda said with a laugh. She herself was finally starting to feel a semblance of joy on her personal happiness scale and relished every piece of this blissful jigsaw puzzle.

'I've no idea what you're on about, you toad, Magda. I've got something to tell you all, and God knows, I've been puzzling over how to break the news for days.'

She stood by her desk unpacking her bag with clear excitement; a few items slipped from her hands and fell to the floor. Gosia's attention was caught by a small pink notebook. She hadn't even noticed how she'd risen from her desk, walked slowly to Alicja and picked up the fallen item. At that moment, Krystyna's hand flew to her mouth. At first, she wanted to rush over to Alicja to congratulate her, but she was stopped by Gosia's icy and very alien gaze. That moment, when it dawned on Gosia that Alicja standing beside her was pregnant, struck her like a lethal blow.

'You're pregnant?' she asked with the coldest, most distant tone she could muster. Her voice sounded almost offensive.

'Yes, Gosia,' confirmed Ala quietly. 'It wasn't planned, one foolish evening and such is the result ...' She closed her eyes. Only after saying it did she realise how it sounded. Krystyna and Magda stood as if petrified, waiting for what would come next.

'Well, congratulations then. See how lucky you are? Just once and there you are. Pregnant. Bloody pregnant! First try, and there it is! And I, despite thousands of attempts, cannot have such a splendid pink booklet. I can't go for an ultrasound and hear my child's heartbeat,' Gosia spoke softly, almost in a whisper, yet her voice was sharp, full of anger, swollen with emotions, helplessness and incomprehensible pain. She opened the pregnancy booklet. 'Look at that, one kilogram gained, isn't that a bit soon for putting on weight? Aren't you afraid you'll get fat? Oh, so it's the ninth week and the heartbeat can already be heard ...' Resigned, she handed back the booklet to Alicja and stepped back a few paces, still looking at her with a cold gaze.

'Why? Fuck, why must you always have everything that I want? I've tolerated everyone paying attention to you, that you have everything I've ever wanted. But this? You never wanted a child! You didn't want to be pregnant! You said it didn't interest you! You don't deserve a child! You've fucked half the town, you might not even know who the father is! You surely don't!' Tears were streaming down her face, but her voice remained icy. She looked at Krystyna.

'Why is she pregnant and not me?' she asked almost in a whisper, then spun on her heel. She sat at her desk and started to rock. She was unresponsive to Krystyna's and Magda's voices. Alicja was afraid to approach her, not wanting to do more harm.

'Krystyna, what the hell is going on, what is it?' asked a terrified Magda.

'Shhh …' Krystyna walked over to Gosia, caressing her face. 'Little one, what is it? Gosia, can you hear me? Please, say something …'

Gosia's gaze was cloudy. She looked without seeing, heard without being able to respond.

'Magda, ring her husband. Have him come at once. Ala, leave the room. Go to the secretary's office and have them call for an ambulance, but do not return while Gosia is here,' she commanded. Seeing that Alicja was petrified, she yelled, 'Get out!' She drew closer to Gosia, embraced her and began to gently rock her. When they were alone in the room, Gosia whispered, 'I always envied her that charm, that allure, the way she always looks like a million dollars. I consoled myself with just one thought – that she had no child. That she would not have one soon, for she had no man in her life and did not want one. And now … I've miscarried again, I haven't the strength to endure this another time. I see also how much it costs my husband. Do you know how he wept when I miscarried last time? He sobbed, truly, sobbed in the bathroom at night. He thought I was asleep. But I was not, I was listening. And I wept, too. Over being a lesser woman, one who cannot conceive and carry to term, give birth to just one child. We do not want more, just one! Nothing more. Just that. And now …'

She began to cry again, her sobs seeming to originate from the depths of her fragile body. Spasms tormented her and seemed endless.

'All I see is the surrounding darkness, drawing me in. I want to hear nothing, see nothing, I do not want to live. I never want to see Ala and her vile brat again! It was supposed to be my child, not hers! She had no right to take it from me! Because it is through her that I lost my child. She took it from me! Exactly when I lost it, she received it! Because it hurts, you know, it hurts so much when the only thing you dream of is beyond your grasp and even fucking medicine can't help you … I must leave, leave everyone, you and my husband. If I do, he'll still be able to have a life and have the child he longs for. Because I am unable to give it to him'.

She was crying more quietly now, yet her anguish became more pronounced – not masked by spasms or sobs, but laid bare in raw emotion that struck a chord of fear in Krystyna's heart. She continued to cradle Gosia, rocking her gently back and forth.

Minutes passed, and then the door swung open to reveal Piotr. His face turned ashen at the sight of her distress. He looked to Krystyna, a question on his lips, but she shook her head, signalling him to refrain from speaking. Piotr approached, lifted Gosia into his arms, and sat down with her in a chair. Shortly after, a doctor accompanied by a paramedic entered the room. Krystyna quietly explained the situation to them, ensuring Gosia was out of earshot. The doctor approached Gosia and her husband, inquiring if they wished for her to be taken to the hospital. Gosia vehemently shook her head, requesting only a sedative injection and promising to see her own doctor the next day. Krystyna was not convinced by this course of action but respected their autonomy, silently hoping Gosia's breakdown wasn't as severe as it appeared. Leaving the room to them and the paramedic, she stood by the door, waiting. Employees occasionally peeked into the corridor, eager for details of the commotion, but Krystyna declined to provide any explanations. After some time, the ambulance crew emerged.

'This is Mrs Małgorzata's sick leave note. For now, it's for a month, but I fear her absence may be significantly longer. Her mental state is quite serious. Mrs Małgorzata's husband asked me to pass this on to you,' the paramedic addressed Krystyna. 'He also requested that you ensure they can leave the room undisturbed. That's all I can do. Goodbye.'

With brisk steps, they departed. Krystyna returned to Gosia and Piotr.

'The way is clear; you can leave undisturbed. Are you certain this is wise?' she asked, her voice laden with genuine concern for Gosia's current state. She feared the worst was not yet over.

'I'm certain of nothing,' he confessed, his voice trailing off uncertainly. 'I'm merely fulfilling Gosia's wish. I'll take her home, stop by work to hand in my leave note, take some time off, and then we'll see. If anything …'

'You can always reach out to me … to us,' Krystyna corrected herself, 'at any time, no matter the hour. Gosia can always count on our support.'

He nodded in gratitude, took Gosia by the hand, and led her towards the exit.

Krystyna lingered in the room for a moment longer, needing a moment to gather herself. She took several deep breaths before heading to the secretariat. She wanted to congratulate Alicja and express how truly happy she was for her joy.

Piotr settled Gosia into bed. After the injection she'd received at work, she seemed so tranquil. He removed her shoes, positioned her head on the pillow and tucked his wife under the duvet.

'Darling, I must step out briefly, just for an hour or so. Have a nap – you won't even notice my absence. I'll drop off the sick note at work and return as soon as possible. We can plan our dream holiday then.'

He caressed her head tenderly and left the bedroom. Momentarily, he returned with a glass of water and placed it on Gosia's bedside table. Once assured she had fallen asleep, he quietly exited the flat.

Gosia was not asleep. She lay in bed waiting for Piotr to leave. She felt the encroaching darkness, although it was only nearing midday, as evidenced by the sun piercing through the curtains. She sat up, drew a piece of paper and a pen from the drawer, and scribbled a few words. Placing the paper aside, she reached into the drawer again, retrieving a vial of small tablets. She examined it closely and opened it. Spilling its contents into her hand, she began taking the tablets one by one, intermittently sipping water.

'I cannot stay with you, though I love you more than anything in the world. I wish for your happiness, yet I can't give it to you. I cannot give you a child,' she articulated slowly, as if explaining to someone. After a few tablets, her head began to droop, and her words became increasingly nonsensical. 'You'll have them … but alone … will you cry?'

She no longer knew if it was morning, noon or evening. Had she cried all her tears? She was at the very bottom, in an abyss so black and dense that only tar could compare with the consistency of her pain. The more she tried to escape, the more the depths engulfed her. She could no longer distinguish truth from illusion.

She envisioned herself and Piotr with a child, and then, in an instant, saw only herself, alone. She wanted nothing more than happiness, to build a home, to finally have a family, a child. The memory again constricted her with pain so intense it seemed to block the air from her lungs. With the last of her strength, she lifted her head from the pillow and reached for the remaining tablets. A long moment had passed before she swallowed the last one and washed it down with water. She fell back onto the pillow. 'I don't have to do anything anymore,' she thought. Then there was only silence. The spectre that had been creeping along the walls drew nearer, enveloping everything in its path. Darkness fell. And only the cuckoo clock cheerfully announced noon.

When Krystyna received a call from Piotr in the evening, she couldn't believe what had happened. She was terrified. She quickly rang Magda, and after consulting with her, she also called Alicja. As she had feared, Alicja took all the blame on herself. She was deeply troubled by it over the next few days. Unfortunately, a frenzy of project work began at their company, and it was not until the weekend that the friends could find the time to meet and talk things through. As was their custom, they gathered at Alicja's home. However, this time they decided to forgo the wine. As they sat on the sofa in the living room, with Coleman Hawkins's music softly weaving in the background, they returned to the topic of Gosia.

'It appears thus, girls,' said Alicja, tucking her legs under her on the sofa. 'I feel responsible for what has happened. I should have somehow prepared Gosia for the news of my pregnancy, rather than bursting into the office and announcing out of the blue that I was expecting.'

'You said nothing because, frankly, you had no chance! Gosia noticed your maternity book and drew her own conclusions,' said Magda.

'You can't take the blame on yourself, Ala. Gosia wouldn't even admit to herself how poorly she took her last miscarriage. You all saw that two days later she was back at work. She didn't allow herself to mourn, to truly grieve her loss. All that sorrow was bottled up inside her. I, consumed by my own grief, failed to help her when she needed it most,' Krystyna wiped away a tear that was rolling down her cheek.

'Stop! Enough, or I'll go mad,' Magda reacted more loudly than she had intended. 'This is all heading in the wrong direction. None of you is to blame for what happened. It was unforeseeable. I spoke with Piotr today. Gosia is in good hands. They are using quite unconventional methods, at least in our country, but Piotr sees positive changes in Gosia. Let's stop this self-reproach, shall we?' Magda looked at the girls with a wry smile.

'Yes,' both confirmed, yet it was evident that they did not entirely agree with Magda's opinion.

'I would just like to add that I really could have handled it differently, and ...' Alicja attempted to interject further, but Magda swiftly cut her off.

'There was nothing you could have done, nothing you could have foreseen. Damn it all! Gosia is an adult, so is Piotr. Both made their decisions. I don't blame either of them,' Magda added, her gaze flitting between the two women. 'They simply didn't cope with their pain, didn't allow themselves to feel, and that led them to where they are now. Gosia didn't want to commit suicide. She simply wanted to sleep, to not feel the pain. That's all. None of us are responsible for Gosia and Piotr's fertility issues. It's nobody's fault. End of discussion. Gosia is in the care of specialists and, most importantly, her family. We will support her as soon as she feels better and returns to us. Of that, I am certain. That's the end of it. Or I'll start biting. Alka, didn't you mention you went to the shopping centre today? Knowing you, you've bought out half the shops,' Magda switched to an old topic that always worked at their gatherings.

'Not half, I didn't have the funds,' Alicja threw back, visibly relaxed by Magda's diversion. 'You know how it is. You enter the shop for toothpicks, and suddenly a huge banner screaming "Sale" catches your eye. Involuntarily, you're drawn over. It started with handbags, with belts lying next to them. Especially one looked splendid and would match that coat I just spotted. In a moment, I'd paired them. Once I'd picked a scarf to go with the coat, I realised I had no matching shoes. Then came the dilemma. Which to choose? Loafers, wedges, or should I go straight for boots? When I finally made my choice, it dawned on me that I was actually there to buy cotton pads. Heading to the other end of the shop, I stumbled on new candles, such delightful scents. You can smell them now. I simply had to purchase them, didn't I?' All three burst into laughter.

'Have you bought those cotton pads?' Krystyna asked with amusement.

'Of course not. I forgot,' Alicja admitted honestly. 'Thanks, girls. I needed you today. Aleksander is a wonderful man, he loves me and spoils me rotten – especially now that I'm pregnant – but he doesn't always understand what I say to him. It's as if he's from another country, or perhaps a different planet.'

'Because they are from another planet, although in my opinion, they're from an entirely different universe. Supposedly parallel, but on a very cosmic plane,' Krystyna quipped, sipping her strawberry and spinach cocktail.

'A very apt cosmic comparison,' Magda observed. 'And I have to agree with you. Sometimes, it's the same with Tomasz. We're seemingly speaking the same language, yet it's as if we're from different worlds. But if it's similar with your blokes, then it must mean they're just like that by nature.'

'I don't want to pry, but how are things between you two? You keep such a distance at work, I doubt anyone would realise that there's more between you,' Krystyna said, eyeing Magda, whose cheeks had turned a shade of pink.

'It's good,' Magda said, embarrassed, and looked away.

'You don't think such answer will satisfy us, do you? I'm not asking for the most intimate details about Tomasz, but surely you can tell us something. How do you feel with him, are you happy, what's he like? Does he look after you? Is he affectionate? Does he know what films you like to watch in bed? You simply must satisfy my pregnancy curiosity,' Alicja pressed.

'Are you using your pregnancy to interrogate me?' Magda teased her.

'Yes!' Alicja replied with disarming honesty, and they all began to laugh.

'Okay, then I'll tell you. I even wanted you to quiz me because who else can I tell everything if not you. It's wonderful. It feels as if there haven't been years of separation. I enjoy spending time with him, he pampers me, listens, and at night, when dreams still sometimes trouble me, he holds me close and is there. He's incredibly tender and for the first time, I've truly experienced that sex can be a marvellous thing.'

'Do you have orgasms?' Alicja inquired. Noting Krystyna's slightly terrified expression, she added, 'You know full well that satisfaction in bed is just as important as satisfaction in love or conversation.'

'Of course it's important,' Magda said. 'I do have orgasms, sometimes two or three in one evening. It happens.'

'Perhaps I asked somewhat indelicately, but in my experience, people pay far too little attention to satisfaction in bed, and then there are affairs, problems.'

'And there I must agree with you, Alicja. Just look at me and my husband. No improvement, still no time for me. He's always very busy with everything else but me. Lately, I've started wondering if it would affect me in any way if, for instance, he left me or I left him. And the thought didn't frighten me, on the contrary – I think I would feel relieved. But I don't want to talk about it now, I need to sort it out in my head,' Krystyna concluded, seeing the interest in Alicja's and Magda's eyes.

'I should be going. The twins are home alone. I want to spend some time with them. Especially now, as Krzysztof has no time for us at all.' Saying this, she rose from the sofa and made her way to the hallway to get dressed. Magda got up to follow Krystyna.

'I'll be off as well. Tomasz is waiting, and Aleksander is bound to turn up soon. Take care!' Magda approached Alicja to peck her on the cheek in farewell.

'Would it be terribly rude if I didn't stand up to see you out? I'm so comfortable that I just don't feel like getting up,' Alicja said, ever so straightforward.

'Don't worry, darling, we'll see ourselves out and even close the door behind us, so you won't have to move your pregnant belly from the sofa,' Krystyna sent an air kiss towards Alicja and mimed a belly rub. Moments later Alicja was alone, comfortably settled on the sofa, covered with a blanket, and she drifted off to sleep.

The sky was shrouded in steel-grey clouds. They hung heavily over the city, utterly obscuring the sun's rays. After another row with Krzysztof, Krystyna had no energy left to deal with the paperwork related to her father's flat. Unfortunately, the deadlines were relentless, and time was not on her side. The last thing she fancied was a trek through the bureaucracies.

She sat at the kitchen table, staring blankly ahead, pondering what had become of her life. How had they become such strangers to one another so suddenly? Her husband had helped with the arrangements for her father's funeral but did absolutely nothing to provide emotional support. Only on the day they learnt of the death did Krzysztof hold her, allowing her tears to flow freely. But that was the only time. Afterwards, he retreated; present, yet behind his own invisible wall. Last night, as they lay in the bedroom watching a film, she had simply wanted to snuggle up to him. He pushed her away, got up and spent the night on the couch, without a word, without an explanation.

The television in the bedroom was his idea, too. They had never needed one there before, and now, as soon as Krzysztof came home from work, he would shut himself in the room, flipping through the channels before falling asleep under his own duvet. This new arrangement had materialised abruptly, without any discussion with Krystyna. She could have sworn that when the new bedding arrived, Krzysztof breathed a sigh of relief as he covered himself with his duvet. She never questioned him about it, and he was in no hurry to offer any explanation. He left her without answers, and she was frightened to demand the truth.

She could no longer put off leaving the house. She slipped on her coat, pulled on her boots and grabbed her umbrella. The tram arrived promptly, sparing her from waiting on the tiny island amid the sea of vehicles that had sped past her that morning on her walk to the stop. She could have asked Krzysztof for a lift, but after last evening, the very thought was unappealing. It frightened her.

Sitting on the tram, she began to ponder when they had become strangers to each other. When had it begun? She could not pinpoint the moment in time. It felt as if it had been happening since Christmas, and now it was October. So for at least ten months, they had been behaving like strangers. There was no closeness, no love, to say nothing of intimacy. She alighted from the tram, immediately opening her umbrella. The pelting rain seemed endless, the dark clouds remaining ever oppressive and heavy.

Huddled into the collar of her coat and shielded by the umbrella, she navigated the streets to the office. Standing in the doorway, she turned to shake the raindrops from her umbrella. She felt droplets on her cheeks, their coolness piercing her to the core. She shook her head, intending to move forward, but unexpectedly she stumbled into a pair of a man's arms. The first, quite irrational thought that struck her was: she knew these arms. Moments later, she also heard a voice that was all too familiar to her.

'I do not believe it is a mere coincidence that I am holding you in my arms,' said Antoni, embracing her more tightly.

'Antoś,' she whispered and, against her will, began to cry. They stood like that for a moment, blocking the entrance and exit, until impatient patrons began to express their discontent rather loudly. Antoni took Krystyna by the hand and led her to a nearby café. He ordered tea with lemon and raspberry syrup, her favourite for such days, and waited in silence for her to compose herself. Only after a few minutes did she wipe her eyes and look at him. His black hair was slowly turning delicately grey and wrinkles were beginning to etch his face. He looked even better than she remembered from the last time they had seen each other, just before her wedding.

'I apologise for my outburst. I don't know what came over me. Or perhaps I do, but it's hard to admit even to myself how bad things are,' she said, noting his concerned look. 'My dad passed away a few weeks ago, and my marriage is virtually non-existent. I'm sorry, I shouldn't speak of my marriage this way in front of you. It's unfair to Krzysztof. Don't ask, okay?'

'As you wish. But know that I am always here if you need to talk. I won't let you disappear from my life again like last time. Give me your number, and from now on, I want to know at least every few days that everything is alright.'

His smile remained unchanged, bewitching her once again. Antoni's eyes still twinkled mischievously. Without thinking of the consequences or how Krzysztof might interpret it, Krystyna gave Antoni her number and saved his contact in her phone. She watched him with curiosity.

'Tell me about yourself first, and then I'll tell you about me – within reason, of course. Do you have a wife, a girlfriend, children?'

'Okay. The answer is: no, no, no. Since that marriage, I've not been involved with anyone seriously enough to consider spending the rest of my life with her. There have been women in my life, true, but none was what I was looking for.'

'And what were you looking for that no woman could match? You are incredibly tanned, have you been on holiday?'

'I lived in Egypt for a few years, then in Spain. I haven't sunbathed in a long time. It's just that my skin has taken on this colour. And to answer your first question: none of the women was you. I've spent hundreds of hours on dates, only to realise each time that someone like you is unique. And even if I searched the ends of the earth, I would not find another. A few weeks ago, I returned to Poland and today I stumbled upon you. God, you're so beautiful, ethereal and fragile ..."

'Above all, I am decidedly older than when we last saw each other in the centre.'

'I saw you once more ...'

'Where, when? Why did I not see you?'

'Because you were walking down the aisle with your now-husband. It's not difficult to find out the time and place of a wedding. A few hours on the phone was all it took. I called every church in the city. The forty-fifth time was lucky. You were a stunning bride. I waited for the priest to ask, like in the movies, if there was anyone who objected to this marriage, but the priest said nothing of the sort, and I was too scared to speak up. I could only sit and cry that I wasn't the man next to you'.'

'Antoni ...'

'I know, calm down, I'm not the same man I used to be. I realised that after all that's happened, you had every right to build your life, and I must come to terms with that. And okay. I've accepted my fate. I only want to be able to call you once a week or fortnightly, to talk, or like now – to have tea together.'

'Speaking of tea, it's my favourite in this kind of weather.'

'I remember, I know.'

He looked at her, and Krystyna felt as if time had stood still. He took her hand and began to gently massage her knuckles with his thumb.

'Please ...'

She wanted to snatch her hand away, to leave quickly, to get away from him. But instead, she began to tell him about Krzysztof, about their relationship, about feeling so alone, how he treated and insulted her. She told him everything, even what she hadn't dared tell the girls from work – that one day she caught Krzysztof in the bathroom in the evening, looking at something on his phone and masturbating.

'He's an idiot. That's all I can tell you. How can someone behave like that? Have you asked him about it? Has he said anything? Or is he just pretending there's no problem? Okay. Masturbation once in a while is fine, but for nearly a year? Something doesn't add up.'

'We don't talk about it. Whenever I try to find out more, he immediately starts calling me names, saying that's all I have in my head, that I act like a whore. The worst part is that I'm beginning to think the same about myself. Maybe in marriages of this duration, eroticism fades?'

'No! And no again! Do you believe that people over forty don't do it? That they don't make love? Intimacy between two people is all about giving and receiving pleasure. And I'll tell you more, without sex, after some time, other forms of closeness fade, and what's left is two strangers. Just like you and Krzysiek now. He should be close to you, especially when you really need him. Has he held you recently to show that he's there, that you can count on him?'

'The day my dad died. Since then, all I've been hearing is that I should be strong or that I shouldn't act like a slut. Good heavens ...' She lowered her head into her hands, sitting motionless for a moment. 'I shouldn't speak of my husband like this ... it's wrong ... to a lover. Even worse ...' She began to laugh. 'That's a mere slip of the tongue, of course, pay it no mind.' She blushed slightly. She didn't want Antoni to think she expected anything more than just meeting him for a coffee.

'No, why? Your slip of the tongue was quite prophetic, actually. Freud would've had a field day with that. We meet after years, and you're immediately suggesting specifics.'

'Stop making fun of me.' She glanced at her watch. 'Is it already noon? I must go to the housing cooperative to return the keys to Dad's flat. I hope there won't be a barrage of questions I don't wish to answer.'

'Do you want me to come with you? As a friend, of course.' He glanced at her from the corner of his eye, smiling mischievously.

'Would you? I don't know if you're not otherwise engaged today. And here I am, monopolising your entire morning.'

'Nothing is more important than you. Come on. But afterwards, you'll owe me.' He gave her a warm look that promised much. 'You'll join me for lunch.'

For some reason, Krystyna felt a twinge of disappointment and letdown. Exiting the café, Antoni held the door open for her, and as she stepped out, he took her hand, and together they walked towards the opposite building.

The formalities of handing over the keys did not take long, with just a few signatures in several places, and they were nearly ready to leave the room.

'Madam, you've written that you are returning two sets of keys for the cellar and three sets of flat keys, but I only see two sets of the flat keys here. Shall I note that you are handing in two sets each?'

'Oh, I beg your pardon, I forgot to detach my father's keys from my own.'

She reached into her bag, extracted a bunch of keys and began to fiddle with the rings, which stubbornly refused to cooperate. Antoni, observing her struggle, took her hand, took the keys and calmly detached the correct ones.

'Which other one?'

Krystyna pointed. Tears streamed down her face uninterrupted. After a moment, Antoni took her by the hand and led her out of the office. Just around the corner, he put her in his car and drove her to his flat. They did not speak during the journey. At every conceivable opportunity, he held her hand, but said nothing, giving her the space to cry. Once they arrived at his flat, he seated Krystyna on the sofa, then went to make tea.

'With honey and lemon?' he called from the kitchen.

'Yes, please. Is this your flat?'

She looked around. The room was dominated by two colours: white and grey, with touches of black. The flat was tastefully decorated, yet it seemed more suited to the pages of an interior design magazine than to everyday living.

'Not mine, I'm renting it, but I've just decided that I'll buy it. I was to stay only a few weeks, but I've resolved to settle in Poland permanently.'

He handed Krystyna a mug of hot tea and sat down close to her. She felt a flush of warmth, and it was certainly not from the tea. A heat slowly spread throughout her body. Rising from the sofa with the intention of placing her mug on the coffee table, she walked a few steps and then settled into an armchair across from him.

'Why have you sat over there?'

'To be able to look at you calmly,' Krystyna responded quickly. Too quickly.

'And you think I'll believe that?'

'It all feels so surreal now. For years, I tried not to think of you. And honestly, I nearly succeeded, save for a few moments. I thought I'd moved on. That I'd forgotten you. And then you reappear in my life. The worst part is that

I don't want you to disappear from it again. Not now. God! What am I rambling about?!'

'Steady on, I'm not going anywhere. I'll always be close by. I expect nothing from you, no declarations, no promises. I just want to be able to call you, to meet with you for tea, or …'

'That will be difficult,' Krystyna whispered.

'I know. I feel it too. I'm trying to sit here with you, to have a normal conversation and not think about the bedroom next door, with its vast bed, where I'd rather be with you right now. And by God, I don't mean to sleep. But I also know you're married, and the next move is yours. But –' he stressed '– I won't wait long.' Looking into her eyes, he rose from the sofa. Krystyna shifted nervously in the armchair.

'Don't come any closer.'

'Why?'

He was so near she could feel the warmth of his body. The desire to touch him seemed endless. His hand caressed her cheek, his thumb teased her lips. He leant in and lightly touched her lips with his, allowing her the choice. The passion with which she responded surprised her most of all. She pressed into his warm lips, one hand entangled in the hair at the nape of his neck. The world ceased to exist. Nothing else mattered. Only him, her and a closeness she had never felt with anyone. As if she had never been touched, caressed, loved. She desired him with her entire being.

'Are you certain?' whispered Antoni, as he attempted to unbutton her blouse. His voice, or rather the question, brought her back to reality.

'No, I'm sorry. I am not certain.' She moved away from him to maintain a distance. She fastened the buttons of her blouse, smoothed her skirt that, for some unfathomable reason, had ridden up to the height of her thigh, revealing her garter belt and stockings. She picked up her jacket from the ground.

'Antoś, it's not that I don't want to be with you. I've dreamt of it since I saw you this morning. God!' She buried her face in her hands. After a moment, she began to put on her shoes. 'But it can't be that at the first sign of trouble, I jump into bed with you. Damn it, I am a married woman, I have children. It's all not so simple. Despite the breakdown of my marriage and that I'm sure I don't love Krzysztof, I must act decently. Out of respect for myself. Simply. Do you understand?'

'Yes. And although it's hard for me to act like a man, and not a fool, at this moment, I will wait for you. But believe me, it won't be easy, because I damn well want you. And even more for you to always be by my side. But I understand that I must wait, and I will wait. I don't want to mess this up like last time. I won't let you go again. Perhaps next time we could meet in town, not at my place. Because I can't promise that I'll have the strength to act like a gentleman.'

'I wouldn't have the strength either,' said Krystyna tenderly, 'but I want to do the right thing, unlike my husband. Shall we text tonight? Life being what it is, I'll likely be alone. But now I must leave, because the longer I stand here and look at you, the harder it will be for me to go.'

Already wearing her coat, she approached Antoni, embraced him, kissed him and left promptly.

Outside, the rain persisted, yet curiously, it didn't bother her in the least. Glancing at her watch, she was startled by the hour – it had already struck past five. Hastily, she found a taxi rank and slid into a cab. For a moment, she hesitated over whether to ring Krzysztof, to warn him she'd be later than usual, but soon concluded it was pointless. She could scarcely recall when the last time that they exchanged messages or called over some trifling matter was, just to hear the other's voice.

Navigating through the clogged veins of the city in the taxi, she began to scroll through her phone, locating her exchanges with Krzysztof. The last message from her end concerned groceries. A mere, dry text message with a shopping list, nothing more. An earlier one mentioned she would be late due to a prolonged meeting at work. Reviewing the correspondence with her husband, she noticed how, over many months, perhaps even years, they had been drifting apart step by step. And now, after so many years of marriage, with grown children and a chance to finally breathe, it seemed they were just two strangers.

The taxi trudged through streets and traffic lights, coming to a halt beneath her block of flats after twenty-five minutes. Krystyna paid her fare and got off. Out of the corner of her eye, she caught sight of another taxi departing with Krzysztof. He waved at her, in the manner one acknowledges a neighbour one is not particularly fond of but feels obliged to greet nonetheless. And he drove off in his direction. She swiftly climbed the steps to her flat and was home in moments. The scent of hot pepperoni pizza greeted her as she crossed the threshold.

'Hello, young ones. Are you having pizza?'

'Hi, Mum. Yes, Dad ordered it. He said he had to go away for a week and wouldn't be back until next Sunday. Did you know he was going to be away that long?' Patryk inquired. She didn't know how to respond to the children. She was herself taken aback by Krzysztof's departure, especially that he had left for over a week without giving her a prior notice.

'Yes, he mentioned it,' she lied. She saw the glances the children exchanged. 'I'm going to get changed. I hope there's a slice of pizza for me.'

'Of course, Mummy, Dad ordered two pizzas, so there would be some for you,' Patrycja chimed in.

Krystyna proceeded to the bedroom and closed the door behind her to change in peace. On the chest of drawers, she noticed some documents. She was tempted to look closer, but then decided that the paperwork could wait. She slipped into her tracksuit, grabbed her phone and returned to the children.

'How about a film night? We'll make popcorn and watch something on Netflix?'

'Great. But no romantic comedies,' Patryk protested.

'Okay, how about the new film with Cruise, is that alright?'

She wasn't fond of action movies, but she knew the children adored them, and she wanted some time to herself to think things through.

'I'll make the popcorn,' Patryk declared. 'Patrycja will set up the movie-watching area, and you, Mum, just enjoy your pizza in peace. See how nice it is to have grown-up children?'

'Bloody brilliant,' Krystyna laughed, delighting in the surprise on the children's faces upon hearing a swear word from her.

'Mum!' They both exclaimed, bursting into laughter. 'You never swear!'

'Time for a change. From now on, I shall live on pizza, watch films, and swear. Do you approve of this new Mum?'

'Yeah, cool. It'd be nice if Dad could change too because he's always absent. He never has time for us. And he's been acting so odd, all secretive. The other day when you weren't here, some bloke came to see him, dressed rather oddly, a bit like a woman, and they had a chat on the stairwell. They were even shouting at each other. Dad said something like, "Don't come here pressuring me, I've promised and

I will keep my word. Everything will be as you wish soon." And then that fellow said something odd: *Wmiestie nawsiegda*, and Dad repeated after him: *Nawsiegda*. When he came inside, he had this strange smile on his face and only after a moment noticed I was standing in the room. He asked if I had heard anything, but I quickly told him I'd been in the bathroom, though I couldn't have been because Patrycja was having a bath. Pati and I even talked about it and concluded that perhaps Dad is a spy, and that man was in disguise, because he's someone working undercover. Though on the other hand, undercover agents shouldn't be so conspicuous, right, Mum?'

'No, you're right. It must have been one of Dad's mates having a laugh.'

She knew they didn't believe her. She didn't believe what she'd said herself. But now, the situation with Krzysztof was beginning to clarify. Various stories associated with him were gradually emerging from the recesses of her memory. She had once paid them no heed. She recalled odd remarks from Krzysztof's extended family suggesting they probably wouldn't have children. Or before the wedding, questions about whether she truly knew what she was doing. She tried to remember any instances where he'd talked about finding another woman attractive. But there was nothing. Instead, she remembered Krzysztof's evasive gaze when they happened on a bodybuilding competition at a fair. She was certain back then that he simply envied their appearance. Now she realised he hadn't looked at them with envy, but with desire. She had mistaken envy for desire. And though it pained her that after all these years he hadn't mustered the courage to simply tell her the truth, a thought had been smouldering in the back of her mind for some time that there was something amiss with Krzysztof.

She watched the film with the children, laughed and joked with them, but in truth, after watching it, she didn't even know what it was about. When she went to the bedroom in the evening, she looked again at the documents on top of the drawers. She picked them up. Their contents were quite a surprise. Mostly bills. Hotel bills. On days when he was supposedly away on business at the other end of the world, he was actually at the other end of town. He had been deceiving her for so long that she didn't even have the strength to be angry with him, yet tears streamed down her face regardless. At first, she thought of Antoni, but she dismissed the idea. It wasn't the right time to go to him. She took her phone and called Magda.

'Hello, sunshine, good of you to call; we were just thinking of you. Ala's over here. Fancy dropping by?'

'I can't be bothered to change, so I'll be in my tracksuit. Have you got wine? I need a lot of wine today.'

'You, in a tracksuit? Wanting a lot of wine? What have you done with Kryśka?'

'Very fucking funny. I'll bring a couple of extra bottles just in case and I'll be right over.'

She hung up. She walked into the living room where her children were watching another film.

'Will you watch with us, Mummy?'

'I need to dash out to see the girls from work. You two can manage, right?'

'Yeah, Mum, we're almost grown-up,' Patryk replied, with Pati fervently nodding in agreement.

'You're darlings. I love you very much. Maybe we could pop to the cinema or go shopping tomorrow?'

'Brilliant idea, Mummy. We'll be fine, don't worry about us.'

'I'm off to Magda's, I'll be available on my phone.'

She kissed them both, grabbed her sports bag with two bottles of wine and Krzysztof's receipts, and left the house. She caught a taxi quickly and, a few minutes later, was knocking at her friend's door.

'Oh my! You really are in a tracksuit,' Magda exclaimed, surprised.

Alicja peeked out from behind her. Seeing them both, Krystyna broke down in tears again. They didn't ask any questions, just let her cry it out. Knowing her well, they understood something terrible must have happened for Krystyna to react so out of character. They settled her into an armchair, Magda poured her wine, and they both waited patiently for the worst to pass.

'I'm sorry, but since this morning I've been confronted with such ludicrous situations that I've lost control over everything. And since yesterday's row with Krzysztof, everything has been throwing me off balance. The office, Antoś, the bills ...'

She paused to take a sip of wine.

'Antoni? Did you see Antoni? Your love? The one who kisses so passionately?' Alicja seized the moment to ask a few questions.

'And still kisses.' If Krystyna had declared that she'd joined the circus to become a trapeze artist, it wouldn't have made as much of an impression as the fact that she was kissing Antoni.

'Bloody hell! What's happening? Can you start from the beginning?'

Thus, Krystyna began recounting everything that had happened since the day before: the argument with Krzysztof, the television in the bedroom, the extra duvet, finding him in a compromising situation in the bathroom, what her son had overheard, and finally the hotel bills. And at last, to Alicja's delight, she talked about Antoni.

'Are you suggesting Krzysztof is bisexual? There's no other rational explanation. What are these bills for? Have you checked them online?' Magda inquired.

'No, I haven't checked; I couldn't bring myself to do it.'

'Okay, give them to us; we'll check everything now,' Alicja offered.

'Will you help me? I'm overwhelmed by all of this. I don't have the energy to check everything myself. And I know there's probably more I don't know about Krzysiek.'

Each took a few bills and with a phone in hand, began to check Krzysztof's expenditures. After a moment, Alicja spoke up with a hint of hesitation.

'I've got something, but I'm not certain it's a good idea to delve into it.'

'Show what you've found,' said Magda, approaching Alicja. She tilted her phone to display her findings.

'I'm going to check later at home anyway. Show me!' Krystyna demanded sharply.

'It's a bill for a hotel in Warsaw.'

'I knew as much myself.'

'Yes, but this hotel is notorious for hosting weekend gatherings for gay people who are into rather extreme sex. I'm sorry, Krysia.'

'Well, that at least confirms what I suspected. I understand now why he's been avoiding me and why there's been no intimacy, no tenderness between us for a year. I don't have a bloody penis!' She spread her arms, smiling sarcastically though she felt far from amused. 'I found bills for leather collars and whips. Bloody hell! Do you know what really infuriates me? That he didn't come to me and tell me about it. He didn't say that something had changed, he just kept deceiving me. He deliberately made me feel guilty. I'm livid! That he demeaned me, calling me a whore. Hell! He made me feel like a whore, begging for his love and attention. For at least a year! And now I'm certain, probably since always. He didn't have the balls to say he liked men too. I know! He has no balls because he likes being fucked by others!'

'Ha, ha, ha, I've never heard you curse so much in one go. You're changing.'

For the first time, Magda saw Krystyna in such a state. For the first time, her friend truly revealed herself, exposing her darker side.

'He always told me that we shouldn't stick our necks out, that there was no need to stand out unnecessarily. But it wasn't about me; it was about him. He was the one who needed the camouflage, a family, to pretend to be normal.'

'Do you have any ideas? Do you want a change?' Magda inquired.

'Oh, I'm absolutely craving a change! From today, no more uniforms, no conservative suits, I shall not stifle myself. And I know Dad would forgive me, but enough of the black! He wouldn't wish me to spend my life mourning him. He'd prefer that I begin to live. Especially now. I won't give Krzysztof the satisfaction. Tomorrow I'm off shopping, I'll take the children, and I'll buy something I've never dared to wear. Because I was too conservative. And then I'll arrange to meet with Antoś.'

'And how will it be now? Will you continue to see him?'

Magda was taken aback by the entire situation. She could have anticipated anything, but what had transpired completely shattered her perception of Krystyna and Krzysztof. She had known them for years. At first, she thought they were unnecessarily posh. Sometimes she even felt like telling Krystyna to remove that stick from her backside and start living a little more freely. That was when they just met, but as she got to know her better, she came to accept that Kryśka was just that way and nothing would change it. Until today.

'I don't know what will happen now. I need … some wine, would you pour me some?' she asked Magda, waving an empty wine glass. 'And besides, I need to replace my entire wardrobe. Do you know what it's like when you find out your whole life is one big sham? You build something, think you have a strong foundation, and nothing will shake it, only to find out you don't even have a ground floor, just directly a first floor. Bloody hell, the house has collapsed, only an idiot, I mean the site manager, immediately erected a ballroom full of glitz meant to mask the muck and pile of dung. Exactly! That's what my life looks like now. I'm smeared in manure!'

That evening, Krystyna talked a lot about herself and drank a lot of wine. None of the girls interrupted her, and Magda topped up her glass every few minutes. Sometimes there comes a day when you just have to let go and allow yourself to release your brakes.

'Krystyna, I'll call you a cab, alright?'

Magda rose to make the call, while Alicja assisted Krystyna to her feet.

'Am I drunk?' Krystyna inquired with curiosity.

'Yes, you've got a bit pissed today.'

'It's all because of that deceitful witch!' She shrugged. 'I suppose I'll have a hangover tomorrow,' she giggled, 'and nothing cures a hangover like a good romp!'

'I think I'll just take you home, you know?'

'Splendid idea, we could swing by Antoni's on the way. Though no, because he's all mine, you won't be able to shag him, you know?'

She tried to stand erect but was barely keeping on her feet. She glanced sideways at Magda, who had already booked the taxi.

'You know I've never been drunk before? Because apparently, it's not done.' She shrugged. 'And is it proper to shag your mates when you have a beautiful wife at home? That's not either, yet they do it. Well, from now on, I'll drink and shag too. But not with you, you know? Only with my hero Antoni.'

'I regret not having recorded this,' Alicja remarked with a laugh. 'I have a feeling we're going to be laughing at this for years. Put on your shoes, miss, and we're taking you home.'

'Okey-dokey. But first, we pick up Antoni. If my still-husband can frolic with anything that comes to hand, then so can I.'

'When we wrote those plans for this year? Have you noticed none of it has come true?' Alicja said to Magda, watching her help Krystyna put on her shoes. 'Krystyna's legging it in tracksuits; all she's missing is a bottle of wine in hand; I wanted peace, and instead I'm pregnant; you met your love when you wanted to be alone; and Gosia can't have the child she longed for.'

'It's all topsy-turvy with us. But I never expected such a Krystyna.'

'Neither did I, and I least of all expected that I would be the drunk one. Alka would have suited that role better.' Krystyna pointed at her friend and began to snigger under her breath.

'Thank you for your frankness; now let's get our arses moving and head to your home.'

'Well, mine may not be as tempting as yours, but I can certainly give it a good twist.' In a bid to demonstrate, Krystyna tried to sway her hips, but her head spun, and she steadied herself against the wall. 'Looks like I won't be dancing today.'

'Definitely no dancing for you. Let's go, boss lady.'

'Oh, see, at last you're talking sense. After all, I am the boss lady of our room.'

Magda got into the taxi with Krystyna and Alicja. Together, they got her home. They helped her out of the car and to her building entrance. There, Krystyna assured them she could manage on her own and headed for the lift. The girls then went to their own homes.

The next morning, Krystyna awoke with a monstrous headache. She felt every millimetre of her body. Her head throbbed, she was parched, but the mere idea of getting out of bed made her nauseous. She feared any movement. Lying with her eyes closed, she felt the pounding between her temples, blood rushing. It seemed her head might explode at any moment. Her phone vibrated. Without even glancing at the display, she answered the call.

'Hello!' she said with a wasted voice.

'Hey, beautiful!' greeted her Antoni. 'I can only imagine how you're feeling today after yesterday's drinking. I know you probably haven't got the energy for anything, so take my advice. Ask the kids to make you a hot tea with plenty of sugar and lemon. Drink the hot beverage in small sips, then head to the bathroom, take a shower, have more hot tea prepared the same way, and only then have breakfast. Scrambled eggs with butter, sausage and lots of tomatoes would be ideal, or if you have tomato juice at home, then have the juice with the eggs.'

'How do you know?' she asked in surprise, as she couldn't remember speaking to him since she had left his place.

'You texted me. I'll give you some time to recover. We'll talk later. Bye!'

He hung up before Krystyna could fully grasp what he had said. Slowly, making no sudden movements, she made her way to the kitchen. She turned on the electric kettle and waited for the water to boil.

'Hi, Mum, how are you feeling?' Pati greeted her warmly.

'Hey, Pati! I'm not feeling the best, I must admit. I'll try to sort myself out but I need a little time,' her mother responded, sounding under the weather.

'There's no rush, Mum. It's still early. Why don't you go and have a bath, and I'll sort out breakfast? You were quite funny last night,' Patrycja remarked timidly.

'Oh dear, did you both see me in that state?' A crestfallen Krystyna stared at her daughter.

'Ha, ha, ha, don't be so horrified, Mum. We know something's up with you and Dad. You probably just needed that kind of reset. I promise I won't tell a soul,' she lifted two fingers in a gesture of oath.

'There's no excuse for my behaviour. Nothing justifies what I did last night …' Krystyna mused, her thoughts muddled. She was unsure if she was referring to the amount of wine consumed, the kiss or the awakening desire within her. Wanting to conceal her guilt, she rose from her chair to retrieve her tea from the counter, brewed according Antek's special recipe.

She hadn't anticipated the surge of bliss from a sip of the hot, sweet-and-sour beverage. Slowly sipping her tea, she pondered over the previous day's events. Initially, she thought to check her phone, but concluded she wasn't ready to confront her embarrassment. Knowing she had written to Antoni, she decided she wanted to remain ignorant for the moment. She placed the empty mug down and headed to the bathroom.

Turning on the water, she stepped into the shower. The hot water was effective in washing away the prior day's negative emotions, leaving behind a tumult of blood that centred in the core of her being. She wasn't sure if she was acting consciously as her hands began to move with a mind of their own, actions she wouldn't even admit to herself. She closed her eyes and once again saw Antoni, felt his hands on her flesh. The image was persistent. She took some shower gel, applied it to her hands and began to lather her body. One hand, seemingly of its own volition, traced circles on her breasts, causing her nipples to swell with the touch. The other hand moved down her stomach, finding her lips and the sensitive spot. With short, firm movements, she quickly brought herself to climax. Leaning her forehead against the wall in spasms, she couldn't recall the last time she felt so good. Long-suppressed tension had found a release.

After a moment, she regained enough composure to finish washing. As she rinsed off the shampoo, her hands once again brushed over her nipples, eliciting an involuntary response. Surprised by the previous intensity, this time she sat down in the shower tray, propping up her leg for easier access. Both hands quickly found their way; one massaged her lips while the other with swift movements slipped into the increasingly warm, moist area of her femininity. The orgasm arrived even more swiftly and intensely than before. Spasms wracked her wet body. She needed several moments to be able to stand up calmly. The smile that spread across her face spoke more than a thousand words. She turned the water to cooler, patted down her body, and stepped out of the shower in decidedly better spirits. In the kitchen, the twins were preparing breakfast – freshly made scrambled eggs with chives felt very inviting.

'Mummy, take a seat, we'll serve you everything.'

'It smells divine. Listen, I've saved some money and really have no idea what to do with it. How about we significantly dwindle those savings? We could go to the shopping centre, do some shopping, perhaps a cinema visit? I fancy a trip to the hairdresser's for some sensational highlights, what do you think?'

'Really? You're going for a sensational hairstyle?' Patryk asked.

'Absolutely. I'm in the mood for something wild, and I invite you to join me in some retail madness.'

'How many zeroes does this madness include?' Pati inquired. 'Is it more like one top and one t-shirt or a complete outfit?'

'A complete outfit for everyone, how about it?'

'I don't know what's happened, but don't change, Mum, stay just as you are,' said Patryk, with Pati nodding in agreement.

After breakfast, the children quickly cleaned up – surprisingly without arguing about who had how many square centimetres of plates to wash – and calmly waited for Krystyna to be ready to leave. She put on a shirt and the navy-blue jeans she once bought on Alicja's urging but probably never wore. They called a taxi and the trio went to the nearby shopping centre. They entered every shop she'd previously ignored. Thus, she became the owner of two jumpsuits, a short skirt, a lacy dress, playful underwear, and – in a moment of desperation – a new hairstyle. Patryk, having received a new tracksuit and several games, left their company because – as he pointed out – he did not feel like watching his women change their image at the hairdresser's for an hour and a half, and happily walked away with some friends he bumped into. Pati secretly told Krystyna that Patryk had planned this, but both concluded that he indeed would have been bored with them.

And so, after several hours, a completely new Krystyna stood at home, looking at her reflection in the mirror. For the first time in many years, she saw in herself the old Krysia. The one who liked to splurge, sometimes surrender to the moment. Looking at her reflection, she was amazed at how she had allowed someone to take control over her. She allowed herself to be dressed in a coat of good manners, alien rules, views on what's proper and what's not, when in fact, it was only she who adhered to those rules. It dawned on her that what was will never return. With a decisive move, she reached for the phone. At first, she wanted to call Krzysztof, but concluded that she did not want to hear his lies once more. She sat down in the armchair and wrote a message. She wanted to give him time, not to surprise him, so she wrote:

> *I know everything. About where and with whom you spend your time. Our marriage has not existed for a long time, and I see no reason to remain in limbo and lies. I am not calling because I do not want to hear more lies and insults. I'm only sorry for one thing: that you didn't have the courage to tell me everything. I want you to move out as soon as you return. K.*

She pressed 'Send' before fully realising what she was doing. The almost instantaneous reply from Krzysztof took her by surprise.

> *I have no excuse for my actions. I never intended to hurt you, yet I inflicted the worst kind of pain. Can we meet during the week when the children are at school? I'll collect my things and we can talk. Honestly, this time. K.*

She pondered over the content of her next message for a moment.

> *OK. I expect the truth, the whole truth. I will try to draft the divorce papers by then. If you confess to everything in court, we can be divorced immediately. I'm sorry that we both lacked the courage to be honest. We*

both made mistakes. You, by not speaking, and I, by not demanding the truth. Please let me know when you will come for your things. K.

The response came as swiftly as the previous one.

I can come for my belongings on Wednesday around 10. That's when the children have their longest lessons. I'll have enough time to pack and we can have our talk. K.

At that moment, she realised that Krzysztof had planned this all along. His supposed trip, the way Krystyna would 'accidentally' find the incriminating invoices. Once again, he had done things his way. Even left her in his own cowardly manner. She felt an urge to hurl her phone against the wall, but just then, another message arrived. A flashing envelope icon and an 'A' appeared on the screen. She smiled involuntarily and once again delved into her smartphone.

Hey, Princess Krystyna! How's your Saturday going? Still think I'm the sexiest man alive? Because if so, we could arrange a dinner with wine and … ;)

When she read that message, she recalled she was meant to read what she'd written to Antoni the previous evening. She muttered 'once in a blue moon' under her breath and began to search her phone. Thankfully, there was just one message to Antoni and one to Alicja:

Antoś, but you do turn my head! You're the most handsome man in this vale of tears. I'd shag you standing up.

The message to Alicja, fortunately, was more composed.

I've written to Antoś. Oh, there will be sparks flying! But first, I must get some sleep.

At first, she wanted to write to Antoni, but she decided it would be simpler to ring him and explain away that unfortunate text. He answered after just one ring.

'Hello, beautiful! How's your health? Notice that I'm enquiring after your well-being first and foremost.'

She could visualise him smiling, the corners of his eyes crinkling in anticipation of her response.

'Don't make fun of me. After our meeting, I had a traumatising evening yesterday. In short, I understand why my husband, well, nearly ex-husband I should say, behaves the way he does.'

'Do you want to talk about it?'

'Yes, but not today. On Wednesday, we're settling the divorce terms. I'll have everything sorted by then and will know where I stand. Or rather, what I expect from myself.'

'Has he found someone?'

'Yes, but it's far more complicated than I thought. I don't want to meet with you until then because I don't want to be carried away.'

Saying this, she changed her tone. She was aware she was treading on dangerous territory, but she needed the attention, the flirtation, the tension that come with new relationships, when the magic of desire circulates between lovers, creating an incredible chemistry of attraction.

'Carried away? How could you possibly be carried away? Will you tell me about it?'

His purring voice teased her, arousing her to the limit.

'Oh, for instance, like this morning when I was in the shower. The hot water awakened me as never before. Though no, I remember now. Do you recall our morning together at the hotel in the shower? That was twice in a row, too.'

She never suspected herself capable of such candid conversation. Antek groaned into her ear.

'Please, don't tell me such things. I've had a permanent erection since yesterday. If I could, I would have made love to you a hundred times over by now. And now you're telling me about your shower shenanigans ...'

'Should I refrain from telling you what my hands get up to?' she teased with full intent.

'Give me your address, I'll be there in a few minutes.'

'The children could arrive at any moment. They've extracted an indecent amount of cash from me, but I never know when they'll run out.'

'Then come to me. The bedroom and I are waiting.'

'But what of it? Am I to come to you for a quick tryst?'

'Just one?'

'Madman!'

She laughed, and despite being fully aware that she was acting in direct contradiction to what she had just told Antek, she responded:

'There's a certain logic to it. I'll call the children and let you know, OK?'

'OK, I'm waiting.'

Before she chose Pati's number, the intercom signalled that someone from the household was entering the building. Minutes later, they both stood at the door, expressions uncertain.

'Hey, Mummy!' Patryk said and quickly added: 'But Mummy, you really do look fantastic.'

'Ha, ha, ha, thank you for that unforced compliment. Now out with it, what do you want? Because it's more than obvious you two are up to something.'

'Well, we've got a bit of money left, and it's raining, so we thought maybe two or three people could come over ... We'd order pizza and put on Netflix or some music, but not too loud. So as not to disturb you in the bedroom ...'

'So as not to disturb me in the bedroom?' Krystyna laughed. 'Invite your friends over, don't leave them loitering in the hallway. I'm heading out anyway, I have matters to attend to. I'll be home before ten.'

'Really, Mummy?' Pati inquired, while Patryk was already swinging the door open, nodding to friends who had been waiting patiently outside. 'But Patryk is so gentle and tactful. I must have told him a thousand times how to broach everything with you.'

Krystyna glanced at her son and his friends. She recognised all six from school trips and was acquainted with their parents as well.

'Hello! You'll be on your own. I'll just order pizza for you lot and disappear. Do your parents know you're here?'

'My parents are aware, they just ask for a short text to confirm your consent,' replied Pati's friend, whom she had been close with since their first school day. The rest of the youth confirmed their parents had agreed but asked for a confirmation from Krystyna. She quickly sent a group text, ordered and paid for the pizza, and twenty-five minutes after speaking with Antek, she was ready to leave. She beckoned Pati over.

'I'll be back around ten. Call if anything happens. I trust you.'

'It'll be fine, Mum. We didn't want to wander in the rain, and with Dad not here, we thought you'd surely agree to let our friends come over. You look beautiful in that lace dress.'

'Thank you. I promise, many changes are coming so you can feel at ease at home, but we'll discuss that in a few days. Now I must dash; my taxi is waiting, and you have a good time.'

She pecked her daughter on the cheek and, not waiting for the lift, hurried downstairs.

The journey to Antek's was significantly shorter than on Friday afternoon, and just a few minutes later, she was standing in front of his door. A fleeting thought crossed her mind. *What the fuck am I doing here?* But it vanished as quickly as it had appeared, and Krystyna confidently knocked. Antek answered, clad only in tracksuit bottoms, took her hand and almost pulled her into the flat. He shut the door, kissed her and took off her coat all at the same time. Within minutes, they lay in bed, exhausted as if after a marathon.

'I hope next time will be significantly longer, but I couldn't hold back. Since yesterday, I haven't been able to stop thinking about our kiss. I've never reacted to a kiss before as I did to yours yesterday.'

'Well, welcome to the club, because I felt exactly the same. I am astounded to find myself here with you, lying in bed, and feeling as content as I haven't felt in a long while. It's barely been thirty-six hours since I met you, and so much has happened that it's beyond comprehension.'

'Do you regret it?' he asked, gazing into her face. 'I've imagined this moment so many times, you being right beside me, that I could touch you, kiss you.'

'I only regret that it didn't happen sooner.'

'Are you thinking of your husband?' Antoni inquired, and Krystyna burst into tears against her will.

'Don't think I'm such a cry-baby, but it's all been too much for me,' she began once she had calmed a little. 'I hadn't yet come to terms with my dad's death when it hit me that my husband had been unfaithful for a long time. But not with a woman. Then you appeared yesterday. A million emotions and I think I can't sort them out.'

'Not with a woman?! Are you saying he's been cheating on you with men? Have you considered a good psychologist? It could help. I don't know your stance on therapy, but trust me, it can work wonders.'

'I think that's a good idea. While I know what the grieving process looks like and how to get through it, I have no clue how to sort out everything that's to do with Krzysztof. And then there's you. What I care about most is not to fuck this up.'

'So you're entertaining the thought that I'll be in your life for more than a week or two?'

'Are you joking? I can't imagine lying like this with anyone else. And though my life is now as twisted as Russian ice cream, there's one thing I know for certain. I love you; I've loved you all along, I just tried to drown it out with my relationship with Krzysztof – the marriage and pretending not to see the signs about my husband.'

'I've loved you too, from the moment I saw you on the tram. From the first kiss. In Egypt, I would wake up at night because you appeared in my dreams now and then. There was even a time when I did everything to forget you, but it was futile. Until one day, I met this guy and over a drink … after decidedly too many drinks, I told him about you. And do you know what he said?'

They were still lying in the bedroom, embraced, marvelling at how much joy could be had from a conversation alone.

'What?'

'He quoted Winston Churchill to me: "Never give up on something that you cannot stop thinking about even for a single day." And then he introduced another quotation, this one from Disney.'

'The Disney associated with Mickey Mouse?'

'Yes, the very same. The quote goes: "If you can dream it, you can do it." And it was then that I understood that if I believed that we'd be together one day, it would happen.

Of course, considerable time had elapsed before the meaning of those two quotations dawned on me, but I knew there was something to which I could anchor myself to stave off madness. I found my goal; I was resolved to return to Poland to meet you. And what happened? A week later, I went to the office to register my temporary address and there you were. I had a premonition that morning that something significant would occur, that if I felt at ease, you'd be part of my life too. I must ring Karim and report to him that he was correct about it all.'

'And who is Karim?'

'My comrade, tutor, guru, mentor – he's all of these one after another.'

He gazed at Krystyna, and then he kissed her.

'I'm utterly bewildered. I've had no time to process any of this. On Thursday, there was yet another fight with Krzysztof; come Friday morning, life seemed bleaker than ever, yet it's Saturday evening and I'm lying with you in bed after some phenomenal sex. And that's not all; I'm now aware that my marriage doesn't exist, Krzysztof wants a divorce just as much as I do. I need to untangle all these thoughts. I can scarcely recall when my life last moved at such a velocity. This time, it's Alka who'll envy the cosmic speed of it all.'

She smiled at the thought of Ala's and Magda's facial expressions. She pined for Gosia too. She even considered texting her, but Antek had a somewhat different plan for the remainder of the evening, and because he was so compelling, it was only shortly before ten that she stepped into a taxi.

Alicja was roused by an urge to consume a sandwich. Even in slumber, she could feel her teeth sinking into the fresh, crusty bread. Acting on impulse, she woke Aleksander to tell him about her craving. He had once heard from a friend that pregnant women can have peculiar cravings at the most absurd hours, yet he had never witnessed that firsthand, so Alicja's admission caught him off guard.

'My love, where am I to find you fresh, crusty bread at two-thirty-seven in the morning? No chance. Go back to sleep, we'll figure something out in the morning.'

'But what is there to figure out? There's nowhere here that has bread like we used to have. Like we ate when we were children when our only worry was whether the sandcastle would crumble.'

'You simply want homemade bread with a crunchy crust, correct? Come here, cuddle up to me and let's get back to sleep.'

He wrapped an arm around her and began to stroke her head. Before long, she was sound asleep. He reached for his phone, reset the alarm for a different time, and soon fell asleep as well.

In the morning, Alicja was awakened by the scent of bread being baked. She stirred but did not yet open her eyes.

'This pregnancy will be the end of me, how on earth can I smell bread for hours on end, it's absurd,' she murmured to herself. Slowly, she slid out of bed, put her robe on and followed the aroma to the kitchen. There, on the countertop, was a beautiful, fragrant loaf of bread. Beside it stood Aleksander, bursting with pride like a titan after a victorious battle. The sight deeply moved her. She approached and hugged him tightly, her way of thanking him for what he had done.

'You're a darling, did you get up especially for me to go to the bakery?'

'Woman, what bakery?' he feigned indignation, puffing out his chest like a stallion after a triumphant race. 'I baked it especially for you. You're lucky Grandma taught me to bake. She believed that every man should be able to provide for his family, and that bread should never be in short supply. And I was an apt pupil. Would you like to try?'

'Are you even asking? Hand over the end piece, quickly!'

'What are you after? You mean the heel of the bread?'

'It could be the heel, the end piece, the crust – whatever you call it, I'm asking for it, just quickly, I'm drooling here!'

Indeed, she wiped her mouth with one hand, while the other reached out towards Aleksander, though perhaps more towards the bread.

'Please give me the bread and don't starve a pregnant woman!'

'I'm not sure, it might need to cool down still, it's quite warm …'

Teasing Ala, he handed her a crust of bread. She took it eagerly and popped it into her mouth. And then, for her, the world stood still. The bread was perfect. The crusty exterior tantalised her palate while the soft inside melted in her mouth. She felt like a little girl again, dashing home for a slice of bread before running off to her childhood pals. She savoured the white inner part, leaving the fresh, crunchy crust for later. She ate with her eyes half-closed, her joy evident in every part of her being.

'Do you like it?' asked Aleksander.

'Really, you need to ask? I can't recall when last I had such delicious bread. Perhaps when I was a nipper, scampering through the woods and by the river with the neighbourhood kids, each clutching a slice of bread. All those prawns, noodles and other flavours can take a back seat. From now on it's all about simplicity. I don't remember when last I enjoyed something so thoroughly … that is, until today.' She approached Aleksander and embraced him tightly. 'I've never loved anyone quite as much as you. Well, unless it was the divine Leo from *The Beach*,' she said with a mischievous glance from beneath her lashes.

'But he never baked you bread for breakfast.'

'That's why you're the one living with me, not the heavenly Leo. Could you fix me about three sandwiches?'

'Of course, what would you like in them?'

'Do we still have those beef tomatoes?'

'With tomato, then?'

'Yes, and plenty of butter. Don't spread it; just lay thin slices on the bread, then add tomatoes, onions, and a bit of cream.'

The combination somewhat surprised him, but he complied with her wishes.

'Would you like something to drink with breakfast? Coffee, tea?'

'No, it'll only spoil my taste of childhood. I think I fancy some warm milk. Do you happen to have a cow on the balcony?'

'Not on the balcony, no, but if you wish, we could drive to my family home, and I can promise you not just milk, but homemade butter, and there's home-cured ham to be had as well.'

'Stop,' laughed Alicja, her stomach rumbling already.

'You little glutton, do you agree then?' My parents are quite insistent on meeting you, as is my grandmother. And I've promised we'd visit them this weekend. You know, they are simple folk, and soon we'll be parents to their grandchild.'

His gaze lingered on Alicja's gently rounded pregnant belly.

'That's why they wish us to come as soon as possible. They're eager to bask in the company of me, you, and the prospect that, after all these years, I've finally –' he mimicked with a smile '– settled down.'

'Do you promise there'll be food, proper homemade fare?' She looked at him like Puss in Boots in *Shrek* and Aleksander wrapped her in an embrace.

She was at a loss for words. On one hand, she recognised this as the natural course of events when two people decide to live together. They meet, fall in love, share moments, and inevitably there comes the time to meet the extended circle of friends and family. Her only concern was how Aleksander would take to her parents, to the reality that they lived in a modest wooden house nestled by the forest. Since she left her family home, she'd never told anyone where she used to live and who her parents were. To any curious friends, she would offer the vaguest of responses – yes, she had parents who lived a good distance away, but she spared the details. She strained to remember when she saw them last time. It must have been half a year or maybe more. She spent the previous Christmas in the mountains with Krystyna and her family, which meant it had been about nine, perhaps ten months since she was last home. Suddenly, she was consumed by an urge to embrace her mother, to converse with her father. This yearning ignited a fire within her, etching a pattern that spelt out the word *home*.

'I'll just ring home now to ask,' Aleksander said, retrieving his phone, pressing the speed dial and turning on the speakerphone. A moment later, the room was filled with the merry timbre of an elderly lady's voice.

'Please just don't tell me you've had second thoughts and that you won't be coming! Have you baked bread for Ala? Did the poor dear have something to eat for breakfast?'

'Hello, Grandma, I've got you on speakerphone. Ala has a question for you. It seems the only thing on her mind is food. Will there be anything to eat?'

'What sort of question is that? Everything's ready, your father smoked the ham yesterday, the butter's prepared, and the bread's just finishing up. For dinner, I'll make your favourite cold beetroot soup and dumplings …'

'Good morning, this is Alicja. And what will those dumplings be filled with? Sorry to keep asking, but when I heard about the dumplings …'

'Good morning, Alunia, and what do you fancy? We're making some with blueberries. There'll be ones with meat and sauerkraut as well. The cabbage isn't quite pickled to perfection yet, but we can eat it. And you, Alunia, what do you prefer in your dumplings, what are you craving?'

'Those will be perfect, Madam, thank you …'

Aleksander's grandma cut her off swiftly and assertively:

'Grandma. Call me Grandma. In a few months, you'll be the mother of my first and only great-grandchild, so that alone necessitates a closer bond. How long till you arrive?'

Aleksander wanted to say something, but Alicja beat him to it.

'We'll be there in an hour, Grandma.' Alicja's voice quivered slightly. Perhaps it was the anticipation of homemade dumplings, or perhaps dormant emotions were stirring in her memories.

'Grandma, it will be an hour and a half, as we need to travel, and I don't want to drive too fast while carrying my greatest treasure. See you soon.'

He placed the phone on the kitchen counter. He wanted to ask something, but Alicja looked just as she used to, and there was no sign of the earlier emotion. She slid off the bar stool, approached Aleksander, kissed him tenderly, hugged him tightly with a swift movement, and before he could react, she was already running to the bedroom.

'Give me ten minutes and I'll be ready.'

'Ten minutes? That would be a miracle. What's brought about this change in you? Is it the desire to meet my family?' he inquired, preparing sandwiches for the road. He preferred to play it safe. And seeing how much Alicja was enjoying her breakfast, he was almost certain the sandwiches would come in handy. 'With a pregnant woman, you never know,' he muttered under his breath. 'Do you want to meet my parents, or has the prospect of blueberry dumplings truly motivated you?'

'I want to meet your family and eat dumplings. Loads of them, smothered in cream or fat with onions.'

Ten minutes later, they were driving towards Aleksander's family home. Alicja didn't know what to expect. They had never talked about their family homes. True, Alek tried to probe, but she didn't particularly want to discuss her childhood. She didn't know how to describe her parents, simple yet honest folk. She feared Alek's reaction when he found out that until she was ten, the toilet was outside, a tiled stove still stood in the kitchen, and her parents refused to change any of it. They didn't believe they needed anything more in life, and what they had now was worlds better than what they had years before. Ever since she started working, Alicja has sent them money every month. Perhaps this was her way of repaying them for enabling her escape from the village. She wasn't sure herself. And she didn't particularly want to think about it now.

The sandwiches, of course, came in handy. No sooner had they left the city than Alicja began to complain about all the good bread left at home, wishing she could have just one more, well, perhaps three more sandwiches made with that delicious bread.

'We are approaching the house. I know this forest like the back of my hand – or perhaps even better,' said Aleksander.

'That's quite remarkable. I've been silent the whole journey because I wanted to be certain. Now I am absolutely sure. Did you know we had lived close to each other all our lives?' asked an exhilarated Alicja.

'How come? Why didn't you say anything?' Aleksander asked, astonished.

'You idiot, you never told me exactly where you lived either. After we visit your parents, we shall stop by mine, alright?' Alicja proposed.

'Of course, I would be delighted to meet your parents,' Aleksander replied, slowing down to turn onto a forest path.

'Do you live in the forest?' she inquired, surprised.

'One might say so. Is that bad?'

'No, it's actually quite intriguing because I also lived with my parents near the woods. I even knew a hare that would come up to our house in the winter.'

'Then you'll feel right at home. Look, you can already see the roof of the house over there on the left.'

Alicja looked on with interest. Before her was a wooden, renovated nineteenth-century house, strikingly similar to the one she had grown up in and had felt ashamed of her entire life. They drove onto the premises enveloped on three sides by the forest. At that moment, Aleksander's parents and grandmother emerged from the house. His parents appeared to be in their sixties, the quintessential residents of a small homestead by a wood. Aleksander's father was a tall man, his face weathered by the sun, wind and rain, and Aleksander bore a strong resemblance to him – it was visible in his features and stance. Beside his father stood a slender woman dressed in a summer floral dress, looking charmingly quaint with an air of mysterious delicacy. But it was Aleksander's grandmother who captivated Alicja's attention. Dressed in an apron with a scarf wrapped around her head, she looked as though she had stepped right out of a Brothers Grimm fairy tale. If there was an archetypal grandmother, Aleksander's was the epitome.

Aleksander brought the car to a stop, glanced at Alicja with childlike excitement, opened the door and got out. He walked around the car and assisted her to alight.

The parents and grandmother moved closer to greet the arrivals. Aleksander sprang towards his father with a swift movement, gave him a bear hug, embraced his mother, then, with ease, lifted his grandmother, spun her around thrice and gently placed her back on the ground. The grandmother laughed heartily.

'Your Ala may well think we've lost our marbles with these antics,' she remarked, her curiosity piqued as she began to scrutinise the future mother of her grandchild.

'My dears! Mum, Dad, Grandma! Allow me to introduce Alicja, my beloved, and soon to be the mother of my child. Ala, these are my parents.'

Grandma seemed as if she had been waiting for this moment. She swiftly approached and hugged Alicja tightly, paying no heed to formalities.

'At long last, he's brought you to us, how much longer could we keep asking? But I must admit he was right about one thing: you're as pretty as a picture! Come inside. Surely Alunia must be hungry?'

'Mum, perhaps you'll allow us also to greet Alicja? After all, she is to be our daughter-in-law shortly,' Aleksander's dad chimed in. He approached Alicja and embraced her warmly, planting a fatherly kiss on her head. His wife did precisely the same: first an embrace, then a kiss, this time on both cheeks. Grandma wouldn't wait any longer – she took Alicja by the hand and led her inside.

And there, Alicja felt as though she had returned to the time of her childhood, like the true Alice in Wonderland. The mere sight of the wooden house was a foretaste of what awaited inside, yet what she saw with her own eyes, she had not anticipated at all. The long hallway stretched along the length of the house; she could see a window on the opposing wall. It was kept in a rustic style. White dominated the walls. The floor as well, though it was simply laid with black and white mosaic patterns. To the left was a white coat rack with a bench. Here one could leave their coat and sit while removing or putting on shoes. The seating was cushioned, and Alicja was certain that either Grandma or Aleksander's mum had handcrafted the cushions. In the distance, white stairs led upstairs. Behind the coat rack, there were wooden doors, a metre and a half wide. Further along that wall, another set of doors could be seen, as wide as the former. To the right, just past the entrance, was a smaller door emblazoned with the letters WC, and just beyond that was the open doorway to the kitchen.

Here Alicja experienced an even greater astonishment. On entering the kitchen, she felt as though she had stepped into her family home. Dominating the foreground and of utmost significance to her was the old tiled stove — a restored version of the one she remembered from her childhood. To the left of the room was a colossal tiled heater, on which two cats were comfortably ensconced in sleep — one a complete ginger, the other striped. A wooden table had been draped with a linen tablecloth. White lace curtains fluttered gently at the windows, while various herbs had been hung to dry beneath the ceiling. In stark contrast to the old-fashioned kitchen were modern, white high-gloss kitchen units complete with an induction hob. Alicja felt compelled to speak, yet she remained spellbound into silence. The kitchen looked nearly the same as the one in her family home. The home she had once felt ashamed of, considering it too humble, too impoverished. She felt ashamed because she realised how deeply she had hurt her parents. At the same time, she was profoundly grateful to Alek for bringing her to his family home – it helped her understand that she could easily fix her mistake. She was moved and knew her voice would betray her emotion, but in a true Alicja fashion, she ignored it.

'It is so wonderful here, I feel as if I am at my own home. And it smells beautifully of home … I can't quite name the scent, perhaps it is the herbs. I feel as though I have returned home. To my parents …'

Her voice failed her, and she felt tears on her cheeks. She stood in the middle of the kitchen, looking around, as the cry that was once deeply buried in her heart finally found its release. Aleksander's grandma approached her first, although her parents intended to do the same. Meanwhile, Aleksander stood as if bewitched. He knew that Alicja was a delicate woman, but he had not anticipated that she'd reveal herself so soon. He thought her protective shell would shed slowly, that he would have to peel it away layer by layer like the skin of an onion. He heard the soothing voice of his grandmother, this time calming Alicja, not him.

'There, there, Alunia, calm down, calm down …' Grandma was stroking Alicja's head, allowing her to cry it out.

'I'm sorry, but these pregnancy hormones are absolutely bonkers. I wake up brimming with energy in the morning, and a few minutes later I'm weeping in the bathroom because I've an advert with a little child. It's complete madness,' explained Alicja, trying to compose herself. 'It's so lovely here. Aleksander baked bread for me this morning and that probably triggered this stream of tears …'

'Stream? You've clearly never seen a stream,' Aleksander said with a laugh. He knew well that what Alicja had said was just a fraction of something much larger, and that the true reason for her reaction lay much deeper.

'Let's give Ala a break. Are you hungry? Everything's ready, we just need to set it on the table. Oluś, show her your bedroom and bathroom upstairs, and we'll get the table ready in the meantime.'

Aleksander took Alicja by the hand and led her upstairs. He didn't ask anything; he knew her well enough to understand that her facade had returned to its place, and Alicja was once again in full command of her realm of ice. That's why he was all the more surprised by what she said when they were alone.

'I'll tell you everything, but let's do it calmly, back at home. I don't want to cry anymore at your parents'. You have a beautiful home and I'm very grateful that you have brought me here.' She hugged him tightly. 'Now come on, let's go downstairs quickly because I'm really hungry.'

'Hungry again? Surely that's impossible,' Aleksander remarked cheerfully.

'What's impossible is to push an elephant through the eye of a needle. And there I agree with you – unless the eye of the needle is as big as my hunger, then the elephant would easily fit through, and his mates too. Downstairs, sir, and don't starve the pregnant lady!'

She pulled him by the hand and they went downstairs. There, the crackling of bacon could be heard in the pan, the scent of ham and homemade horseradish filled the air, and in a clay jug, homemade sour cream was on display.

'May I help? Prepare something?' Alicja asked Grandma.

'No, darling, today you're our guest. Tomorrow we'll put you to work chopping wood for the fire, but today you rest,' Aleksander's dad spoke in place of Grandma.

'What are you on about, she might take you seriously. Where is a pregnant woman supposed to chop wood?' Alka's mum was indignant. 'You must be starving, my dear? What would you like to eat first?'

'Honestly? Everything. It smells divine. But I think I'll start with the dumplings with cracklings.'

'With meat and cabbage?' enquired Grandmother.

'Can you actually eat dumplings with berries and cracklings?' Aleksander expressed his surprise.

'You'd be amazed at what pregnant women can eat,' Grandmother declared. 'Ala, will ten be enough for you?'

'Yes,' Alicja responded with a beaming smile, reaching for the plate of dumplings.

Everyone was seated at the table, with only Grandmother fishing out the last dumplings from the pot. Alicja took a fork and eagerly attacked the dumplings. The delicate, almost paper-thin pastry concealed a delicious, perfectly seasoned meat filling. The cracklings, with a subtle hint of garlic and onion, added a distinctive flavour to the dish. Alicja noticed everyone was watching her and blushed slightly.

'I apologise for not waiting for everyone, but I couldn't help myself. I can't remember the last time I had such delectable dumplings,' she said by way of explanation. This made everyone laugh.

'Ala, it's not about that; we've not seen anyone eat with such enthusiasm and relish for a long time. Eat all that you want and crave. You don't realise how overjoyed we are that you're here with us, that you're with our son. And perhaps what delights us most is that we shall soon have a grandchild, be it granddaughter or grandson,'

Aleksander's mother said. Her eyes perilously filled with tears. In an attempt to prevent another tearful outburst that day, Aleksander's father looked at his son and loudly suggested:

'I reckon it's the perfect moment to bring out Grandma's homemade liqueur. What do you say, son? You're staying the night, of course?'

Aleksander confirmed while Alicja merely nodded, her mouth full of dumplings.

Then they went for a walk in the nearby woods. Only Grandma excused herself, remarking that because of her age, the times when she briskly roamed the forest had long since passed. When they returned home, Alicja once again sat down to enjoy the dumplings. That evening, as they went upstairs, she was fast asleep so quickly that she didn't even notice when Alexander lay down beside her.

On Sunday morning, Alicja was awakened by the scent of cream being fried with vanilla. Before she opened her eyes, she stretched with pleasure and snuggled up to Aleksander. He embraced her tightly and kissed her forehead.

'Good morning, darling.'

'Can you smell that?' she asked dreamily.

'I said "good morning", but if you like, we can go straight to breakfast. I suspect Grandma is already wreaking havoc in the kitchen warming up some blueberry dumplings with sweet cream for you. Do you like them?'

'Like them?' She tried to rise from the bed too quickly, felt dizzy and sat back down.

'Easy there, little one, what's the rush?' asked Aleksander, though he knew the answer full well.

'How can you lie there so calmly when there's such a feast downstairs? I'm off to the bathroom first and then running down to eat. God, I adore this house, your parents, your grandmother. I love you, but I love your grandmother's cooking even more.' With that, she kissed Aleksander on the tip of his nose and vanished. When Aleksander went downstairs twenty minutes later, Alicja was sitting at the table, her leg tucked under her, devouring dumplings with cream.

'Good morning, everyone. Darling, I see you're already onto your portion of dumplings?'

'The second helping. This is my second helping. And do you know what's the best part? Grandma is preparing a stash for us to take home. We can enjoy them in Warsaw too,' she announced joyfully, biting into another piece.

'Grandma, I have a question. Will Alicja always eat this much?'

On the journey back, Alicja took Aleksander to visit her parents, who hadn't anticipated their arrival. It had been quite some time since she had made them such a surprise, especially on a Sunday. As the car drew up, her parents came out of the house, curious to see who was visiting. Alicja jumped out of the car and rushed to her parents, embracing them with all her might.

'My girl, what's with this warm greeting?' asked Alicja's dad, just after he regained his speech from his daughter's tight embrace.

'Daddy, Mummy, I love you so much and I'm sorry that I haven't visited more often … And I'm sorry for not being there when you probably expected me … And because I'm going to have a baby, and I want it to know its grandparents …'

Alicja either ran out of strength or was overcome with emotion, because she cried again. Aleksander got out of the car and approached slowly.

'There's no need for tears, my child. It's a wonderful piece of news; don't cry, my dear,' Alicja's mother soothed her as she held her. 'Hush now, be calm. Instead, tell us who this gentleman that has come with you is?'

Alicja wiped away her tears and, with a smile her parents had never seen before, she said:

'Dear ones, this is Aleksander. We've been together for some time and recently found out that I'm pregnant. Aleksander, these are my parents. Mum and Dad.'

A momentary consternation and surprise flitted across the faces of Alicja's parents. While their daughter's unannounced and sudden visit was a big surprise, the news of her pregnancy was a real shock to them. They didn't want to cause a disappointment in their daughter's eyes, so after a brief silence, it was the father who spoke first.

'Come in, come in. It's not proper to keep guests on the doorstep. And soon enough, half the village will gather to see what sort of limousine has pulled up to our house,' said Alicja's dad, gesturing for the young couple to enter. Inside, everything was as Alicja remembered. The old brick stove was next to the electric cooker. Dried herbs were hanging above the stove, and a cat was sitting on the windowsill. Perhaps for the first time in her life, Alicja felt immensely proud of her home and that she could show it to someone. She noticed the flyers by the stove – they depicted her family home.

'Mummy, do you have flyers?' asked a puzzled Alicja.

'Yes, my dear, a teacher from the nearby school recently visited us and suggested we organise workshops for the city children. So that they can see what life was like in the old times. Most homes are modern, but ours remains as it was a century ago. We agreed, and now at least once a week we're having visits. We demonstrate butter churning and meat smoking. The children are delighted, we have something to occupy us, and a little money comes our way. They say our home is like a living museum.'

'What a brilliant idea. I must mention it to my parents; they'll be thrilled.' Aleksander wanted to add more, but Alicja interjected:

'Mummy, is that the scent of sour cucumber soup on the stove?'

'Yes, would you like a bowl each?' Alicja's mum asked and, without waiting for an answer, she went to the cupboard to get bowls.

'Yes, please,' said Aleksander while Alicja was already sitting down at the table with a spoon in hand.

'Do tell, my daughter, what are your plans? And what of this pregnancy of yours? You don't look at all like an expectant woman.'

'Perhaps I shall answer. Of course, we're planning a wedding and will have it as soon as the baby is born,' said Aleksander. 'For my part, I can only say that I have never loved any woman as I love your daughter. And I assure you, I will do everything within my power to make her the happiest woman on earth. What are you doing in two weeks' time? My parents will be in Warsaw and would certainly like to meet you. I could pick you up on Saturday morning and drive you back on Sunday evening. It would be an opportunity for us to get to know each other better.'

'Why make a fuss? We can come by coach,' replied Alicja's father.

'There's no point. By car, it's less than an hour's drive, by public transport it's over three and a half hours. It's a waste of time. My parents will be around at ten, so I would come for you at about eight-thirty.'

'And your parents, how will they arrive?' Alicja's mother was curious.

'Dad has a car, so it's no trouble for them.'

'Excuse the interruption, but, Mummy, are there seconds?'

'Daughter, do you want more?'

'Ever since Alicja got pregnant, she just eats second helpings.' Aleksander laughed.

'Quite right, let her eat as much as she needs,' said the father. 'Darling, we still have dumplings with cabbage and mushrooms, would you fancy a few?'

Alicja's mother stood up to warm up the homemade dumplings with cracklings. And though Aleksander had had his fill of dumplings for the weekend, he did not let on. He even helped himself to seconds.

As they were leaving, the boot was laden with more provisions – dumplings, sour cucumber soup, and home-cured meats. Alicja had also managed to coax her mother into baking a yeast cake with apples and streusel topping.

'We're returning home like true pantry jars,' Alicja remarked as they drove into the city. 'The most splendid part is having such a stash of dumplings. I can hardly wait to tuck into them.'

'Really? After this weekend, you're still keen on dumplings?' Aleksander asked, shaking his head in disbelief. 'By my rough count, you've eaten a hundred.'

'I know, but my pregnancy craves it.'

'If you say so, then eat. I just hope you don't give birth to a dumpling, my dear.'

'Be silent, sir, if you have naught wise to say. Dumplings are sacred, just like my pregnancy.'

They laughed together. One thing they were certain of – there would be no shortage of supplies after this family weekend, especially dumplings.

She lay on the sun lounger, enveloped in the sun's warm embrace. For the first time in ages, Gosia felt truly safe. The smile on her face was genuine, not feigned. Piotr watched his wife with delight; her tanned skin and the playful swimsuits they had bought in Punta Cana added a spark to the atmosphere. If it wasn't for Gosia's parents being around, they would happily have stayed in bed all day.

Gosia's thoughts drifted to recent events. Weeks ago, she had swallowed an entire bottle of sleeping pills. Not to kill herself but to kill the tumultuous thoughts in her head. She didn't want to remember that it was her best friend, not her, who was pregnant. She felt betrayed that someone close to her was having a baby. In the hospital, after having her stomach pumped, she tried to bury that feeling deep within her subconscious, labelling it 'Do not open, fuck!' And she'd probably have succeeded not to open it for a while. But Piotr found a person who could help her. For two weeks, every single day she met with a therapist, and every single day she got into her thoughts so that she could confront her inner demons. She started each day with tears and ended it with laughter. The daily purification was unparalleled. She began to notice that the sun was shining, that she had wonderful people around her. But, most importantly, she started to notice herself. She realised how many beautiful moments she had wasted because she was fixated on something that she couldn't have at the time. Now, lying on the beautiful beach, she was grateful for who she was, for being alive, and for being able to share this beautiful time with her loved ones.

Piotr's voice brought her back from her thoughts.

'Gosia, shall we take a walk along the beach? I feel like I've gained at least five kilos with all this all-inclusive food. Breakfasts, lunches, desserts, coffees, and the evening rum with your dad isn't helping either. Imagine what is going to happen when we leave here in a week. I'll be overweight.'

'Ha, ha, ha, who's making you try every rum drink? You and Dad seem to know every bartender in the hotel. Speaking of which, where are my parents? Have you seen them?'

'When you napped after breakfast, your dad winked at me and said they were off for a siesta. Though I'm pretty sure he wasn't talking about sleep,' Piotr explained with a laugh.

'Stop! I don't want to hear this! In my eyes, my parents end at their shoulders, both of them!' Laughing, she got up from the lounger, draped a delicate *pareo* around her hips and looked at Piotr. 'Come on, let's burn off all those rum drinks.'

They took each other's hand and strolled along the Caribbean Sea.

'You know, I can't get over how soft the sand is. Almost like flour, yet it's sand. Such a strange combination. And the colour of the water … When I was in the orphanage, I could only dream of this. I once saw a picture of the Dominican Republic in a magazine; it looked incredible, especially since it was November back home, raining, and the orphanage was what it was. The Dominican Republic seemed as real as the chance of my parents coming back to life.'

'You rarely talk about your parents. Do you remember them?'

They walked along the shore, the warm water occasionally washing over their feet. Gosia had to squint as she looked at Piotr, the sun dazzling her eyes.

'You look beautiful when you scrunch your nose. Did you know you have freckles on it?

'I feel like I do remember them. They died when I was five. Sometimes, it seems like I just imagined them so vividly that I retained that image so that I could recall it when I missed them too much. I remember being in a car with them, but I can't recall the accident. I vaguely remember a hospital bed. Then there's a blank and I don't remember anything until the first day of school in year one. I never felt as alone as I did then, seeing my classmates with their parents while I was by myself. No one was straightening my collar, patting my head or asking how I felt. That's a hard level of loneliness. I don't know what it's like to play ball with a dad, bake with a mum, or get scolded and punished for jumping in puddles. I never experienced the closeness and belonging of childhood. There were "aunties" – the caregivers in the orphanage – but it's not the same as having a real family.'

'So, is this why you wanted to have your own family so badly?' Gosia asked, showing interest in Piotr and his feelings for the first time. For years, she had only focused on her own experiences.

'Yes, it has always been and will always be important to me. But you're forgetting one thing. A family isn't just about having a little child; it's also about me, you, your parents, grandparents. I've received more than I had ever dared to hope for while I was still in the orphanage. Look, fifteen years ago, I left the orphanage. I was given a seventeen-square-metre flat with a bathroom in the corridor. Luckily, not long after, a private developer bought the building I lived in. They wanted to demolish it, so I got a flat in a new block. A normal studio with a kitchen, bathroom and one room. I had basic furniture, a place to sleep and something to eat. I never told anyone, but when I moved into that new flat, I set up a Christmas tree, even though it was April. A Christmas tree was the only real memory of home I had.

I remember sitting under it, admiring the lights, baubles and everything else on it. Those were my most beautiful memories. When I knew I'd soon be able to move out on my own, I started collecting everything related to Christmas. When I left the orphanage, the aunties and everyone else gave me a huge Christmas tree as a gift.'

'Is that the one we have at home?' Gosia asked, surprised. 'I always wondered where you got such a beautiful tree from. It must have cost a fortune.'

'The same one. For the first week, I sat under that tree and couldn't get enough of the fact that no one was telling me to go to sleep, that I couldn't sit there any longer. I knew I was luckier than others. Then, I decided to never give up and always believe that dreams do come true. It just might take a while. And so, I finished my dream studies, then did another degree, found a good job and met you.'

'Why have you never told me this before?'

'At the beginning of our relationship, there wasn't the right time, and I didn't want to spill everything about myself. What had happened shouldn't affect my new life. I thought I was doing the right thing. Then, when we were trying so hard to have a baby, going through all those tests and so on, I didn't want to burden you with my past. And things turned out as they did. We both shut ourselves off instead of supporting each other when we needed it the most.'

'Now it's my turn. I heard you crying in the bathroom at night after the last miscarriage. And I can't forgive myself for not going to you, even though I wanted to. I wanted to cry with you, but I was afraid you'd reject me.'

'I would have never done that. I remember that night. It's a pity you didn't come. I couldn't hold back my pain any longer. I couldn't bear how much you were suffering and that I couldn't help you. That's why I cried. Out of helplessness.'

'We should talk more about important things, not just everyday problems. Where are we, actually?'

Gosia looked around. There were no hotels in sight, and she couldn't remember the last time she had seen anyone. In the distance, tiny silhouettes of holidaymakers were visible. Palm trees gently bowed to the beautiful, almost white beach and the azure water.

'Shall we head back?'

'I think we should. It's getting close to lunchtime, and I'm starting to feel a bit peckish.'

They turned around and, hand in hand, started walking back towards the hotel. For a while, they walked in silence. Gosia pondered over a question for a long time before finally asking it.

'Do you want to have a child?'

'I do because that's the natural order of things. Two people meet, fall in love, get married, and then the fruit of their love joins them. But I don't feel as strongly about it as you do. You want it, so I want it too because your happiness is what's most important to me.'

'Oh God … I thought, since you talked so much about family, you wanted a child soon.'

'I spoke about family because it's very important to me. But my family is you, your parents. That's important to me. But whether we have a child now or in five years, frankly, I don't care. I wanted a child because you wanted it so badly.'

'And I wanted it because I thought you did. Of course, each miscarriage was hard for me, and all the tests and procedures convinced me that I needed to have a baby right now. I got carried away thinking you wanted it! We should have had this conversation at the beginning of our relationship and clarified everything instead of acting on assumptions. We didn't need to go through all of that.'

'No, it was necessary, very necessary.'

'Do you mean that …'

'Listen, if it hadn't been for the IVF attempts, if it hadn't been for your hospital stay and the pills, maybe we would have never got as far as we are now. And I'm not talking about the length of this walk. I am talking about our understanding. If it hadn't been for what happened, we wouldn't be having this conversation.'

'You're right. Will you hold me?'

She stopped. Piotr embraced her tightly and kissed her. They kissed for a long time, the dormant heat in their bodies growing stronger. Gosia was the first to come back to her senses.

'We're on a public beach,' she whispered.

'Mmm, what a shame … Shall we continue?' He reached out his hand to Gosia. 'We'll make up for it during our siesta after lunch. And then tonight after dinner.'

During dinner and the following days, they ate a lot and enjoyed the evening entertainment provided by the hotel. They also spent a great deal of time together alone, whether during walks along the beach or during siestas in their room. One thing they were certain of on the day of departure was that they had made the most of every day, as much as they desired and had the energy for. They joked that if they were to sum up the trip, it would be about sex, food and rum drinks.

Krystyna dreaded the conversation with Krzysztof. She knew it was the end of their marriage, which had effectively ended before she even realised it. He had been cheating on her, been unfaithful. He admitted he was seeing other people, men. Yet she trembled at the thought of meeting with her still-husband. The children had no idea that their father hadn't gone anywhere, that he was still in the city. Krystyna didn't know where, but she didn't care anymore.

The twins left and she took a shower. She relished it, feeling each shower cleanse not just her body. She had the feeling that the water penetrated into her soul, washing away accumulated negative emotions. Initially, she thought of wearing her usual clothes – a conservative grey outfit. An outfit that Krzysztof had accustomed her to. However, realising this, she instead pulled out the new jeans she had bought on her last trip to the shopping centre. They were the latest fashion, slightly stretchy material hugging her form. The light denim with a worn-out look matched her brightly coloured shirt. She tied the ends of the shirt around her waist with a roguish flair. She no longer looked like the old Krystyna. Her new, somewhat avant-garde hairstyle gave her a defiant look. She smiled at her reflection in the mirror, trying to give her image a bit of courage. Hearing the intercom, she knew someone had entered using the code. She ruffled her fringe and headed to the hall to greet Krzysztof. A moment later, they stood facing each other, unsure how to act. Krystyna broke the silence.

'Come in. Would you like something to drink?'

'Yes, if it's no trouble, I'd like some tea with lemon. This sudden change in appearance … You've never dressed like this before; it's not your style, is it?' Krzysztof observed.

'How can you be sure it's not my style? I'm in my own home. Besides, how can you know what my style is when we haven't spoken for a year? We've exchanged opinions, instructions and notifications, but we haven't talked. Don't you think there's a fundamental difference?' she spoke calmly, coolly, without unnecessary emotion.

'Are we going to talk in this tone now?'

'And what did you expect? That I'd be hysterical, crying, begging you for one last chance? That's a joke. After the last few months under the same roof, I have no illusions. And you know what? It's a relief. I'm relieved because I no longer have to pretend everything is okay. I don't have to beg for your attention.'

'So you're happy that we won't be together anymore?'

He looked at her. Each question seemed to be laced with an ulterior motive as if he wanted to hurt her.

'Don't twist my words. I'm happy we don't have to pretend anymore. I'm just sorry that for all these years, you didn't have the courage to tell me the truth.'

She felt her voice tremble despite herself. She closed her eyes and extended her hand forward, signalling him to say nothing, to give her a moment.

'And yet …' Krzysztof let slip something akin to triumph.

'I'm sorry that you've been lying to me all these years.'

'You must have known. Your father knew everything. He saw me with someone before Christmas last year. We even had a chat, and he tried to pressure me into telling you the truth. Then he saw me several more times at a certain place.'

'In which place?'

'In a club, right next to his canasta club where he met with his old friends. There's a special place there. For people like me,' he said dismissively, with a hint of arrogance. 'Also, when he felt ill in the Łazienki Park, he saw me with Aleksei.'

'You were there then? You saw us and still didn't come over? Didn't help us?'

She couldn't believe how far apart they had grown, how despicable Krzysztof's behaviour was towards her, the children and her now-deceased father.

'Don't act so surprised. What was I supposed to say? And how would Aleksei have felt?'

'What? Your lover's feelings mattered more to you than how I and your children felt? Why are you such an egotist?'

'Don't drag the children into this. They don't need to know anything.'

'You must be fucking joking! What do you expect me to tell them?'

'I don't know, make something up. Say that you don't love me anymore and want me to leave the house.'

'Ha, ha, ha, fuck, this must be a dream! You're demanding that I take all the blame? Should I say the same in court?' she asked sarcastically.

'It would be good. You see, I must take care of my reputation,' he brushed off a non-existent speck of dust from his sleeve. 'I don't want this to spread like a rumour. It certainly can't reach my superiors, considering I hold a public office. How do you imagine me going to my boss and telling him about myself? I'll already have to explain why you left me.'

'You're fucking men in brothels, using whips, masks and other things, cheating on me, deceiving me, and when the truth comes out, you expect me to take all the blame? Fuck off!'

'Don't swear like that, it's so passé ...' He looked at her with disgust.

'Since when?'

'Since when what? Your mood swings are strange. One moment, you're shouting and swearing, then almost whispering. Is it your period, PMS or menopause?' he asked, seemingly to irritate her further.

'Since when have you been fucking men? A year, two?'

'Who told you it's only been that long?' he said with a cold smile. 'How can you be sure I haven't been doing it since the very beginning, that our marriage was just for cover? You and the children are just a curtain, a perfect smokescreen for a stupid, backward society. Why should I explain to everyone that I am who I am when I can pretend to have a loving family? But of course, you had to ruin everything. You expected me to behave every day as if being with you was a pleasure. So – whatever you think – we're breaking up because of you. We could have continued pretending to be a couple. If you really needed sex, we could have found someone together and solved the problem.'

Krystyna stepped back in horror – it was sinking in how calculated her husband was. Only now was she beginning to understand that she had spent her best years with such a deceitful man.

'But your daddy was so retarded, so you didn't even hear about this proposal. I told him it was for your good, of course. But since he's kicked the bucket, maybe it's worth considering? I'm willing to accept that you might go on business trips three or four times a year,' he said in a sleazy, hypocritical tone.

Krystyna looked on, incredulous at how two-faced and despicable her husband had turned out to be. She stood up, smoothed out her jeans and calmly announced, 'We will divorce with a fault verdict. You lied to me by hiding your true sexual orientation. I'm not opposed to anyone; to me, everyone has the same value as a human being as long as they are honest and act with integrity. I see no reason to take the blame for this. I expect you to actively participate in raising the children and tell them the truth yourself ...'

'You're joking! What am I supposed to tell those brats?' he retorted, only realising after a moment that he had gone too far.

'Fuck off! Get out of my house! Now, do you hear me?! Out!' She looked at him, ready to explode at one more wrong word. 'I don't want to see you anymore! My lawyer will contact you. Now get lost!'

'And my stuff? I have expensive clothes here. You don't think I'll leave them to you, do you?'

'The boxes are in the bedroom. Take them and fuck off!'

She couldn't even bear to look at him anymore. Turning away in disgust, she waited for him to gather his things. She heard him going to the bedroom, then slowly, reluctantly, carrying out large boxes and closing the door behind him. Only after a moment did she loudly exhale, a breath she had been holding since Krzysztof entered her home. She was glad she had packed his belongings herself, anticipating how their last conversation might end.

She felt cheated. She didn't want to talk to anyone. First, she needed to sort everything out in her head to draw conclusions. She looked around, searching for something to do. After a moment, she smiled to herself. She took off her tight jeans, ran to get some tracksuit bottoms, put on an old tank top, and returned to the living room. First of all, she tore down the curtains. She had always hated them, but Krzysztof had insisted on hanging them. She decided to channel her emotions into action. She knew there would come a time when she'd have to do an audit of gains and losses. But the time hasn't come yet. Life hadn't been easy for her that year. She felt lost, kind of dazed by recent experiences. And even though rearranging the furniture seemed a trivial activity at the moment, she knew this was exactly what she needed. To focus on something other than her emotional life and to devote herself to something as mundane as reorganising her material reality.

The living room, together with the kitchen and dining area, was over sixty square metres. It was enormous. Their entire flat was nearly 150 square metres. Thanks to her father's savings, they had been able to buy it without having to consider a loan. She had always dreamt of a modern decor. Though they had bought new furniture a year and a half ago, Krzysztof hadn't allowed for any innovations – everything had to be placed according to his peculiar taste. First, she moved the dining table, which had been squeezed into a corner between the kitchen and the living area. She placed it in the centre, partially folding it. She reasoned that since it would now be just the three of them, there was no need to keep the table extended for six people. Once she had finished arranging the chairs, she tackled the corner sofa and armchairs, which also seemed to be placed as a punishment. She struggled with the furniture for some time, but after an hour, nothing remained in its original place except for the TV, which she needed to hang on another wall, but she needed help to do that. She thought about Antoni, but she wasn't sure how to arrange it. She felt everything seething inside her, but she preferred to channel her energy into something more constructive than mere anger.

Krystyna pushed away the thought of the inevitable conversation with her children. Glancing at her watch, she realised it was nearing noon. She still had over two hours before they returned from school. She washed her hands, slipped into her jeans and a shirt, threw on her leather jacket and, full of resolve, left the flat. The nearest shopping centre was just a few minutes' walk away. There was an interior design shop where she could buy absolutely everything, from bricks and PVC sheets to furniture and paints, ending with fabrics and accessories. She had long dreamt of adding colours to their grey and white living room. Wandering around the shop, for the first time in years, she could buy everything she wanted in colours she hadn't even dared to dream of a year earlier.

When she checked the time again, she was horrified to find that her shopping had taken much longer than she had planned. She packed everything into a taxi and directed the driver to her address. Calmer now, she had figured out how to tell her children about their father. She knew it would be a blow to them. They had just buried their beloved grandfather, and now their father has abandoned the family. As she approached the block of flats, she saw the children. They ran to help her.

'Hi, Mum! I see your shopping frenzy hasn't passed since Saturday,' Patryk said in disbelief, looking at the bags in the taxi's boot.

'Something like that. Unfortunately, because of my new obsession, I didn't get to cook any lunch, so we'll order pizza, Chinese, kebabs, whatever you want.'

'Something's not right. Is everything okay?' Patrycja asked.

'You're smart kids. We'll talk at home once we take everything upstairs.'

At the word *kids* both of them bristled, assuring Krystyna of their maturity.

'Wow, Mum!' Patryk exclaimed, entering the house and immediately forgetting about the packages. 'You've made everything look super modern. I wonder what Dad will say about all these changes.'

'He won't say anything,' Krystyna replied quickly. The children exchanged knowing glances.

'Will you tell us what's going on? Dad hates such changes, all these colours. The way it is now at home. I mean, I like it, but Dad definitely won't. Why has Dad been gone so long? Are you getting a divorce?' Patrycja asked. She was more mature and aware of what was happening than Krystyna wanted to admit to herself. Krystyna looked at her children. They waited expectantly. She closed her eyes for a moment, took a few deep breaths and nodded.

'Yes, we're getting a divorce. Your father took his things this morning.'

Patrycja quickly got up from the floor and ran to their parents' bedroom. The sound of her nervously opening the wardrobe doors and checking if it was true echoed. She returned crying a moment later.

'Why didn't he do it when we were home? Why didn't he say goodbye to us? Why didn't he tell us anything? You can't just leave like that. First Grandad, now Dad!' Her voice broke, and she sat down on the floor, bursting into tears. 'Grandad would have known what to do!'

Krystyna sat beside her, wrapping an arm around her daughter and extended her other arm towards Patryk, who quickly came and nestled into Krystyna, also crying. They sat like that, all three on the floor amid bags, packages and boxes, each lost in their own grief. Krystyna knew that sooner or later she would have to tell them the whole truth. She just didn't know how to do it. And – most importantly – when to tell them. How to do it most gently, yet in a way they could understand. She didn't want to lie to them. Just the departure of a parent was stressful enough, let alone a situation where the father leaves the family for a man.

Now, she longed to be in Antoni's arms, to seek refuge and support from him. She felt lost, hurt, deceived. Yet she had to be the stronger one and provide support for the children, who were not coping with the onslaught of emotions that had fallen on them in recent weeks. They sat on the living room floor, paying no mind to the surrounding chaos or the fact that, with the onset of autumn, it was getting dark earlier.

Krystyna leant back against the corner sofa, now daringly positioned almost in the middle of the living room, as the twins rested their heads on her shoulders. Patrycja had stopped whimpering, and Patryk, too, had calmed down, but they still craved their mother's closeness.

'I think we should eat something; my stomach's starting to growl,' Patryk broke the silence.

'I agree. Mum, how about Chinese?' Patrycja lifted her head and looked at Krystyna.

'Patryk, could you pass me the phone and the Chinese takeaway menu, please? Let's choose something.'

Patryk stood up and walked to the countertop where the phone was. In the drawer next to it were the menus they often used. He picked up the phone and, for a moment, looked at the screen, then quietly said, 'I'm sorry, I didn't mean to read your messages, but when I picked up the phone, part of a message came up. Who is Antoni, and why does he write that he loves you? Is that why Dad left?' Patryk's last two sentences carried a stronger, more aggressive tone.

'No, your father left because, for over a year, he's been with someone else, and he wants to be with that person. It happens that people fall out of love. It's a natural thing.'

'Why did he lie to us, then? Why didn't he just say he wanted to be with another woman? Is that why Dad has been so distant with us? Are they going to have a new baby?' Patryk bombarded her with questions, and Patrycja simply nodded, echoing her brother's sentiments.

'I don't know why he lied to us. I can't answer that because I haven't received an answer myself.'

'And who is Antoni, and why does he write that he loves you?' Patryk persisted.

Krystyna knew that, sooner or later, she would have to tell them the truth. She took a few breaths, closed her eyes for a second and then addressed the children.

'Alright. Let's do this: we'll order dinner, as it's really getting late. You must have homework to do ...' Seeing Patryk's look of dissatisfaction, she quickly clarified, 'Patryk, we will talk, I promise. But what you're about to hear might upset you, and I don't want our home situation to affect your studies.'

'Mum! Our life is falling apart, and you're only thinking about homework! Seriously, in many countries, young people our age are fighting for freedom, are forced into labour, into prostitution, and you want us to do doodles. Damn! This is mine and Patrycja's home, and we want to know the whole truth! Now!'

Krystyna saw the frustration on her children's faces. She didn't plan to tell them about male brothels, her husband's escapades, or her new erotic life, but she realised that secrets had a way of revealing themselves at the most unexpected times.

'We'll order dinner, and I'll tell you what I know. Then you'll sit down to do your homework. Although I still believe the order should be different. But I also think you should know the truth, as you're old enough to have that right. You will always be my children, and I'll always want to protect you and ...'

'Mum! Can we finally order that dinner?! Please! Just because you keep avoiding the topic doesn't mean we'll forget about it,' Patrycja stated firmly. 'I want the five-flavour chicken with noodles. Patryk, how about you?'

'Beef with five flavours for me. Mum, what are you ordering?'

'Prawn noodles.'

Krystyna picked up the phone and dialled the number. The friendly Chinese lady who took the order promised that the delivery would be in about thirty minutes.

'Just going to the toilet and then we'll sit down for our talk.'

Krystyna was trying to delay the moment. She gained maybe three minutes. She took the phone to the bathroom to reply to Antoni's message. She read his text in peace.

Hi, beautiful! I know you're having a tough day. I'm with you in spirit and energy. Just know that I'm missing you and love you more than anything in the world.

Sitting on the toilet, Krystyna typed her reply.

The kids have found out about Krzysztof. I'm terrified by what's happening and what I still have to tell them. I'll call you after our talk. Love and miss you.

She washed her hands in cold water, splashed her face, gave a forced smile to her reflection in the bathroom mirror and walked out. The children were sitting at the dining table in the living room. They were looking at her expectantly but with uncertain expressions.

'We can start. What I'm about to tell you is hard. I ask only one thing of you: don't judge anyone because that's not what this is about. None of us has the right to judge Dad. I don't, and I ask the same of you.'

She took a deep breath and continued, 'Listen. As I told you, your dad has moved out. It was a mutual decision. For a long time, things haven't been working out between us, which you must have noticed. Over the past year, it just intensified, and in reality, we only shared occasional meals together. Each of us had their own friends, separate dreams, and ...'

'Mum, you're avoiding the subject again,' Patryk interrupted. 'Does Dad have a new baby? You can tell us; we're really sensible, grown up and can accept the truth.'

'Your dad hasn't left for another woman, and he certainly doesn't have any other children besides you two.'

'I don't understand ... You said yourself that Dad has left because he has someone else, and now you're saying he hasn't left for another woman. What is actually happening?'

Patrycja stared at Krystyna, then at Patryk, who started to laugh.

'Pati, please, think! If Dad hasn't left for a woman, who could he have left for? He's gay, or if you prefer, a homo!'

'Patryk!'

'Mum, but that's right! Dad's left his family, his kids and a cool woman – you – because he prefers to be with a man! Great that he's happy, but I don't want to know him! What am I supposed to tell my friends? "Hey, my dad's moved out to be with his male lover, and now I have two dads"? He should've told us himself! Shame he didn't have the courage and acted like a kid! He always said we should take responsibility for our actions! And what? He runs away like a coward! Not only a coward but a liar and he's gay! Fucking brilliant!'

'Patryk!'

'Mum, but Patryk is right! It's not about the swearing, though I feel like doing it too … but I'll stop myself. Dad behaved terribly. How can we trust him now when he's let us down so much. He deceived us and left us. I also don't want anything to do with him. Not because he's different, but because he didn't tell the truth! Damn it! I'm angry! I'm outraged and disappointed! I swore, sorry.'

'I know you're disappointed with Dad's behaviour, the fact that he didn't trust us enough to tell the truth. It would've been completely different if we had known from the start.'

'You mean Dad has known he was different for a long time? Then why did he marry you?'

'Patryk, I don't know, I can't answer that.'

'You did the right thing, Mum, finding yourself another man!'

'It's not like that, Patryk. Antoni came back into my life last Friday. We were very close once. Certain things happened, and we had to part ways. After some time, I met your dad, and we got married. I hadn't been in touch with Antoni for a very long time until last Friday when we bumped into each other at the office. He helped me with the paperwork for returning the keys to Grandpa's flat, and then we went for lunch. We also met on Saturday, that's all.'

'Mum, please, at least you don't lie to us! I saw the message; he wrote that he loves you! You don't write *I love you* to someone you've just met again, whom you supposedly haven't seen for many years!'

Patryk spoke with a raised voice. Krystyna was startled by how he seemed so grown up suddenly.

'That's true. We were very important to each other once. Even though I was with your father, Antoni remained important in my life, and I was important to him. External factors meant that we had to separate years ago. But that didn't change our feelings. Trust me, you can love two people at the same time. Each love is different. I love you differently than I love Patrycja, but that doesn't mean I love either of you less. You're a young man, and I treat you differently from how I treat Pati. I can't expect her to participate in sports like you do, nor can I expect you to go to every drama club like Pati. You're very different, so my love for each of you is also different. It's the same with loving others. You love me differently than you loved Grandpa.'

She used this comparison on purpose to divert Patryk's thoughts from Krzysztof at least for a moment.

'The fact that you love me and Pati differently doesn't mean you love either of us less. One day, you'll love a girl, then a woman, and those loves will also be entirely different. You'll see for yourself that you can love in different ways. I'm not lying to you. I've always believed and still believe that truth is a hundred times better than a lie. I know you feel cheated. And you have the right to be angry. The truth also affected me badly; I took it worse than you did! I went to Magda's, and there was too much wine, and then Saturday morning was tough …'

'Saturday was actually nice. That shopping spree in the shopping centre was really cool. And I like how you've changed now. You're more relaxed.' Patryk relaxed a bit.

The intercom rang, and Patryk went to answer it to receive the order. During this time, Patrycja said to Krystyna, 'Mum, I also think you look better now and act differently, more relaxed. Before, there were days when you were very uptight. Only around Alicja and the girls did you forget about etiquette and were yourself. Unless Dad was around. With him, you were very tense, but now you're more approachable.'

'Really? I hadn't noticed that.'

Patryk listened to the conversation while unpacking the food boxes.

'I agree, and you look really great in those jeans – like you've shed a few years,' he observed.

'Mum, can you tell us about this Antoni? Who is he? What's he like?' Pati asked, eating her chicken.

'Antoni is a very old acquaintance of mine. He was and is my friend.'

'Will we be able to meet him?' asked Patryk. 'I have an idea – maybe you both could come to my match on Saturday? Dad never had time for it. After the match, we could go for pizza or ice cream.'

'Alright, I'll ask Antoni. I don't know his plans, but I don't think he would mind.'

'Can you ask him now?' Patryk insisted.

'Why this sudden desire to meet Antek?'

'Will you be upset if I tell you?'

'No. You see, we're talking about everything. I've trusted you in telling everything, and it will be good if that trust is mutual.'

Krystyna looked at Patryk, wanting to assure him of her love and that she wouldn't let him down like his father had. Patryk took a deep breath before speaking.

'I'd rather say at school that my mum's found a cool new guy and left my dad than that my dad is gay. They wouldn't let me live it down at school. The same for Patrycja.' Both of them fixed Krystyna with gloomy looks.

'Can you call him and ask?'

'Now?'

'Yes. I want to know who I can really rely on. Because I definitely know I can't rely on my own father, and I've known that for a long time. He was never there for me, always just demanding from us. Will you call?'

'Yes, of course. I don't know his plans, but I'll call now.'

She picked up the phone and chose Antoni's number. He answered after the second ring.

'Hey, beautiful! How did the talk at home go?'

She knew he was waiting for a message from her, but she didn't want to talk about the children in front of them. So, she quickly asked:

'It went as I had expected. But that's not what I want to talk about. You see, Patryk has a match on Saturday, and we were wondering if you'd like to come with us.'

Even if the question surprised him, he didn't show it.

'Great, what position does Patryk play?'

Patryk heard the question and immediately answered that he was a striker.

'Fantastic! We'll give him support worthy of the Champions League. Then I invite you all for pizza and ice cream after the match. Is that okay?'

Krystyna relayed the question to her children, and they eagerly agreed. After exchanging a few words with Antoni, Krystyna hung up.

'Your guy seems nice, Mum!'

'Patryk, he's not my guy. I've already explained this to you.'

'He's cool. He agreed right away and didn't make excuses about why he couldn't come with us. And he knows what proper support in the Champions League should look like. Not like that gay!'

'Patryk! It's your father. You can't talk about him like that.'

'But it's true, Mum! My father is gay, and I can't accept it. I don't want to know him. Now, excuse me, but I'm going to do my doodles.'

He pushed his chair back from the table and started clearing up after the meal. Patrycja joined him, and they gathered the containers together.

'Mum, I'd use different words, but I feel the same way as Patryk. I don't want to talk about … Dad right now.' Then she turned to Patryk, 'Shall we do our homework together?'

'Sure, sis! Mum, you take a break.'

They both hugged her and then went to Patryk's room together. Krystyna was well aware they were not really going to do their homework, but she lacked the energy to react. She was mentally exhausted after the day's events. She went to the fridge, took out a bottle of wine, poured a glass and sat on the sofa with her phone in hand. She browsed through her emails. The girls had sent her a summary of the day and reassured her that the office was still there and she still had a job to return to. Regardless of her mental state. Alicja's emails always lifted her spirits. They contained all the vivacity that the girl had inside her. And some funny comparisons only Alicja could come up with. She had also received a text from Antoni.

Glad to hear the kids want to meet me. Have they learnt the truth?

Krystyna replied immediately.

Yes. I told them. They don't want to know Krzysztof. You should've heard what Patryk called him. Now they're in the room, supposedly doing their homework, but I know that's not true. I need to give them time. They've decided they'd rather tell their friends that I left Krzysztof for you than that their father left us for a male lover.

Antoni continued writing:

It doesn't surprise me at all. Can you imagine how their classmates would react to such news? They would have several really terrible months, if not years. People are very keen to judge, too keen. Which doesn't change the fact that it must be hard for the kids. So, I got the role of your man :-) Quite interesting, I must say.

Doubts began to grow in Krystyna.

Aren't you mad at me? Patryk insisted, and I didn't really think it through. Maybe you just don't want to meet my kids or even to go to my son's matches. Which I would fully understand.

Are you crazy? Finally, I will have someone to watch the matches with. I always wanted a son to watch a game with and go to training. And I am very happy that I will have the chance to meet your children. Then pizza afterwards. The world is beautiful! But the most beautiful thing is that you are in my life. Speaking of invitations, my friend Karim really wants to meet you, and he will be in Poland in three weeks. Do you think you can make it to dinner with us?

Sure. I'd love to meet him. I don't know how I would cope if I didn't have you now. I wouldn't have anywhere to draw strength from.

You would. The children are your strength. You yourself are incredibly strong. You just have to believe in it.

What I've always loved most about you is that I can talk to you about everything, just like now. I didn't even realise how much I missed it.

I thought you loved me because we had fantastic sex.

Ha ha ha, that too. I'm going to see what the twins are doing. I'll be in touch later. Bye!

She put down the phone and approached Patryk's bedroom door. They were sitting on the bed, engrossed in conversation. They didn't even notice her. They were very agitated. She noticed that Patrycja was crying. Krystyna didn't want to interrupt them. She realised that she had to give them time to process everything and accept the facts they were not yet ready to agree with. She quietly retreated to the living room, not wanting to disturb them. Surprised, she discovered that evening had come, and it was completely dark in the living room. Only the streetlight illuminated their living room. She remembered that the children had once begged for colourful LEDs, but Krzysztof, of course, wouldn't agree. So she quickly ordered a set of LEDs for the living room and returned to exchanging text messages with Antoni.

Just as I thought, the kids aren't doing their homework. And I don't blame them. This day has shaken me, let alone them. Fortunately, they don't know everything, and I don't think they need to know the whole truth. It turned out that Krzysztof had been lying to me throughout our marriage and was meeting men. It's hard for me to endure this blow, the worst possible. My sixteen-year-long relationship is one big failure. Built on a lie from the very beginning. Alright, I won't mope anymore or you'll think I'm a grumpy old woman, and you'll never speak to me again after this elaborate text I'm finishing.

She waited a moment for a response from Antoni, but since it didn't come, she decided to call Magda. She answered the phone after the first ring.

'Hey, I was just about to call you. What's the situation with Krzysztof? Did you sort things out?'

'Do you mean the fact that he expects me to take all the blame or that he's been cheating on me throughout our marriage?'

'What?!' exclaimed Magda over the phone. 'What a bastard! Fuck! Just a motherfucker and nothing more. What do the kids think of all this?'

'At first, they were devastated, but since they found out who Krzysztof left for, they don't want to know him. Right now, their father doesn't exist for them. They don't want to talk about him or listen, as if he's not there. They've also decided to tell friends that I left Krzysztof for a cooler guy. And that's why they want to meet Antoni.'

'What? What happened to your stable life?'

'Magda, please, my life was one big sham of which I had no clue. It turns out even my dad knew about Krzysztof, just not me.'

'Seriously, I'm speechless. What are you planning to do?'

'File for divorce on the grounds of fault and ask for alimony. And then build a normal life. Alright, I don't want to talk about it anymore. How was the meeting today?'

'Sure, I understand. The meeting was just another meeting. Though there were minor conflicts between the director and Tomek. Our esteemed director decided to take credit for the schedule of upcoming works and announced our work as his own idea at the board meeting. Tomek has connections up top, so he found out. Today, during the meeting, he asked the director about his contribution to the project and requested a detailed description of tasks and who does what – officially, to be put on the project's website. The information has already been posted. And I know for sure there will be bonuses for this project. Unofficially, I also know that the director got a notice for what he had done. I don't know about the manager, but there are rumours that he will be transferred to another department. He never raised any objections to the director's conduct, though he should have. As a result, the board is considering various options …' She paused for a moment as if thinking. 'Tomorrow will be a good day,' she added.

'Hopefully. I need something to effectively occupy my mind for a longer time. How's Alicja? How many times did she eat today?'

'She's really weird. If I ate as much as she does, I'd weigh a hundred kilos. And Alka still looks fantastic. Today, she only ate four times – for her, that's practically a food ration. And she just announced that her mum was coming today, and tomorrow we shouldn't bring any food because Alicja will supposedly bring the best dumplings ever.'

'Good Lord, what's with her and these dumplings? She practically eats nothing else, and every one is the best ever. I understand pregnancy and hormones, but how many dumplings can one eat in a day?'

'As it turns out, quite a lot, and for dessert will be … Guess …'

'Yeast cake, of course, the best in the world.'

'Not "the best".'

'What do you mean "not the best"?' asked Krystyna with feigned outrage.

'It's "epic"!'

'Look at that, how could I get that wrong. I guess I need to go to confession.'

'You don't stand a chance, darling, for absolution.'

'Why?'

'Well, you know! Your husband is part of the LGBT community, and you're not yet divorced! Another societal tragedy, and on top of that, you're having an affair with a man! You're doomed to live in sin.'

Both started laughing. After a while, Krystyna said:

'Thank you for such a perfect summary of my current situation. You nailed it. Tomorrow, when Alicja asks about today, I'll tell her just that. Thanks, you've cheered me up.'

'No problem. I'm always here when you want to chat, drink some wine or gossip about the wicked, too-happy and lovestruck Alka. Rest up, and see you tomorrow. Tomorrow will be a good day.'

'Bye, love,' said Krystyna, ending the call. The twins entered the room.

'What's up?' asked Krystyna.

'Mummy, we've decided that we don't want to see Dad right now. We need time to accept all this, to come to terms with the changes. And while we can accept that you have someone else, we can't come to terms with the fact that Dad's left us for a man. See, I can keep the level of discourse,' said Patryk to Pati.

'Yeah, especially that last bit. But I must admit, you said it masterfully, and I'm proud of you,' Pati praised her brother.

'Did you hear that, Mum? Pati is praising me! What has the world come to, a sister singing her brother's praises to the skies!' He raised his hands to the heavens, thanking them for the miracle that had occurred.

'You're exaggerating, brother. Seriously, you're overdoing it with the praise,' said Pati, shaking her head and turning to Krystyna. 'Mum, one more thing. Can we take a day off school tomorrow? It's really complicated, it's late, we haven't done our homework, and we need time to adjust to the situation.'

'I should say no, but I myself feel like taking a day off tomorrow.'

'Great, we'll go shopping again!'

'Are you crazy?' laughed Krystyna. 'We need to slow down on the spending. We've indulged too much. Now there will be only one salary. And I need to figure out how to manage the household budget.'

'We can help with that,' offered Patryk.

'Okay. We'll sit down over it this weekend, but until then, let's not go too wild with the money, okay?'

'So, are you staying home with us to play truant?' asked Pati.

'Unfortunately, I can't. Changes are happening at work, and I need to be there. But you deserve a day off life.'

'You're the best mum in the world. And I'm not saying that because you let us stay home, but because we can always come to you with a problem, and you never laugh at us. Not like … you know who.'

Patryk approached Krystyna and hugged her tightly. Then Pati did the same.

Eventually, Krystyna was left alone again with her thoughts, problems and thousands of question marks that had been appearing in her head since morning. Now, they formed an overwhelming image of the truth that hit her with full force. She curled up on the couch and let the tears of the day flow down her face.

'Mummy, get up, Mum!'

Krystyna felt a gentle tug on her arm. She opened her eyes. Pati was standing over her with a worried look.

'You didn't get up, and you said you were going to work. It's already seven-thirty.'

'What? Good thing you woke me up. Damn, I overslept. I need to get ready quickly and take a shower. Damn, there's so little time!'

Krystyna jumped up from the couch, where she had fallen asleep the night before, and whirled around the flat in confusion.

'Calm down, Mum, I'll prepare your clothes. Patryk will make breakfast, and you take a shower. By the time you're done with your makeup, we'll order a taxi, and it'll be okay. You always say meetings start at nine so that everyone can make it. We'll handle this situation in no time.'

'Have I told you I love you guys the most in the world?'

'Not today,' Pati truthfully answered.

'Well, I'm telling you now, in advance, in case I don't have time later. I'm off to the bathroom.'

'And I'm off to your wardrobe. Any requests?'

'Something optimistic,' said Krystyna and disappeared into the bathroom. She needed a cold shower, but the desire, awakened by Antoni, was pulsing in her again. She wanted to return to her room for her vibrator, but Pati was already browsing through her wardrobe. *I might as well go to Antoni's after work*, she thought and turned on the cold water. To wake up and to cool down the desire – her first two goals for the day. After a few minutes under the cold water, she felt decidedly more alert. Drying off, she heard a gentle knock on the door.

'Mum, I have your clothes. If you want, I can hand them to you. There's also clean underwear.'

'Sure, come in, I'm in a towel.'

After a moment, the door cracked open, and Pati slipped Krystyna's clothes to her. Before her eyes was a dress she had bought about a year earlier and had never worn. Krzysztof thought its colour was too provocative for a work dress. Once, she wanted to wear it for a family outing, but her husband's look effectively discouraged her, and the dress hung in the wardrobe under the section *Not Allowed to Wear*. This wasn't the only piece of clothing that had met such a fate. The dress was a dark wine colour, fitted, with an asymmetrical slit that accentuated the length of the leg, reaching a few inches above the knee. The neckline was a delicate boat shape edged with red and gold thread. The three-quarter sleeve was suitable for almost any season. Pati had paired it with a silk scarf in gold and black tones. Krystyna also found nude stockings and lace lingerie. She smiled to herself. Clearly, her daughter wanted her to understand that since the father had left the family, he should leave the wardrobe too. She happily put on everything Pati had prepared for her.

In the kitchen, the twins were busy making breakfast. She could smell the coffee already brewed and the bacon omelette sizzling in the pan. Krystyna's makeup bag and mirror were set on the table so she wouldn't waste time running around the flat.

'I thought it would be simpler and faster this way,' Pati said, seeing Krystyna's look.

'Sure, thank you so much. I see you've also chosen a different style in clothes,' Krystyna noticed, glancing at the children. They were dressed as if they were about to go to school, though today, their outfits were far from their usual ones.

'Yes. We need a bit of change. Is it okay?' Pati spun around. She was wearing a grey, white and pink plaid skirt with a little pink jumper. Patryk was wearing a trendy tracksuit with flame motifs on the jacket and trousers.

'You look perfect, absolutely ideal. So, I take it you're going to school after all and not playing truant?'

'Yes, Patryk has a football practice, and I have maths club. Besides, we were planning to go to Czesiek's birthday party in the evening.'

'Right, I totally forgot about that,' said Krystyna. Czesiek was a friend of Patryk's from the team. He was the goalkeeper, and both believed they were the core of their football world.

'Ah, Mum, we thought we'd go to Czesiek's after my practice and Pati's club. Then Czesiek's dad will drive us home in the evening. We'll be home by ten, okay?'

'And the homework?'

'Don't worry, Mum, we'll do it between the classes and the practice. We'll make it, I promise,' Patryk reassured her.

'Of course. I promised you this earlier, and now I remember that even homework had been planned. I hope today will be much better for you than yesterday. Do you need money?'

'Some cash for pizza after school would be good, right?'

'No problem. I'll give it to you now.'

They had breakfast and left for school in much better spirits. Krystyna was worried about the lack of messages from Antoni but didn't want to seem desperate and decided to wait. She wanted to meet him in the evening. She planned to call or text him around noon and, until then, focus on work.

Nearly an hour late, she entered the room where all the girls were already gathered. Even Gosia, who had returned to work after the traumatic events.

'O la la! Phew, phew!' Alicja whistled, seeing Krystyna enter.

'You said things had changed, but I didn't think it would be this much! Krystyna, you look stunning. And you're not wearing anything grey. Wow! I need to hug you!'

Gosia hugged her friend warmly.

'Ladies, I was away just a few weeks, and look at these changes. Can I get a quick summary before we go to the meeting?' Gosia suggested.

'In a nutshell, it's like this: I met Antoni, then found out Krzysztof had been cheating on me for years. And not just with anyone, but with a whole bunch of guys like him who are into sado-maso. Krzysztof moved out, and we're getting a divorce, and I started an affair with Antoni. That's about it, I guess ...' Krystyna looked questioningly at Alicja, who started to laugh.

'Sorry, Krysia, but it sounded so unreal that I couldn't help it. If someone had told me three months ago that you'd be standing here talking about your life in clothes that make you look like a million dollars, I would have never believed it.'

'Me neither. I didn't realise how suffocated I felt living under Krzysztof's thumb. Finally, I don't have to pretend and I can shag. Damn, the world is beautiful, Alicja, you were right.'

'What the fuck is happening here?' Gosia laughed. 'We definitely need to meet up on Saturday to catch up. I mean, catch up on my end. By the way, Krystyna! I've been trying to call you since yesterday, but every time it says the subscriber is unavailable. What did you do with your phone? Did you decide to throw that out of your life, too?'

'I can confirm that your phone is off, or you've changed some settings. I called after 8 a.m., and it was the same situation.'

'Damn,' said Krystyna, checking her phone settings. 'And here I am, sitting like an idiot, waiting for a text from

Antoś. Instead of turning off the sounds, I completely turned off the card.'

Within moments, Krystyna's phone rang, and for several seconds, the sounds of text messages and other notifications filled the air.

'Someone's popular,' observed Magda, noticing the flurry of messages on Krystyna's phone.

All eyes were on the new Krystyna, a face they knew but couldn't quite recognise. She had always been hidden under the mask of what was appropriate and what wasn't. This barrier had been created by Krzysztof, and Krystyna had to submit to his demands and expectations, receiving nothing in return. They watched as her face transformed while she was reading the texts, how she smiled to herself.

'Is that really Kryśka?' asked Gosia.

'I'm in shock myself, but yes. That's our Kryśka. You should have seen her at Magda's, all pissed, talking about what she would be doing at night with Antoś,' said Alicja, laughing, with Magda adding funny anecdotes about Krystyna from that day. Soon, all three were laughing together.

'You meanies, I'm right here, and I can hear you, so please don't make fun of me.'

'How I missed our mornings together! The Dominican Republic was wonderful, but I was so looking forward to returning to you,' said Gosia, approaching Alicja. 'I know I've already apologised, but I need to do it again. You have no idea how sorry I am for how I acted then. There's no excuse for my words. After my last miscarriage, I should have gone away and taken a break. Listened to everyone telling me I just needed to grieve. I'm really glad you're so happy, in love, pregnant. See? I can talk about it without crying. Those therapy sessions gave me absolute power! Will you ever forgive me?'

'You silly, I forgave you a long time ago. Almost immediately after you left. I missed you so much. Come here, let's have a hug, my dear Gosia.'

They hugged and stood together for a while in the middle of the room – until Krystyna snapped back to reality.

'Damn! The meeting started fifteen minutes ago! Let's get our butts in gear and head to the conference room. This is unprecedented. Why didn't the manager call us?'

The whole office team came to support Patryk at his match, helping Antoni bond with Krystyna's children. Alicja brought Aleksander, and Magda came with Tomek. Gosia and Piotr were there, too. And this way, for the first time, Patryk had a massive cheering section. They gathered near the stadium an hour earlier. Since everyone was wearing sports clothes, the men couldn't resist what they called a 'kickabout'. They split into two teams: Patryk and Antoni on one, Aleksander and Tomasz on the other. Though the men were nowhere near Patryk's level, the fun was great. The girls from the office sat with Patrycja on a nearby bench.

'Mum, look how Antoni passed the ball to Patryk. Thanks to him, they're leading 3–0. He's good. Patryk likes him. He always complained about not having anyone to play with, and now look how happy he is. Oh, there's Szczepan and his dad. They'll probably join the warm-up.'

Krystyna noticed other fathers with their sons, who were on Patryk's team, approaching. The small warm-up turned into a big match. Everyone who arrived early joined in. Just before meeting with the coach, Patryk managed to run over to Krystyna.

'Mum, I know you don't like it when I say this, but it's bloody brilliant. The guys on the team are thrilled with my idea to warm up like this. Even the coach praised us for our spontaneity. And sorry for saying this, but Antoni is a hundred times cooler than Dad. He's already made plans with the other dads for cheering and the next match. Don't be mad at me, okay? But really, that's how it is.'

Glancing to see if his teammates were watching, he quickly hugged Krystyna and ran back to the rest of the team. The seniors, tired from the warm-up, took their seats in the stands.

'Oh, darling, your fitness isn't up to par,' Alicja said to Aleksander, who was trying to catch his breath, just like Tomek, who sat down on the grass, panting heavily.

'Patryk has a great talent. And incredible speed. He's a good striker,' stated Aleksander. 'Too bad my fitness is at zero. It's hard to keep up with him in running, passing and accuracy.'

The rest of the men heartily agreed. As the match began, they cheered the loudest, as if Patryk was fighting for the first place in the Champions League. Later, during a meal, they analysed every detail of the match with Patryk, who blushed with excitement. The ladies were unusually quiet that day, giving the floor to the men. They quietly agreed that it was good for them. Krystyna was delighted with how the day was going. The most important thing for her was that the children had accepted Antoni and seemed comfortable in his company. Once they had finally planned all the matches for the season and said their goodbyes, the children clearly let Krystyna know how much they had enjoyed the day. To her surprise, they also said that she deserved some time for herself and should spend it with Antoni.

Gosia was sitting in the waiting room at the gynaecologist's surgery, a place she had become all too familiar with. She had visited almost every room in the clinic, especially those for pregnant women, multiple times. She was seated in one of the comfortable leather chairs in the corridor. There were potted flowers on every table and windowsill. She really liked the orchids. She also knew they were the doctor's doing as he dedicated every spare moment to his plants.

For years, Gosia had been on various medications, hormones and injections. She was aware that the sheer number of pills she had ingested over the time had not been without impact on her body. One concerning symptom that had emerged was the absence of her period since her trip to the Dominican Republic. Over the last few days, she had spent time searching for information. She knew for certain that she wasn't pregnant. After years of unsuccessful treatments, she instantly dismissed that possibility. She didn't even do a pregnancy test. What worried her more were the heartburn and frequent vomiting. She should have visited a GP first, but she trusted her gynaecologist more and made an appointment with him at the earliest opportunity. Now, she was sitting outside his surgery and waiting for her turn. A few minutes later, she heard her name. She entered the room bracing herself for the worst.

'Good morning, Mrs Małgorzata. What brings you in today?' the doctor asked as she entered the room.

'Good morning, doctor. I haven't had my period for a while, and I've been experiencing some worrying symptoms like heartburn and vomiting ...'

'Have you and your husband been trying for a baby at another clinic?'

'No, doctor, you advised us against trying for the next two or three years after what happened last time.'

'Did you take a pregnancy test?'

Gosia looked at the doctor as if he were an alien, almost offended by the question.

'But you said we couldn't have children ...'

'I said I didn't know why you couldn't have children,' the doctor emphasised each word. 'I also mentioned that it might be a psychological block that might one day lift. Have you sought therapy with a psychologist, as I had suggested?'

'Not with a psychologist, but I've had a form of therapy. Just talking with someone who helped me understand where my blocks were coming from.'

'Have you seen an improvement?'

'Yes, definitely, I feel better mentally. After therapy, it was like a dam had broken. My friend is expecting, and I can finally talk to her about it and share in her happiness.'

'That's wonderful, I'm very pleased. Now I need to examine you. Have you gained weight recently?'

'Yes, and I can't seem to shed those few kilos.' She looked embarrassed at the doctor.

'Alright. Let's proceed with a transvaginal ultrasound scan to get a complete picture. When you're ready, just call me.'

Gosia went into a small adjacent room, undressed, lay on the couch, and covered herself with a green sheet.

'I'm ready,' she called out. She was scared of what her doctor would discover. Her mind was racing with fear of the worst.

'Very well.' The doctor worked swiftly. He picked up the ultrasound probe, put a condom and gel on it, and started the examination.

'When was your last normal period?'

She had to think for a while before she gave the exact date.

'Nothing since then? No spotting, abdominal pain?'

'I had some stomach pain, but it stopped. I thought my period was delayed due to some stress. But it's been too long. Can you see anything?' she asked anxiously.

The doctor looked at her oddly.

'I can. And you will see something in a moment, too. And you will hear.' He turned on the monitor in front of her. She saw a black screen with two pulsating dots. A heartbeat echoed, but it sounded strange.

'Is that my heart beating? Is something wrong?' she asked, terrified.

'Please look closely. What do you see?'

Gosia turned her head uncertainly towards the monitor.

'I'll say it out loud, and you will correct me.'

Slowly, the reality of what she was seeing began to dawn on her. 'I see a foetus. I mean, I see … But that's impossible! I see two little ones!'

Tears streamed down her face.

'Calm down …' the doctor comforted her, himself moved by what he saw. He had known Małgorzata for several years and was aware of how much she had put into trying to have even one child. 'We need to measure everything, check it all out … It's time to start a pregnancy record, do all the necessary tests and treat that period in a special way. You've never had a twin pregnancy before. This can happen after such a long time of hormonal therapy. As I can see, the babies are developing almost by the book. All indicators are at a very good level. I would recommend prenatal testing, but looking at the development of the babies, I see no indications for it. We have very sensitive equipment, so any concerning issues would have shown up during the examination. But I see nothing worrisome. If you decide you want to do prenatal testing, we certainly can. Please discuss it with your husband and let me know. Now, please come to the office; we'll call the midwife and discuss the next few weeks.'

'Excuse me, could I get an ultrasound picture for my husband? I don't think he'll believe me.'

All the while, she was gazing at the monitor hanging in front of her, at the two tiny beings that looked a little like aliens.

'They're already printed, and I've also recorded a video for you where you can hear the heartbeats. Nothing could beat such a Christmas present. Does your husband know you're here?'

'No, I suspected everything, but not that I was pregnant. And with twins.'

She took a deep breath, like someone coming up for air after being underwater for a long time.

'I'm leaving, please get dressed and then come to the office.'

Once he had left, Gosia slowly started dressing. Only now did she notice that the trousers she had bought a month earlier were practically too small for her. She couldn't fasten them. She decided to let her shirt hang out to hide the fact that the zipper and button of her jeans were undone. She entered the office, where the midwife she knew from previous visits to the clinic was already waiting.

'Good morning, Mrs Gosia. Congratulations, really!'

'Thank you, I'm so happy ...'

She put her hand on her stomach, as pregnant women do all over the world do, and burst into tears. The midwife came over, sat her down and patted her head until Gosia calmed down.

'I'm sorry, but this is so new to me. I've never got this far in a pregnancy. Can I go to work as normal? We have a lot of projects going on, and I don't want to leave a mess.'

'Of course, there are no contraindications. Since you've been working up to now, there's no reason you can't continue as before.'

'That's good. I just need to pop into a shop for some larger trousers because the ones I'm wearing mysteriously won't fasten.'

'That's normal. Often, for example, a bride who's pregnant suddenly can't fit into her clothes the day after the wedding. That's how our subconscious works. You didn't allow yourself to believe you were pregnant, and your body followed suit. I recommend buying some larger clothes and maternity trousers, so they won't press on your stomach, as that will lead to a lot of discomfort. Across the street, there's a well-stocked maternity shop.' The midwife smiled warmly at Gosia. 'Shall we begin?'

The visit lasted several more minutes. Gosia left with an armful of pamphlets, samples, books and a list of tests she needed to do soon. In her hand, she also held the pregnancy record book she once envied Alicja for having. For the first time, she walked down the same long corridor she knew so well with a smile on her face. She exchanged a few joyful glances with the women sitting outside the surgeries, waiting for their appointments. Some were further along in their pregnancies, others less so, but they all shared that special aura that connects expectant women.

After leaving the clinic, she stopped by a nearby maternity shop. She bought trousers, called a taxi and headed to work.

The office was buzzing with life and chatter. That's the way it is at the end of the year when the penultimate day before the Christmas break centres around the company's Christmas party. And so it was on this day. When she entered, Gosia could immediately smell the distinctive scent of tangerines.

'Hello,' she said, seeing Alicja munching on the citrus fruits. Dressed in a red-and-white tunic with fur trimmings, she looked as though she had stepped out of an illustration depicting Santa among his Snowflakes.

'Hello, you seem exceptionally radiant today, as if you've snagged a bargain at Molier?' As she said this, Alicja glanced at Gosia's shopping bag and froze. As her gaze shifted between her colleague and the bag, she recognised the logo of the shop she herself had been shopping at for months. Initially, Gosia had intended to tell the girls everything only after talking to Piotr and her parents, but her joy was so immense she couldn't contain it. She removed her coat and gently revealed her belly, still small but noticeable enough that Alicja jumped to her feet and rushed to her friend.

'Gosia, are you pregnant?!' Alicja looked at her, and Gosia only burst into tears, nodding enthusiastically. Alicja's squeal was so loud it must have been heard on the other side of the city, but moments later, she was already embracing Gosia. They both wiped their eyes only to laugh, cry and stroke their bellies. This is how Krystyna and Magda found them.

'Alicja, what have you been up to now? You can be heard from the other end of the corridor. Gosia, good that you're here … What happened?' Krystyna tried for a moment to understand what was happening. She noticed that both were tearful yet appeared immensely happy. Gosia, lacking the strength to speak, lifted her shirt, revealing a gently outlined pregnant belly.

'You mean to say you're pregnant? How many weeks? What do Piotr and your parents think?'

'They don't know yet. I went to the doctor, expecting it to be some illness or complications from using hormones for so many years. But it turns out I'm having twins!'

'Twins?!' exclaimed Krystyna. 'My goodness, what wonderful news! After so many years of trying!'

'Don't tell anyone in the office, okay? I told you because I trust you completely. But neither Piotr nor my parents know yet, and I should probably start with them, only I couldn't help myself. I want to tell my parents on Christmas Eve, but I don't think I can wait. I'll call them and ask them to come over today. This year, the presents will be early because I absolutely can't wait any longer.

'Gosia, now we can swap clothes and go for walks together,' Alicja said, delighted.

'Didn't you suspect anything?' Magda asked, having been the quietest on hearing Gosia's news.

'No, I thought I was ill or stressed. But now that I think about it, I probably just ruled out that option before I allowed it to materialise. You know, a kind of denial before I realised that such a possibility existed.'

Gosia's phone rang.

'It's Mum. I sent her a message that I had something important. Hello, Mum. Yes, it's important. I'm glad you called back. Can you and Dad come over today? It's very important that you're there. Yes? That's great, six o'clock? Okay, Mum, see you then.'

She hang up.

'I won't even call Piotr because nothing will stop me from telling him over the phone, and I know he's swamped at work today. Besides, I want to see his face when I play him the ultrasound video and he hears two little hearts.'

'You have a video? And pictures, too?' asked Ala. She and Aleksander had spent countless hours over every picture, marvelling at every tiny detail of their unborn child.

'I can hardly imagine your happiness, Gosia,' said Krystyna. 'It's simply unbelievable.'

'You're going to give your family a Christmas present like no one has ever seen before.'

The door opened. The manager almost burst into their room.

'What are you all chatting about? Everyone's waiting for you. Quick, to the conference room!' He opened the door wider and began ushering the girls so that they could start the company meeting promptly.

The director delivered a pleasant speech, emphasising that he couldn't imagine working without any of the current team members. He thanked everyone for the year spent together and wished them a happy Christmas break. As per tradition, between Christmas and New Year's Day, only skeleton staff was present, and usually, this time was spent gossiping and indulging in post-Christmas cakes. Only the accounts department was busy preparing the annual balance. The girls stayed with the rest of the employees for a while, but after an hour, they served themselves portions of cake and fruit and slipped away to their room to talk in peace.

'I feel like these tangerines have made my belly grow even more,' said Alicja, sitting in the armchair at the desk and putting her feet up on a nearby chair to give some relief to her feet, which had recently started to swell. 'But I think I'll take one more tiny piece of cake.'

'You're crazy,' Magda said, laughing.

Alicja looked at her and asked, 'And how are you spending Christmas this year? You've been quiet and not boasting about anything ...'

'Well, next to your news, my Christmas Eve with Tomasz seems really modest.'

'Big love?'

'Yes, but as you know, I need time. The most beautiful thing is that those terrifying dreams have stopped. Right after I decided to report the rape case. I'm going to travel to my hometown and meet Franek face-to-face. Sort out matters related to my flat. Tomasz will go with me. For the first time, I can breathe deeply and wait to see what the next year brings. I never felt this way before. And how are your Christmas preparations?'

'This year, I'm turning into the lady of the house, and we're inviting our families to our place for Christmas Eve. Then, on Christmas Day, we're going to Aleksander's parents, and on Boxing Day to mine. Just last year that would have meant the end of the world for me, but now I can't imagine it any other way. This year really took off for me and is completely different from what I imagined last year,' Alicja said, stroking her belly and looking at Krystyna.

'You think your year took off? Look at me. My dad is dead, my husband turned out to be bisexual and left me for a man, and now I have a lover. Antoni is the only man I truly love. It seems only Gosia got what she wanted.'

'My only dream will come true twice over. And how are the children, Krysia?'

'The kids don't want to spend the holidays with Krzysztof. They're still upset with him. Patryk has a problem with Krzysztof leaving us for a man. He says he doesn't want to have a gay for a father. On one hand, I feel sad because I know it's not Krzysztof's fault for being who he is. But there's the betrayal that lasted our entire marriage, the constant deception and so on. And that's not okay. I feel sorry that they don't have contact with their father, but on the other hand, he brought it upon himself. Then there's the situation with Antoni. Here, it's better than good. They like each other and get along, and Antoni spends more and more time with us, and it's okay. But I have no idea how it will be in a month or three. We have a challenge ahead, as Antoni will be with us for the entire holidays, then for New Year's Eve and New Year's Day. Speaking of which, are we still on for New Year's Eve?'

'Absolutely. Aleksander says it will be our last New Year's Eve together because next year, we'll be sitting in nappies.'

'Me too. And in double the amount of nappies,' Gosia noted with a laugh. 'We can be together and drink Piccolo.'

'We have a plan. Magda, are you also coming to Krystyna's?' asked Alicja.

'Just as we decided. Hey, do you realise it's almost four? We should head home, girls.'

'I'm in for a wonderful afternoon,' Gosia mused dreamily.

In high spirits, they left the office, parted ways outside the building and each went in her direction.

Gosia opened the door to her flat. She was surprised to find Piotr already there.

'Hello, love, your parents called, they're on their way. What's this secrecy about?' He approached her for a welcome kiss. 'What's happened that you're suddenly organising a family gathering?'

'Is the DVD player plugged in?' Gosia asked, starting to rummage through the shopping bag, which contained the trousers, all the flyers and papers from the doctor.

'Yes, but can you tell me what's going on?'

'I want to show you something before my parents arrive. That's all.'

He looked at her intently. He approached the DVD player, turned it on and reached out for the disc Gosia held in her hand. He pressed play and instinctively looked at the screen. Gosia approached and turned up the volume. Both stood and watched the monitor with two tiny bodies on the video. Piotr looked at Gosia. Tears streamed down his face unceasingly.

'Does this mean that ...?' His voice failed him. He covered his face with his hands. She saw his shoulders rise from crying. Meanwhile, the video recorded by the doctor had ended and Gosia played it again.

'We'd never reached this moment before and now we're going to have two babies, not just one ...'

Piotr swept her into his arms, hugging her long and tight. After a moment, he gently pushed her away and bent down to her belly.

'Hey, kiddos, Daddy here. You kept your parents waiting quite a while.' He turned his head in such a way as if expecting a response from the babies. They stood there for a long time: Piotr on his knees, nestled against Gosia's belly, both absorbed in the video, listening to the beating hearts of their twins.

'Piotr, I need to sit down. It's uncomfortable standing like this, and I really need to pee.'

'Darling, of course; go to the bathroom, and I'll set up a cosy spot for you on the sofa.'

'It's just pregnancy, relax!'

She was already on her way but turned to see Piotr's expression as she said it aloud. He jumped up to embrace her one more time, hugging her tightly.

'Pee!' Gosia exclaimed, and just then the intercom rang. 'I'll pee, you get the door.'

She felt she had made it to the bathroom just in time. She heard Piotr greeting someone through the intercom, resetting the DVD to the start of the ultrasound video and, after a few minutes, there was a knock at the door. It was Gosia's parents.

'Hello, Piotr, what's the emergency? What's so urgent it can't wait till Christmas? Is something wrong?' they inquired.

'Hi, come in. Just wait for Gosia to come out of the bathroom and we'll tell you.' Piotr turned towards the room and the TV. Gosia's parents followed his gaze and almost simultaneously noticed the image. At that moment, Gosia emerged from the bathroom, not expecting such a reaction. All three stood there, staring at the screen.

'Hey! I'm here! Can you see me?'

Piotr was the first to recover, feeling immensely proud that his wife was pregnant. His father-in-law quickly embraced his daughter.

'My dear girl, I'm so thrilled about your double joy!'

Gosia's mum, after a moment, managed to respond. She approached her daughter and husband, joining in the embrace. Meanwhile, Piotr picked up the remote and played the short recording showing the twins and emitting the distinct sound of their heartbeats.

'Okay, I don't know about you, but I've had enough of standing and hugging; I just want to sit down.' Gosia had been trying to break free from her parents' embrace for a while. 'Gosh, I'm happy to be pregnant too, but I need some air, and I'm hungry, and there's nothing to eat at home. Now that we've watched the Film of the Evening, let's go get something to eat.'

'You shouldn't be going out now! You've obviously taken time off work, right?' Gosia's mum quickly switched from "mum" mode to "doctor" mode.

'I haven't taken any time off. I'm planning to work till the end. Why shouldn't I go out? Pregnancy is a natural state. You always said that, Mum. And please don't stress me out now. We're going out.'

They all went to a nearby restaurant to celebrate this amazing occasion.

Right after Christmas, Magda set off on the journey of a lifetime with Tomasz. She was confronting her worst demon. A pain no one she knew had experienced, a pain no one should endure, even in their most terrible, nightmarish dreams. They spoke little on the way. Everything had been said before. Knowing Magda, Tomasz didn't press for conversation – he knew that the journey itself was terrifying enough for her. He didn't want to exacerbate it.

Their first steps were directed towards the police station, as advised by the lawyer they had consulted a few weeks earlier. When they entered, they were greeted by a kind older police officer at the reception. From that moment until their return home, Magda felt as if everything was happening outside of her. As if she were watching the events unfold from an observer's perspective rather than as one of the main characters.

'Good morning. I would like to report a crime. Specifically, the rape of me, which took place fifteen years ago and dragged on for more than four years. When it started, I was just over fourteen years old,' she said in a cool tone.

The initially indifferent officer reacted promptly when Magda provided her address and her stepfather's name. They were ushered into a room where three police officers were seated. After a brief greeting, the officers got down to business.

'Have you come to report a crime?' inquired the first police officer.

'Yes, I wanted to report that for years I was abused by my ...' she interrupted as if searching for the right words. When she spoke again, her voice was even more matt and devoid of emotion.

'By my stepfather, Franciszek Zbukowski.'

'How old were you when the first abuse occurred?' quickly asked the second police officer.

'Fourteen,' Magda had the irresistible impression that the police officers were just waiting for such information. There was a visible expression of triumph on their faces.

'Do you wish to report everything now, for the record, so we can start the whole process immediately? Do you need a psychologist present during the questioning?' the third officer asked.

'No, I've been in therapy for years; I can handle this. I'm ready,' Magda's voice conveyed incredible confidence and resolve.

'One of us will stay with you,' the second officer indicated to the older colleague, 'and we'll take care of the rest. May we ask your companion to wait outside?' he turned to Tomasz.

'Will you be okay?' Tomasz asked Magda.

'Yes, I want to get this over with. Will you wait for me outside?' she wanted to be sure.

'Of course, my dear. I'll be right here,' Tomasz reassured her. The officers gave him a chair and a cup of coffee, and he stepped outside.

Magda's interrogation began. The police station, which had initially seemed a bit sleepy, was typical of small precincts that rarely handle major cases. Most of the activity occurred in the evenings when the boisterous patrons of the local dive began to deliver their brand of justice outside the bar. Occasionally, minor thefts or domestic disputes would occur. Tomasz, sitting in the corridor, noticed the bustle. Doors slammed intermittently and snippets of conversations were audible.

'We have a statement against Zbuk.'

'What the fuck? From whom?'

'His former stepdaughter's just testified that he first raped her when she was fourteen.'

'Finally!' a loud voice exclaimed. 'When do we move in?'

'Zdzisiek is calling the prosecutor. Probably right away today.'

'That's the kind of delayed gift from Santa that I understand. We'll catch the bastard!'

'Quiet, there's a civilian in the corridor,' someone said. Then the door was closed. Tomasz couldn't hear anything more. He only saw more and more police officers arriving at the station. Just before Magda came out of the room where the questioning took place, the prosecutor himself had arrived. Of course, Tomasz wasn't supposed to know, but again, someone had shouted so loudly in the corridor that the prosecutor was already downstairs.

The interrogation lasted over an hour and a half. When Magda came out of the room, her face showed traces of many tears but also incredible relief. Tomasz quickly embraced her. They stood hugging for a moment.

'Shall we go?'

'The officer asked us to go with them. Because it's only my flat and as the owner, I have the right to enter any time. And they want to go in. They have reports that there is abuse of other children in the home, but they lacked hard evidence. They want my help to enter the apartment. We'll go with them, right?'

'Of course, that's why we came here, to sort out this … person,' Tomasz said, taking Magda's hand. Moments later, the officer who had interrogated Magda appeared, accompanied by another man, who turned out to be the prosecutor.

'Ms Magda, are you ready?' the officer asked.

'Yes, we can go,' Magda said with a firm voice. They went downstairs, followed by the prosecutor and several police officers.

From that moment, Magda and Tomasz felt as if they were in a thriller or crime movie. They arrived at the block of flats, got out of the car and headed to the flat. As they entered the staircase, they heard a scream of a child.

A pleading voice came from Magda's flat. When they knocked, everything went silent. The door was opened by a girl about twelve to fourteen years old. The face of her stepfather blurred in the distance. Magda wasn't prepared for this. She felt like she was going to vomit. She saw the confusion on his face. He spoke first.

'Oh, look who's here. Her Ladyship has graciously arrived. What do you want?'

'I came to reclaim my flat,' Magda said firmly.

'You must be joking!' He began to laugh ironically. 'How do you plan to force me out? You think I'll be scared of your little boyfriend?'

'I've taken precautions; the police are with me.'

The police officers and the prosecutor, who were standing on the half-floor, were waiting for these words. Chaos ensued. Besides the girl there were two other children and a woman in the flat. After an initial inspection, paedophilia-themed materials were secured, indicating that the minors present had experienced rape. The mother, who was also in the flat, didn't react to her partner's actions. Both were detained, and the children were taken to the hospital. Magda learnt that from there, they would be placed in care. If they were lucky, they would end up in a foster family. The flat was secured by the police. Magda would get it back after the proceedings were over. As they stood by the car, getting ready to leave, the prosecutor approached them.

'Ms Magda, I wanted to thank you for your help. Thanks to you, we caught that scoundrel. We will definitely contact you. Please take care of yourself. See you later,' he shook their hands and left.

Magda and Tomasz drove towards Warsaw. Only after an hour did Magda break the silence.

'All my adult life, I've been wondering what I wanted to do. As I stood there and saw those children … Alone, hurt, unloved … I suddenly experienced – no matter how it sounds – an epiphany. Now, I know what I want to do and what I want to devote myself to. There is a lot of learning ahead of me, many training courses, but I want to do it …,' she said in a confident voice and looked at Tomasz.

'I once had a friend from an orphanage. I know what it's like there. I think it's a great idea. It was also my dream. Let's do it together.'

'Really? You want to?' Magda asked, touched.

'Yes. And I know we'll have a better chance as a married couple.' Tomasz pulled over to the side of the road and turned on the hazard lights.

'Are you proposing to me?' Magda asked with a laugh.

'Yes. I've always wanted this. From the first moment I saw you, I knew I wanted to be with you. Will you marry me?' Tomasz asked.

'Yes!' Magda was sure of nothing more in her life. She hugged him, and they sat like that for a long time, wrapped in each other's arms, cut off from the outside world, savouring their happiness.

'We'll tell the girls, but after the New Year, okay? I want to enjoy this moment,' Magda looked at Tomasz.

'Whenever you want. We'll definitely find the right moment.'

When New Year's Eve finally arrived, everyone was happy that the old year was ending and new, better days were coming. Krystyna's flat, with Antoni's help, had gone through a complete transformation. It was festively decorated with garlands, baubles and lights. A huge Christmas tree invited everyone to celebrate every moment together. Considering Alicja and Gosia's condition, everyone decided to abstain from alcohol, only toasting the New Year with a glass of champagne. They had dinner and decided to play charades together. The twins had already assured Krystyna several times that it was their best Christmas and New Year's Eve ever.

'Mum, ten minutes to midnight! We need to get the fireworks,' shouted Patryk. 'The first time we have fireworks. It has to be perfect.'

'We're getting everything. The others will help.'

The men took the fireworks and champagne, and the women took glasses and they all went downstairs in front of the building to join the gathering neighbours.

Together, they counted down the last seconds of the old year and at midnight they made wishes for each other. Each of them was entering the new year with great hope. Krystyna dreamt of a future with Antoni. Antoni finally felt that he had found the perfect haven beside the woman he had loved and her children, who had also stolen his heart. He considered them his family and knew he would do absolutely everything to protect them.

Alicja and Aleksander were expecting a baby together and were planning a wedding shortly after the birth.

Gosia and Piotr, against all odds and expectations, finally got their coolest – as Gosia once put it – pregnancy book and were also waiting for what was soon to come.

Magda faced a challenge. Tomasz was with her, offering his full support.

After a loud and festive welcome to the New Year, the guests returned upstairs. Alicja was cutting the cake that everyone had been waiting for. Unexpectedly, Krystyna's phone rang.

'Hi Krystyna, happy New Year. I wish you a good year. I'm sorry for everything that happened. You and the children didn't deserve it.' Krzysztof's voice sounded very different from what she had remembered. Krystyna felt that something had happened.

'I wish you all the best in the New Year too. It's nice of you to call with wishes,' replied Krystyna.

'I wasn't going to tell you this now, but since we're talking … You'll need to get tested. It turns out I have AIDS. Since I don't know when I got infected, you might be sick too. That's all. Bye.'

Krzysztof hung up, leaving Krystyna stunned. Antoni rushed to her.

'What happened? What did he tell you?!' He hugged her, but she pushed him away.

'I might be sick. Krzysztof has AIDS!' Krystyna exclaimed, looking terrified at her friends, especially Antoni. The thought that she might have infected the people closest to her horrified her. However, she couldn't focus on her own fear, as suddenly her attention was drawn to Gosia, who grimaced in pain, made a strange sound and clutched her belly.

'Piotr! Quickly, to the hospital! Our babies, I think I'm losing them!'

'Well, what a full-on welcome to the New Year. The only things missing are a hooker and a dancing penguin,' Alicja whispered to Aleksander as Piotr and Gosia left for the car, hurrying to get to the hospital.

To be continued …

Title: *She Goes By Many Names*   **Author:** Monique Kristine

Copyeditor: Justyna Bielecka

Proofreading: Agnieszka Anulewicz - Wypych

Style sheet

British spellings

New Hart's Rules and the *Oxford English Dictionary* for reference

No serial comma

-ise endings

Single quotes, doubles for quotations within quotations

Italics for foreign words, thoughts, text messages, film titles

Numbers – spelled out up to 100

Dates – 1 January 1990

Times: spelled out if it is round hours, e.g. one o'clock; otherwise 1:30 p.m./1:30 a.m.<u>Word list (English)</u>

aka

amid

among

apple charlotte (cake)

blond (adj), blond (masc. n.), blonde (femin. n.)

café

cooperate

doughnut

facade

fairytale (adj), fairy tale (n)

further

leukaemia

makeup

mum

medieval

on (not 'upon') in expressions such as 'on entering'

paedophile

passé

polystyrene

thank-you (n)

well-being (n)

wine glass (two words)

while

windowsill

Wmiestie nawsiegda

<u>Word list (Polish)</u>

Adamski

Aleje Jerozolimskie

bar mleczny

Bazyliszek

Białołęka

Ciechocinek

Geńka

Górczewska (street name)

Hala Mirowska

kompot

kopytka

Krasiński Park

Łazienki (The Royal Łazienki)

Piłsudski

Poznań

Rusałka

Sopot

Ursynów

Wąchock

Wołoska

Zagoździński

<u>Characters</u>
Magda Jaśko (she/her) – 26 year old; has lived in Warsaw for a few years; was sexually abused by her stepfather 15 years ago ;

from a small town close to Poznań; secretive about her past; her mother died when she was 18, her father died before she was born (but in the story, Magda doesn't tell her story until later and the girls think her father died when she was little), her mother, who was a cleaner, remarried. In the office, she is in charge of contacts and information flow.

Other names: Magdalena (official), Madzia

Krystyna Dziekańska (she/her) – in her 40s, birthday in February; conservative, secretive, wanting to be 'proper'; the longest-serving employee of the city hall, she deals with the substantive law and drafts contracts and takes care of project documentation.

Other names: Krysia, Kryśka

Gosia Kowalska (she/her) – probably in her late 20s or early 30s; married to Piotr and trying for a baby, two attempts at in vitro; two miscarriages between the 5th and 7th week; slim, petite, delicate; in the office she has the role of an assistant.

Other names: Małgorzata (official name disliked by Gosia), Gosieńka (very diminutive), Gocha

Alicja Nowak (she/her) – in her mid-30s; beautiful and feminine, with long blond curly hair, looking like 'million dollars'; single and independent, doesn't want to settle, dates a lot of men; enjoys life, is optimistic and cheerful, famous for odd comparisons and witty remarks; beautiful and charming; from a small village; parents live 'in a wooden cottage by the wood', but Alicja visits them rarely and is ashamed of her modest rural upbringing; she miscarried after being beaten up in her first serious relationship; in the office she has the role of an assistant.

Other names: Ala, Alka, Alusia, Alunia

Krzysztof (he/his) – Krystyna's husband; has a ministerial role; gay but hid it for a long time.

Names: Krzysiek

Krystyna's father (he/his) – no name revealed, Krystyna usually calls him Dad or Daddy, the twins call him Grandpa; he and Krystyna's husband fell out around Christmas and didn't see each other for quite a while.

Patrycja (she/her) – one of Krystyna's twins, also known as Pati.

Patryk (he/his) – one of Krystyna's twins.

Piotr (he/his) – Gosia's husband; his parents died in a car crash when he was just about 5, he was in the accident as well; grew up in an orphanage; two degrees – IT and the other not revealed.

Other names: Piotrek, Piotruś

Jacek – Alicja's friend.

Kamil (he/his) – a man that Alicja had a date with and who turned out to be quite controlling and aggressive.

Krzysiek – Alicja's neighbour.

Antoni (he/his) – Krystyna's old lover; dark, well-built, blue eyes; got persuaded by his parents to get married to a woman he was with at the time he fell in love with Krystyna, that woman faked leukaemia; he got divorced when Krystyna was about to marry Krzysztof; suffered from depression; spent some time abroad – in Spain and Egypt.

Other names: Antek, Antoś

Aleksander (he/his) – Alicja's new love, a financial analyst at a corporation, with parents and grandmother in the countryside; tall, navy-blue eyes.

Names: Alek, Oluś.

Tomasz Ćwikliński (he/his) – Magda's old friend who appeared in relation to a project at work.

Other names: Tomek.

Henryk (he/his) – the women's manager; in his 50s, tall, slim, pronounced cheekbones; very loud voice like a 'roar'. In Polish 'roar' is 'ryk' so everyone pronounced his name emphasising the second syllable: HenRYK.

Franciszek Zbukowski (he/his) – Franek, Zbuk (nickname he's known under in his hometown); Magda's stepfather who raped her regularly when she was 14–18 years old; her mum met him when Magda was 13; he first raped Magda a week after his and her mum's civil ceremony.

Zdzisiek – one of the police officers.

Karim – Antoni's friend from Egypt.

Czesiek – Patryk's friend.

<u>Places</u>

Warsaw

City Hall – the women's office location.

Room 5 – the women's room.

Magda's flat – with a balcony overlooking the city.

Alicja's flat – the place where their 'witches' gatherings' take place.

Gosia's flat – in a block of flats on a floor with a lift.

Punta Cana, the Dominican Republic

Gosia's gynaecologist's clinic

<u>Timeline/plot</u>

Novel starts during winter school holidays (most probably in February), on Monday. The room 5 team finds an error in the Excel spreadsheets.

Friday – the team from room 5 leaves a memo for the accounts department.

Saturday – the girls meet at Alicja's flat for 'wine, jazz and us.

Thursday – Gosia has an appointment at the clinic for in vitro. She and Piotr go for a fancy lunch.

Friday – Gosia and Piotr decide to go on a little holiday to Sopot.

Friday a week later – Krystyna quarrels with Krzysztof, who announces he will be going away on a business trip and coming back on Monday evening. Krystyna invites the girls from the office for the evening on Saturday.

Saturday morning – Krystyna sees her father together with the twins – they go for a walk and lunch, and the twins stay with their grandpa for the night.

Monday morning – Alicja doesn't oversleep and meets Aleksander on the way to the office.

Tuesday – Alicja tells her colleagues about her new relationship; Tomasz Ćwikliński arrives at the city hall to work on a large project with Magda and her team members.

Saturday in spring – Krystyna is going to Łazienki with her dad and the twins, the dad collapses with a heart attack.

Gosia miscarries on the same Saturday that Krystyna's dad collapses.

Monday – at work Gosia tells the girls about the miscarriage. Krystyna's dad dies.

The evening of the funeral, Krystyna writes the last letter to her father.

Sometime later – Gosia discovers Alicja is pregnant and Gosia has a nervous breakdown, later swallows pills and ends up in a hospital.

October – Krystyna is giving back the keys to her dad's flat and bumps into Antoni, goes to a café, he helps her with the handing over her dad's flat keys and they go to his. She leaves after a little bit of closeness happens between them.

Friday evening – Krystyna and twins have a film night; she discovers Krzysztof's hotel bills and spends the evening with her colleagues. She discovers Krzysztof had been cheating on her with men. She cries, gets drunk and texts Antoni about wanting to have sex with him.

Saturday – Krystyna has a hangover; with her children she goes on a shopping spree to get new, more exciting clothes and an exciting haircut. In the evening, she goes to Antoni and they have sex.

Another weekend in autumn – Alicja craves freshly baked bread and Aleksander bakes it for her. They go to his parents' house where she meets them for the first time, as well as his grandma, and eats a lot of home-made food, especially *pierogi*. They stay overnight and, on the way home, they visit Alicja's parents – it turns out Aleksander's parents lived close by in a similar kind of country cottage.

Gosia and Piotr are in the Dominican Republic having a holiday with Gosia's parents. Gosia feels stronger after having been in therapy. She and Piotr take a walk on the beach and have a conversation about their relationship, having children, and both discover that they overestimated each other's desire to have a baby. They decide to calm down and take things easy.

Wednesday in October – Krzysztof arrives at Krystyna's to talk to her and remove his things. They argue. When he leaves, Krystyna rearranges the furniture in the living room to make it look more modern and goes shopping. In the afternoon, she tells children about what has happened and why their dad had left them. The children also learn about Antoni and Patryk invites him to his football match the following Saturday.

Gosia is at a gynaecologist's surgery and finds out she's pregnant with twins.

Magda and Tomasz go to the little town close to Poland to report that she had been raped by her stepfather and to reclaim her flat; all goes the way they expected; the stepfather is arrested.

New Year's Eve with everyone spending the night at Krystyna's (Krystyna, Antoni, twins, Magda and Tomasz, Gosia and Piotr, Alicja and Aleksander). Krzysztof rings to say he has AIDS; Gosia rushes to the hospital as she thinks she's having another miscarriage.

Trigger warnings: references to rape and child sexual abuse; references and descriptions of sex activities; swearing and obscene language.

Guidance on Polish names

In Polish it is very common for people to use more than one form of their names. All names have their 'formal' version – the version that will appear on ID documents such as passports. Examples from the novel: Małgorzata, Krystyna, Krzysztof.

But very often the very formal names are rarely used in everyday life, except for very formal situations. Instead, people tend to use either shortened versions of their names (e.g. Ala for Alicja, Magda for Magdalena) or diminutive forms, mostly to add a sense of affection or familiarity when addressing the person. Examples of such diminutive affectionate names in the novel: Gosia, Krysia, Piotruś.

Some names can also be made into less affectionate forms that still convey a sense of familiarity – these are also used in less formal everyday situations. Examples: Kryśka, Krzysiek.

Some names have formal versions that sound more formal than others and are more rarely used, e.g. Małgorzata. People who know a woman who is called Małgorzata often call her by her official name very rarely; Gosia then becomes the more neutral/default version of the name. Some formal versions sound more neutral and are more often used, e.g. Alicja, Patryk, Patrycja. In the case of the latter two, people who have those name may never be called by any diminutive version of their name.

To help the reader understand the complexity of Polish names, characters' names are listed below, categorised by the degree of affection and/or familiarity they convey.
Aleksander (formal/neutral), Alek (neutral/familiar), Oluś (very affectionate)

Alicja (formal/neutral), Ala (affectionate/familiar), Alka (less affectionate/familiar), Alunia/Alusia (very affectionate)

Antoni (formal/neutral), Antek (affectionate/familiar), Antoś (very affectionate)

Krystyna (formal/neutral), Krysia (affectionate), Kryśka (familiar)

Krzysztof (formal), Krzysiek (less affectionate/familiar), Krzyś (very affectionate)

Magdalena (formal), Magda (neutral and familiar)

Małgorzata (formal), Gosia (neutral but a bit affectionate), Gocha (less affectionate/familiar), Gosieńka (very affectionate), Gocha

Patrycja (formal/neutral), Pati (affectionate/familiar)

Patryk (formal/neutral)

Piotr (formal), Piotrek (affectionate/familiar), Piotruś (very affectionate)

Tomasz (formal), Tomek (affectionate/familiar)